Praise for
A Babysitter's Guide to Monster Hunting:

"A series opener that melds Goosebumps and the
Baby-Sitters Club with ironic glue."
—*Kirkus Reviews*

"Scary, funny, clever, and filled with heart."
—**Gabrielle Zevin**, *New York Times* bestselling author

"An anthem for female friendship and the
power that comes with it."
—**Ali Bell**, executive producer of *Ghostbusters*

"This shining gem in the campy-monster-drama genre is a step
up from R.L. Stine's Goosebumps."
—*School Library Journal*

"This new series gives babysitting a daring edge and sets up
girls outside of the popular crowd as heroines."
—**ALA** *Booklist*

"An absolute romp of a book that will have kids everywhere
howling for more."
—*San Francisco Book Review*

A Babysitter's Guide to

MONSTER HUNTING

JOE BALLARINI

ILLUSTRATED BY VIVIENNE TO

KATHERINE TEGEN BOOKS
An Imprint of HarperCollins Publishers

Katherine Tegen Books is an imprint of HarperCollins Publishers.

A Babysitter's Guide to Monster Hunting
Text copyright © 2017 by Joe Ballarini
Illustrations copyright © 2017 by Vivienne To

Library of Congress Control Number: 2017932877

ISBN 978-0-06-243784-6

Typography by Joel Tippie
19 20 21 22 23   BRR   10 9 8 7 6 5 4 3 2
❖
First paperback edition, 2019

For my wife
and for every kid afraid of what is
lurking under the bed.

Just so you know, hiding under the
covers can't stop monsters from eating you.
In fact, that just makes you look like a
delicious, tasty burrito.
Didn't know that, did you?

See?
This book is for you.

THE BEGINNING

"'*Hush little baby, don't say a word.*'"

The four-year-old girl blinked awake under her quilted blanket. She froze, listening, wide-eyed. A strange, low singing oozed through the slats of her closet door.

"'Papa's gonna buy you a mockingbird.'"

She had never heard the throaty voice before, but she already knew she never wanted to hear it again.

The closet door creaked open and the girl's white-knuckled fists tightened around her teddy bear, nearly strangling it.

"I'm not a wimp, I'm not a wimp," she whispered under her covers.

She closed her eyes and wished the unseen horrors away. The room fell silent. The whispering vanished.

She drew the covers from her head. The closet door was open just a little.

She didn't like it open *just a little.* It needed to be closed. Now.

She took a deep breath, slid off her bed, and walked barefoot across the carpet to her dark, open closet.

Then she noticed the smell. A combination of wet mud, rotten eggs, and a thousand belches. Her socks smelled bad sometimes, but never this bad.

The hanging clothes swished ever so slightly. Her sweaters parted. A pale hand slithered from the depths, stopping the door from closing. A figure emerged from the closet like an actor stepping through curtains onto the stage.

"Hello, little girl." He smiled.

Fear rooted the girl's feet to the floor. She stared up at the man's wrinkled skull. His elegant suit jacket was covered in soot and corpse-dust.

"Wake up," the girl whispered to herself. "Wake up."

The monster picked a cockroach from the strands of hair cascading down his shoulders and popped it into his mouth, as if it were caramel-covered popcorn. "You think you're scared?" the man said. "I've been in there all night surrounded by your miserable sense of fashion, waiting for you to go to sleep.

2

Horrible, smelly thing you are."

He took a step toward her, and she saw he had brown furry legs, hooves for feet, and a ticking tail.

"Do you know who I am?" the man asked her, placing his hands on his hips. "What am I saying? *Of course you do*. Every child knows who I am." He flashed a vain smile. Bits of half-chewed insect stuck in his mustard-colored fangs.

"Muh-muh-muh . . . ," the little girl gurgled.

"Muh-muh-muh-mommy can't hear you, my dear. She went out with your daddy.

"'So hush little baby, don't you cry . . . ,'" the creature sang. His eyes sparkled with flecks of gold. It was like seeing the Milky Way reflected in the ocean's waves.

The little girl's eyes closed. She swayed on her feet, fast asleep, and tumbled into a large, burlap sack the man had drawn from behind his back. He tied the end with a long, red ribbon.

"There we are," he sneered.

Just down the hall, Veronica Preston, a sixteen-year-old babysitter, was lounging on the couch, talking on her cell phone with her boyfriend, Todd.

"I can't come over, Todd. I'm babysitting," Veronica giggled, absently pulling at the frayed hem of her jeans. "And nooo, you can't come over, either, so don't even try it, *buster*."

Todd was trying to think of a clever, convincing

response when Veronica heard a thud down the hall. "Kiddo?" she called out. "You awake?"

The faint sound of something being dragged across the floor suddenly stopped. She clicked off the phone in the middle of Todd asking her what time the little girl's parents were coming home.

The babysitter closed the blue spiral-bound notebook opened on her lap and placed it by her battered orange book bag. She crept down the shadowy hall toward the little girl's bedroom and quietly opened the door.

"Kiddo?" she whispered.

In the darkness, Veronica could see a large lump writhing under the covers. She reached out and pulled back the blanket.

"Read me a bedtime story?" cooed the smiling face with snakelike eyes.

The babysitter screamed. The monster sprang from the bed, dramatically whirling the covers away.

"Ah, yes. Screaming is the highest form of flattery," crowed the cloven-hoofed demon.

His claws swiped at her long braid as the teenager scrambled down the hall to the kitchen, slamming the door in his face. He kicked it open and saw the kitchen was empty.

"Fast little mouse, aren't we? Where are you, little mouse?" he called playfully.

As the monster sniffed the air in the kitchen, Veronica held her breath and crawled behind a couch. She hid while the creature stalked slowly into the living room, his heavy, black hooves stomping across the carpet, followed by an angry, twitching tail.

Her backpack. She needed her backpack. When he turned away from the couch, she reached over and patted the brown cushions. His hand clamped down on her wrist and squeezed with incredible strength.

"I don't believe we've been properly introduced." He smiled down at her. "My name is the Grand Guignol. Known to many as the Boogeyman."

The Grand Guignol said this with the confidence of a monster that had lived for thousands of years and seen countless poor, helpless souls cower in its presence.

The babysitter, however, had a much different reaction.

"Nice to meet you," she said. "I'm the babysitter. And you're not taking that child."

The Boogeyman blinked for a confused moment. This was supposed to be the part where she screamed in terror. Veronica was holding two ancient Egyptian daggers with emeralds on the hilt. Then she lunged at him.

She ducked, sliced. He dodged her swings and slashed at her with his long, grimy fingernails. They battled across the living room: claw, hoof, snapping tail against two blades and a ponytail.

The Boogeyman's smile raised the hairs on the back of Veronica's neck. His tail lashed out and whipped around her throat. She choked. It pulled her close. His damp, eggy breath huffed against her cheek.

"I've feasted on your kind for a thousand years," he said. "I am the chill down your spine. The nightmare that wakes you, screaming. I'm also a gentleman, but no one seems to care about that."

The babysitter gasped for breath. The scratchy tail coiled tighter around her neck with boa constrictor–like strength. Windpipe crushing, Veronica could feel her face flush purple. With each wheezing breath, she tried to pull away from him.

"Ahaaa. The sweet smell of fear," he whispered.

The girl clenched her jaw and cannoned her fist into his gut. Plumes of dust wafted from his black jacket. He gulped and doubled over. She unwound his twisted tail from her neck and spun away from him, like a professional tango dancer twirling across the dance floor.

Flashes of metal shot from her hands.

The Grand Guignol sidestepped the flying knives and was already clicking his teeth in disappointment as the two blades thunked into the wall beside his head.

"Silver daggers? Really?" he sighed. "Do I look like a werewolf? Amateur."

He clomped toward her. She ran from him, snatched

her backpack, and trampolined off the couch. She dove out the window and into the backyard.

In one swift leap, the Boogeyman followed.

Veronica tumbled onto the grass, landing awkwardly on her right side. A sharp pain coursed through her arm as she rummaged for something in her backpack. She found a glowing vial and worked quickly to uncork it.

Dark hooves slammed down before her. The Grand Guignol towered over her, pinning her to the ground with a cloven hoof on her back.

"Did you not just hear my speech about me being an utterly brilliant, awesome, and magical creature?"

Pressed against the grass, Veronica struggled to look up at him. "Actually, I did. That's why I came prepared."

As the monster paused to consider the statement, Veronica rolled from under his hoof and swung her arm in a circle. He saw that the babysitter had poured a ring of twinkling blue powder on the ground, and he was standing directly inside it.

"Is that—?"

"Ring of Angel Fire? Your only weakness? Believe it is," she said with a smile.

She lit a match and rolled away as the powder caught fire with dazzling sparks. A tornado of ethereal, sapphire flames spiraled around the cloven-hoofed monster, trapping him inside its ghostly vortex. The

Grand Guignol slammed his fists against the shimmering, supernatural wall.

"You can't kill the Boogeyman, babysitter," he warned.

Veronica's grin glowed in the rippling propane-like waves that separated them. The enchanted tornado whirled faster around the Grand Guignol, picking him up off the ground.

"I—I'll return!" he howled. "And you won't be able to protect *her*!"

Veronica watched the Ring of Angel Fire ascend into the sky, stretching into a twisting funnel of light. With a faint whoosh, the vortex vanished into the dark clouds. A cool breeze blew across the grass. The babysitter glanced around the suburban backyard, making sure there were no witnesses. Explaining things to the neighbors was so *boring*.

It was half past eleven on a cold night in Rhode Island. Everyone in this sleepy side of town was most likely in bed.

The babysitter reached into her backpack for a Luna bar and winced. She had definitely sprained, if not broken, something in her right shoulder.

Exhausted, she went back inside to put the little girl to bed.

"Shh, just a nightmare," she whispered, soothing the little girl to sleep with her gentle tone.

As the child nuzzled into her pillow, Veronica inspected the Boogeyman's burlap sack. Fortunately, it was empty. There was no way she could deal with more kids tonight. She shoved the coarse sack into her backpack, then pulled out her blue notebook and flopped onto the couch.

Inside the notebook, elaborate notes were scribbled around a drawing of the beastly Boogeyman. One of the notes, circled in red, was:

Possible weakness: Silver daggers. Angel Fire.

Squeezed into one of the last open spaces, she wrote:

Silver daggers NO BUENO. Angel Fire BIG WIN.

The lock on the front door clicked open, and the little girl's parents entered with the glow of two adults who had just consumed a moderately tasty dinner without the interruptions of a toddler.

"Sorry we're late. How was she?" asked the woman.

"The best," Veronica assured them with a kind smile. As the parents pulled off their heavy coats, the babysitter caught a glimpse of her two silver daggers sticking out of the wall.

"We read," she said, creeping toward her knives. "She fell asleep. I attempted algebra. Pretty chill."

The little girl's dad closed the hall closet door and smiled. "I'll drive you home."

Behind her back, Veronica discreetly pulled the two blades from the wall and slipped them into her backpack before following the dad out to the car.

Had the little girl's parents peered inside Veronica's large, scuffed orange JanSport, they would have seen it wasn't filled with schoolbooks and notes to friends, but rather with exotic weapons, the shard of an enchanted crystal, ten vials of mystical potions all arranged in alphabetical order, and the blue spiral-bound notebook. Written on its cover were the words:

A Babysitter's Guide to
MONSTER HUNTING

1

The cold autumn breeze twisted my frizzy red hair into my face as I ran past pumpkins with carved grins.

"Of course you forgot your hair band, Kelly," I growled to myself.

I tucked my hair under my white scarf and pulled the ends of it tightly under my chin, which made me look like a cartoon character with a toothache. I didn't care. The hair situation was now under control.

But the yellow school bus of doom was already rumbling away from the corner.

"Stop!" I cried, chasing after it, waving my arms. "Larry! Please!"

The bus stopped and the door flew open. A wheezy smoker's laugh greeted me as I ran up the stairs, gasping for breath.

"Looked like you could use the exercise," said Larry the Toothless Bus Driver.

Hilarious.

The bus thundered down the cold, suburban street, passing the rundown movie theater, which was showing eighties horror films all night long for Halloween. I slumped onto the green pleather seat beside my best friend, Tammy Alvaro.

"Could be worse," Tammy said.

She leaned over to one side and showed me a bright neon splotch of gum stuck to her butt.

"I sat in gum," she admitted.

"Oh no, Tam." I covered my mouth and laughed. "Let's move seats."

"What's the point?" she sighed. "If anyone asks, I'll just say I ate an alien and then pooed myself."

Everyone thinks Tammy whispers because she's too shy, but really, it's because she's saying something hilarious and doesn't want to offend anyone. So while everyone else thinks she's this discreet, coy creature, she's actually a raging comedian in the body of a thirteen-year-old mouse.

"Where's your costume, K-Ferg?" she asked.

"I'm wearing it. It's called 'despair.'"

I reached into my backpack and removed a notebook labeled "CAMP FUND." Inside were dollar tallies and a colorful brochure for Camp Miskatonic. The images of cabins and horses took me to my happy place.

Camp Miskatonic.

Magical Camp Miskatonic.

I first heard about "Big Camp Misky" from Deanna. Okay, so Deanna didn't tell me *directly*. I overheard her talking to the Princess Pack during lunch about this incredible place she went to one summer. She rode horses and kissed a boy and won the camp talent show. The camp itinerary even included beach time. *How awesome does that sound?*

Deanna said Camp Miskatonic was where she "found her truth." She said this as she inhaled through her nostrils deeply, as if smelling the memory of the pine trees. Or maybe it was because she needed to take in more oxygen to relieve her overwhelmed brain from all the mature and deep emotions rushing through it.

The Camp Miskatonic website hypnotized me with images of lush lakes, fields, stables, and fabulous teenagers doing Arts and Crafts. I imagined myself sailing down a zip line through evergreen trees, riding on a pony named Freedom, and trading my deepest and truest secrets with my bunkmates while making box-style gimp friendship bracelets.

And then, once summer had ended, having "found

my truth" (wherever it's been hiding), I planned to make my triumphant debut in the vast halls of Willow Brook High School as a newly arrived freshman. It was there, with my tanned chin held high and my spirit brimming with worldly wisdom, that I would no longer be Kelly the Short, Invisible Ginger Girl. From that moment on, I would be known as Kelly the Teenager, who had shed the shackles of eighth-grade obscurity and blossomed into the coolest ninth grader in Rhode Island. All thanks to Camp Miskatonic.

And, for the record, *I don't want to be Deanna*. I want to be me—but like the coolest version of me. I believed that a once-in-a-lifetime experience at camp would help achieve these goals.

But it costs four thousand bucks to go to Big Camp Misky for one summer.

Four thousand dollars is a *lot* of cheddar for a thirteen-year-old. Especially one who cannot ask her parents because they are not rolling in the dough. However, I, Kelly Page Ferguson, worked and saved up a total of *$3,000.32*, which is now locked away in the Life Savers bank in my closet.

I was $999.68 short, and I had already done every job a teenager can do before child services gets involved. No lie. Last summer, I was the CEO of my own lemonade stand. In the autumn, senior rain gutter cleaner and VP of grocery bagging at the Foodtime. In the winter,

I was an executive snow scraper. In the spring, lawn mower in chief. And this past summer, head bouncer (aka ticket taker) at Mulligan Pizza and Golf.

If I was going to make the deadline to get into camp next summer, I had to fork over payment by the end of November to save my spot in Bunkroom C.

I needed another jobby-job. I needed one now.

Tammy slapped her hand on my notebook page.

"I know the perfect job for you!" she exclaimed. "Babysitting."

I stroked an invisible beard on my chin, like a wise wizard considering his options. "Here's the thing," I said. "I don't really like kids. And they don't really like me."

"Aaw. Kids are so cute."

I winced, like I had just devoured a bagful of Sour Patch Kids.

"Have you interacted with a child?" I asked. "Their little raccoon claw-hands are constantly covered in peanut butter. They all have rabies."

Tammy shrugged. "Details."

I tucked my Camp Miskatonic notebook away and shook my head.

"They just watch cartoons and eat cereal and play on their iPads all day," I said. "They don't have to study or get good grades."

Tammy scrunched up her nose. "Kell, are you jealous of five-year-olds?"

Am I peanut butter and jelly?

Yes, I am!

"Bet your butt I'm jelly. I never get to hang out and just watch TV and eat loads of snacks," I said.

"You could if you were a babysitter. And you'd get paid for it. *Boom*." Tammy dropped an invisible microphone and snapped her fingers.

"And"—she nudged closer to me—"my second cousin Shelly posted on Facebook that she just bought a car with all the money she made babysitting. That's *big* money."

I tried to tell Tammy she was crazy, but the more I thought about it, babysitting, compared to my other jobs, sounded like a breeze. I mean, "sitting" is in the job title itself. You play with the kid for an hour, maybe read it a book, plop it in front of the TV, feed it pizza, make sure it brushes its teeth, and then send it to bed. While it sleeps, you're on the phone, bingeing your favorite Korean soap opera on Netflix (*Tears of Flowers and Fish? Soooo good*).

You basically get paid to chill out in someone else's house like it was a minivacation, waiting for the thing's parents to come back and give you some cash.

How hard could it be?

As we walked into school, I tied my scarf around Tammy's waist to hide the gum splotch on her jeans. She wore it well. Not that anyone noticed. In return, Tammy snuck into the yearbook office before class to post about my new career online: "Responsible babysitter: Ready to watch after your child."

She included a picture of me smiling and looking very responsible.

I shared the post with my mom and dad (yes, Tammy is friends with them online), and they shared it with their combined fourteen followers.

By fifth period, no one had responded. No likes. No shares. No online love.

No problem. I wasn't sold on taking care of monstrous

little children. I felt destined for greater things. Relieved, I practically skipped down the row of red lockers, smiling at goblins, super-heroes, and a dude dressed like a banana.

The sea of kids parted for Deanna and the Princess Pack. They were fresh-off-the-pages-of-*Teen-Vogue* shiny, living a music video made just for them. I glanced down at my dirty green puffy jacket, my patched-up jeans, my worn pink Converse, and my nubby knit sweater that I had nicknamed "Itchy," and I tried to blend in with the lockers as, to my total horror, they circled me with satisfied grins.

"Babysitting's the perfect job for you, Kelly," Deanna said.

My stomach twisted, like a bag of cold linguini, but I tried to sound flattered. "Oh, you saw my post?"

"Nothing goes online that I don't know about," Deanna said with a wink.

The three girls that made up the Princess Pack stared me down. One of the princesses crossed her arms and tapped her bedazzled pink Ugg. They all smelled like coconut shampoo and money. I felt like I was living an episode of Shark Week.

"You *have* met the other babysitters, right?" Deanna asked with pointed curiosity.

My stomach sank.

The babysitters?

I looked down the row of lockers to see three of our school's most notorious Invisibles huddled together, carrying their giant, overstuffed backpacks.

How could I be so stupid?

There was Cassie McCoy, whose braces made her spit and whose bangs were so sharply cut they looked like the edge of an ax. She was speedwalking to class, bellowing "Move!"

Then there was Berna Vincent, an African American girl with wild puffy hair and big thick glasses, who constantly chewed gum and wore shirts emblazoned with anime unicorns. It was rumored that she could make one piece of gum last an entire month.

Lastly, there was Curtis Critter. So help me, that was his real last name. One lazy eye, one crazy eye, a crew cut, a chipped front tooth, and camouflage cargo pants tucked into high laced black combat boots. Not exactly

19

mall-crawl material. Kids whispered that Curtis's father hunted squirrels for meat.

They were always together, and it was understood that you didn't hang out with them unless you wanted to become one of the misfits of middle school. I mean, there are misfits, and then there are the borderline mutants that are the babysitters.

And now it looked like I wanted to *be* one of them. *Nooooooooooooooo!*

What have I done?

"They are a total rando trifecta," said Deanna.

"Tooootally." I was happy to shift the attention away from myself.

"They have zero followers on Instagram," said Bedazzled Pink-Ugg Princess.

"Fuh-reak show," said Deanna.

"Totally," I repeated.

For a moment, the Princess Pack and I were united in our collective snarky judgment of a common weirdo. This is not something I'm proud of. I did it merely for social survival.

"They're one step below quiz bowl or Mathletes," Deanna despaired.

"They're so weird!" I said.

"Exactly." Deanna smiled. "Perfect job for you. Ciao." Deanna and friends waltzed away, like they were going to the ball. They were toying with me. Like I was some red-headed court jester. I turned and walked to algebra, feeling each of the babysitters' eyes following me, even Curtis's lazy one.

After class, Tammy took me by the arm and walked with me down the hall.

"Major scoopage! Jesper Tanaka's parents are going out of town tonight, and he's throwing a big-time Halloween party."

Tammy then let out an excited "Eeee!"

I gave her an exhausted look. "But tonight's cookie dough and Netflix at your house."

"*Tears of Flowers and Fish* will have to wait," she said, shaking me with excitement.

"Don't you want to know if Kim Shan ends up with Lee Min?" I was only half joking. If I'm not working, I'm studying. When I'm not studying, I'm sleeping. Cookie dough and *Tears of Flower and Fish* are my go-to escape from my own personal hamster wheel.

"Kell," Tammy said. I sensed a lecture brewing. "We're eighth graders, and we've never been to a party with more than two people."

"We go to parties," I said.

Tammy's eyes shot sour daggers at me. She tightened the knot on my white scarf that was still tied around her butt and then swept her hand across the swarm of students.

"Kelly, it's Halloween. The one night you can be anything you want. Anything in the world."

I looked around at the endless possibilities. Grim Reapers, pirates, witches, superheroes . . .

What did I want to be? A glittering forest pixie? A dark, sad vampire? A unicorn? All three?

"'To be, or not to be—that is the question . . .'"

We were in honors English, and Victor was reading out loud in front of the class. The entire room was silent as we all listened to him recite *Hamlet* with grace and confidence.

Sigh.

"'Whether 'tis nobler in the mind to suffer / The slings and arrows of outrageous fortune, / Or to take arms against a sea of troubles, / And by opposing end them?'" he read slowly and thoughtfully.

Victor has black hair, and these enormous puppy-dog brown eyes, and this little sideways smile that makes him look like he's keeping a secret.

Once upon a time, at the beginning of the school year,

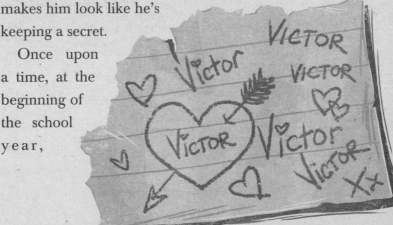

Victor and I sat across from each other in Spanish class. My heart would race whenever he spoke his native tongue. His family moved here from Guatemala when he was two. I know this because he did a report about Guatemala in social studies class (not because I've stalked him online or anything), and he pronounced it "Whaataamaala."

In Spanish class, I made some joke about "*vamanos*ing to the *playa*," and Victor laughed. It was a soft and warm laugh, like his eyes. He glanced at me, as if to say, *Who is this weird thirteen-year-old with wiry red hair sitting across from me?* My blood rushed and my eyelids widened as we held each other's gaze. This is going to sound weird, but I swear I hear echoes of a Spanish guitar playing somewhere in the distance whenever I see him.

Shortly after that, Victor was removed from Spanish class and placed in the *advanced* Spanish class, since he knew the language better than the teacher did. I thought it was really unfair, and I told Mrs. Bowen that yanking Victor out of our class was discrimination against Whaataamaalans. Mrs. Bowen gave me detention for disrupting class and spreading misinformation.

When most kids read out loud in front of the whole class, they fidget or mumble while the other kids doze off or make fun of whoever is reading. Not my Victor. He read with such confidence and power that everyone was in awe of him. I'm not kidding. When he finished, the entire classroom burst into applause. Me included.

"Thank you, Victor," said Mr. Gibbs. He was deeply moved. "Such passion. Such . . . fire."

Victor just gave a bashful shrug, said "*gracias*," and took his seat.

I saw Deanna lean back and whisper to him, "I wish we were reading *Romeo and Juliet.*"

Oh, barf.

The back legs on my chair lifted as I leaned forward to eavesdrop on Deanna and Victor. "Do you need a ride to Jesper's party tonight? My mom can drive us."

NO! SAY NO, VICTOR!

I twisted my number two pencil in my hands, as if it were Deanna's neck.

"*Bien,*" Victor replied.

No bien*! NO* BIEN, *VICTOR!*

"*Bien* it is," Deanna smiled, and winked. *So help me,* she winked. "Wait till you see my costume," she whispered to him.

Victor's eyebrows raised. The pencil snapped in my hands.

After class, I grabbed Tammy by the arm. "We are going to this party."

Tammy gently tapped her fingertips together, like an evil scientist watching her experiment come to fruition. "Yes we are!"

3

"Mom! Major costume crisis!" I shouted over the music.

All my clothes were scattered across my room, making it look like I'd triggered my closet's gag reflex. Tammy's mom was coming to pick me up in *two hours,* and I had zero idea what kind of costume to make out of my limited wardrobe, budget, and time.

My Spidey senses told me that something might happen tonight. I'd see Victor. He'd see me. The eye contact would be strong. And then, after two hours of Tammy psyching me up, I would squeeze up next to him and say something clever, like *"¡Hola, amigo!"*

Okay, not that, but something *super*clever that Tammy and I would have agreed upon after discussing it for the entire night. Then I would tell Victor about the terrible injustice that had been done to him in Spanish class and how things just weren't the same without him.

Again, not that, but something good.

I was going to have *fun* tonight, or at least try. This was a real party—not a pity party.

I rushed into the living room to find my mom pouring a bag of candy into a large salad bowl. She was dressed in a denim shirt, with the sleeves rolled up. She had put a fake tattoo of an American flag on her right forearm. Her hair was tucked under a red bandanna. She wore welding goggles around her neck.

"Mom, I need a costume that says fun but cool, not desperate but cool, and I need it now." I dragged her into my room.

"You could go as Frida Kahlo or Amelia Earhart," my mother said, picking through my clothes.

"I need a costume, not a history lesson."

"Oh! Edith Cavell. In World War One—"

"She helped more than two hundred Allied soldiers escape from German-occupied Belgium and was shot to death by a German firing squad for it," I said, finishing her sentence. My mother is a huge history nerd, which makes me one too. "I was thinking more like a Catholic schoolgirl."

"Young lady. You are thirteen. Not some music video dancer. You don't have to objectify yourself for other

26

people's gratification."

"I know," I sighed. "But once isn't gonna hurt."

My mother stood behind me and looked at our reflections in the mirror. Her hands were warm on my shoulders. We looked similar, but she's much prettier. I like it when people say I look like her.

"Kelly . . . what do you want to be?" she asked quietly.

I shrugged. "Cool?"

"You *are* cool, honey!"

"Doesn't really count when you say it, Mom."

My mom straightened up and threw her shoulders back with powerful pride. "You're right. It only counts when you say it to yourself."

I rolled my eyes. "Just because you read a bunch of life quotes on Pinterest doesn't make them true, Mother."

Her cell phone rang with the dreaded ringtone that she uses only for one particular person: her boss.

"Ice Queen alert," she said nervously. "Why is she calling here now? Focus on my breathing . . ."

"Don't let her intimidate you," I encouraged her. "You're Rosie the Riveter!"

My mother flexed her American flag forearm and answered the phone with a fake cheery voice. "Hiiiii, Mrs. Zellman. Peter and I are just getting ready for the company party tonight! How can I help you?"

She wandered out of my room and paced the hall,

rubbing her bunched-up forehead. I followed her into the living room, where she kept looking back at me and nodding.

"Well, yes, she is very responsible," said my mother. "Sure, she loves kids."

I narrowed my eyes. Something was fishy. My mother kept staring at me and nodding. "Well, I think Kelly's busy tonight—"

Something was definitely up. "Yes! She's very busy!" I said, walking toward her. "She's going to the biggest party of the year!"

"An emergency?" My mother gave me a big apologetic look, and I stopped in my tracks. My fate was sealed.

"Six o'clock? Great. See you at the party. No, thank *you*. Bye, Mrs. Zellman."

I stared at my mother and said in the most dramatic way possible, "Mother. *What hast thou done?*"

"I . . . booked you a babysitting job for tonight?" She winced.

"But—"

"Mrs. Zellman's sitter canceled at the last minute, and she saw your ad that I posted, and she's heard me bragging all about my wonderful, brilliant daughter, and you said you need the money, sooooo . . ."

"So you let her boss you around?"

"She's my boss! That's what bosses do."

I dropped onto the couch and writhed around in agony. "Mom. This was my night."

"I tried to say no, but . . . the big company party's tonight– She planned it, and she runs the company, and she can't just– I can't j-just–" My mother began to stammer, pacing quickly around the living room, pretending to light a cigarette. She quit smoking a long time ago, but she still sneaks a few when she's super-stressed, even though she knows she's inhaling toxic waste.

"She's my boss, Kell. If I call her and tell her I screwed up, then what does that say about me?"

I flopped onto my back and looked up at the ceiling.

"This is the Ice Queen we're talking about," my mom said. "She'd fire me over something like this, and we can't afford that."

I opened my mouth to respond, but I knew what my mother was saying. She needed her job, and if I bailed on the Zellmans, then, well, that job that helped put food on our table and a roof over our heads (but still isn't enough to send me to summer camp) might go away.

"Okay, Mom," I said quietly in my most "I'm being supercool and understanding now, but you owe me later" voice. "I'll go."

She hugged me, squeezing the breath out of my lungs.

29

"Thank you! You're going to make a great babysitter!" she squealed.

"Please don't say that," I moaned.

"I'll tell your father he's got to drive you," she said.

I slumped back into my room and pulled on ole Itchy over my faded NASA T-shirt.

Who was I kidding? Whispering jokes back and forth with your best friend does not prepare you for actual social interaction with a boy.

I may as well become a babysitter.

My father drove me in the family clunker into the part of Mercy Springs, Rhode Island, I call "Storybook Land," because of its redbrick mansions and perfectly manicured lawns. Here, the Halloween decorations looked like they'd been handcrafted by Ralph Lauren. Posh trick-or-treaters strolled down the clean sidewalks.

"Not like our neighborhood, huh, Kell?" my dad snorted. Air wheezed under bits of tape covering tears in his blow-up Godzilla suit. I reached out and pressed down on a piece of tape, blocking one tattered, grimy hole. "And don't tell the Zellmans any of the stuff your mom says about Mrs. Zellman being an ice queen."

31

My father meant well, but my parents' laser focus on everything I do puts a lot of pressure on me to be the perfect kid. I guess that's another reason why Camp Miskatonic appeals to me.

My dad stopped the car in front of a pristine three-story house on the bay side of the street and whistled. "Must be nice."

He waited as I walked up the fancy gravel driveway. A cold rush of air curled off the bay and brushed its chilled fingers across the back of my neck. I rang the polished brass doorbell and heard it echo through the house.

The red door opened.

Mrs. Zellman was wearing a white gown with snowy-gold lace. A headdress of fake icicles clung to her hair. Her eye makeup was arctic blue.

I had to stop myself from having a life-ending giggle fit. Mrs. Zellman was dressed as the Ice Queen.

She glared down at me.

"Hi, Mrs. Zellman," I said with a little wave.

"Five hundred thousand for ten units, Arjun. Final offer," she said.

"Huh?"

My dad honked the horn. "See you at the party, Mrs. Zellman!" he shouted, and waved. "She's all yours." He laughed and then drove away.

Mrs. Zellman gave an absent wave and then gestured

for me to enter. "You can put me on hold, but the numbers aren't going to change, Arjun," she said into her Bluetooth earpiece.

I followed her clacking heels through the flawlessly decorated house. Vast glass doors overlooked the murky Narragansett Bay beyond the rolling backyard.

"Well, well, Kelly Ferguson," she said. "The last time I saw you was four years ago at the company picnic, when you fell into the pool during the potato sack race."

"Yep," I said. "I remember that like it was yesterday."

"HANK, THE BABYSITTER'S HERE, WE HAVE TO GO!" Her scream bounced off the walls as she glided into an enormous kitchen.

"Dinner's in the oven. I took Baby Jacob trick-or-treating at noon."

"Noon?" I blurted out. Mrs. Zellman shot me a stern look. I swallowed under her icy stare. "I mean. Great idea. Very safe."

She pointed to one of fifty cupboards lining the vast kitchen. "We put all his candy in the top cupboard. He can have three pieces: the raisins, the dried-apple chips, and puffed rice cakes."

What kind of neighbors give out rice cakes? This part of town was nice but weird.

Briskly walking down a hallway lined with jagged,

modern art, she snapped a printed-out list in my face.

"Here is a list of no-no's," she said.

BABY JACOB NO-NO's

No ice cream
No gluten
No chocolate
No dairy
No peanuts
No more than 30 minutes of "screen time"
   —this means TV, iPad, video games
No running
No shouting
No discussing global tragedies or current events

"I realize it's a bit much, but it's not without good reason." Her voice lowered into a hushed, concerned tone. "Jacob has these . . . nightmares. Bad ones. We've taken him to doctors, given him medication. . . . We don't know what's causing them. But they're terrifying him."

I shuddered, quietly freaking out inside.

Mrs. Zellman clapped her hands together. "Let's go meet him, shall we?"

We entered a bright room filled with every toy a parent could 1-Click on Amazon. The eyes of a million

34

stuffed animals stared back at me. A red camping tent was set up in the far corner. I could see the hunched shadow of a little boy inside it.

"Where's Liz?" said the shadow.

"Liz can't be here tonight, honey," Mrs. Zellman replied, slowly unzipping the tent.

I leaned down to see Jacob, a pear-shaped little boy in a tight-fitting ninja costume. He was drawing in a large sketch pad on his lap. When Mrs. Zellman pulled back the tent flap, he quickly hid his drawing.

"This is Kelly."

He scowled up at me.

"I want Liz," he demanded.

"Liz LeRue's been his babysitter for years," Mrs. Zellman whispered to me as she checked her phone. "He's got a little crush. Yes, I'm still holding!" she shouted. "Where is Arjun? I'm hanging up and he's going to get nothing in five, four, three—"

I decided to try to make eye contact with the creature.

"We're going to have fun tonight!" I said.

Jacob looked at me again—confirmed that no, I was indeed not his beloved Liz—and promptly kicked his way out of the tent and across a pile of toys like an angry giant stomping through a tiny village.

"Not Liz," he said, marching around the room.

Mrs. Zellman cradled the little pork bean. "If you're nice to her, we'll get you that new toy-thing you want."

Jacob grunted and then ran from the room. Mrs. Zellman shrugged and waved her hand. "Well, that's Baby Jacob."

The muscles in my face struggled to smile. "Cute," I said.

Mrs. Zellman looked at me as if she was really seeing me for the first time. "You *do* have a lot of experience with children, right?"

"Oh, yeah. Of course!" I blurted out. "I've worked with kids a lot. They're—they're the best."

Not *exactly* the truth, but I wasn't going to get fired before I even started the job.

"Not Liz!" came the echoes down the hall.

"Bedtime is at seven thirty. It usually takes a little while to get him to sleep." She paused, staring at his bed. "I don't know what it is; something new these past few months. . . . If he puts up a fight or starts to scream, just read him a book to calm him down." Her lips curled into a proud smile. "He has a *terrific* imagination."

"Oh, yeah," I said, trying not to sound creeped out.

"Finally!" she said. "Thank you. Yes."

"Oh, you're welcome," I said. "I was supposed to go to a party tonight, but—"

Mrs. Zellman walked out of the room, speaking into her Bluetooth headset. "I'll have legal send over the paperwork."

As Mrs. Zellman's heels clacked down the hall, I peeked inside the red tent and saw the sketch pad Jacob had been drawing in. An entire layer of thick, black crayon covered the page. In the middle, two large cruel-looking yellow eyes stared at me through the Crayola darkness. I shuddered and quickly walked out to find Mrs. Zellman.

At the marble staircase, Mr. Zellman waddled down dressed in a penguin costume. If I squinted, he looked like a grown-up version of Baby Jacob, except in a tuxedo.

"You're not Liz," he said to me. I forced a smile. "Don't burn the house down." He was laughing when he said it, but I knew he meant it.

Jacob tugged at his mother's snowflake dress. "Don't go," he whispered.

She held him tight and, for a brief moment, the Ice Queen melted. "I love you so much, Jakey," she said, and gave him a big mushy kiss. "We will be back by one. Have fun."

"Be a big boy, champ," Mr. Zellman said, pulling at his cuff links.

Jacob ran off to the living room. Mrs. Zellman sighed a little and then snapped back into boss mode. "Keep the doors locked. Open them for no one," she told me.

On her way out, Mrs. Zellman taped a sign to the front door:

No Candy.

Don't Ask.

"We'll be back by one a.m. sharp."

With that, she slammed the door. The metal sound of her jingling key turned and twisted in the door with a final *click-clack-click*, locking me inside.

Jacob sat on a large, high-backed chair in the living room, looking like a little king dressed in ninja robes. His big green eyes tracked me as I flopped onto the couch.

"So. You're a ninja?" I tried.

Jacob stared at me in total silence.

"Wanna watch Netflix? There's this great Korean soap opera—"

"I want my candy," said Jacob.

"Candy. Sure," I said. "Let's get some candy."

In the kitchen, I climbed onto the counter, reached up to the highest cabinet, and took down a plastic pumpkin candy holder. I sifted past chocolate-covered caramel bars and fluorescent lollipops and plucked out the minibox of raisins, the dried-apple chips, and the rice cakes. I handed them down to Jacob.

"Mmm. Enjoy that," I said.

I snatched a caramel chocolate nut bar from the plastic pumpkin, and closed the cabinet door.

"Babysitter tax," I told him with a wink.

Jacob stared down at the healthy snacks, which would never be mistaken for candy.

"Sorry, dude. I'm under very specific instructions not to give you the good stuff."

"I wan' all of it," he said.

"And I'd like world peace and a free trip to Camp Miskatonic," I said.

Leaving Jacob to his smorgasbord of gluten-free, sugar-free, and joy-free treats, I plopped down onto the couch again and checked my Instagram. Deanna had posted pictures of her and the Princess Pack getting ready for Jesper's party. Her description read "Party of the Year 2Nite with My Squad. #PrincessPackForLife," followed by fifteen celebratory emojis.

I received a text from Tammy:

Tammy:
Cannot believe UR bailing!

Me:
So sorry. Wish I was with you.

Tammy:

Gonna brave it on my own.

Me:

U R?!

Tammy:

Wish me luck!

Just as I was writing "luck," Jacob swiped my phone from my hand and ran to the bathroom.

"Jacob, give that back!" I yelled, chasing after him.

Jacob held my phone over the toilet. "I want my candy or I'm going to . . . ," he threatened.

"Fine!" I said, holding my hands out, careful not to spook him into dropping it.

"Anna ice cream," he added, glaring. His sticky fingers gripped my most prized possession.

"Your mom said no ice cr—"

Jacob flushed the toilet and lowered my phone toward the swirling water.

I screamed, swallowed my pride, and led him directly to the kitchen.

Three bowls of mint chocolate chip ice cream and five handfuls of real-deal Halloween candy later, Jacob slid my phone back to me. He continued feasting on his sugary booty.

"Don't tell your mom, okay?" I warned him. "And

41

slow down. You just ate a Starburst and M&M's in one bite. Yuck."

He sat back in his chair, doughy legs kicking happily over the edge of his seat. With a chocolate smudge-beard around his chubby cheeks and a look of utter satisfaction, Jacob patted his tummy and smiled at me.

"Thank you," he burbled.

A goober of chocolate plopped off the end of his chin. I handed him a napkin, but he thrust out his mucky cheek for me to wipe. Disgusted, I smushed the napkin over his face. He made a happy sound. I have to admit, it was pretty cute.

Maybe me and the loaf are going to get along fine.

"TAG!" he screamed. He jumped off the chair and slapped me on the back really hard.

Panting, he ran in circles around the kitchen and then chased me into the living room, taunting me to tag him back. He death rolled over the couch and then scrambled into the dining room, but not before knocking over a lamp that looked like it cost more than my house. I dove and caught it an inch before it hit the ground. When I ran into the dining room, I saw that Jacob had jumped onto the table and was wagging his butt in the air.

I was no longer dealing with a child. I was dealing with a runaway rocket.

"Jacob, get down."

"Piggyback!"

"Uh, no."

His head bobbed dangerously close to the chandelier hanging above the oak dining-room table. He shook his rump and sang, "Twerk it!"

I've never liked that expression, and I *really* didn't like it when Baby Jacob used it.

I lunged for the little loaf, but he jumped out of the way. I slipped and hit my ribs on the table, knocking the wind out of myself.

"Ow!" I said, gasping for air.

"Ha-ha!" he said.

Just get through the night, I thought as he went into full tornado mode. *Collect your fifty bucks, and you never have to see Baby Jacob again.*

"Piggyback!" he cried out, jumping onto my back.

"No!" I said. "I . . . have a bad back."

Total lie.

"Piggyback, pleeeeeeeease?" He pouted.

"Look, I'm just not a piggyback kinda person, okay?"

He paused, made his supersad face, and then decided to throw his toys at me.

After thirty minutes of deflecting Legos and G.I. Joes, I finally wore Jacob out. He collapsed onto the couch in a fit of satisfied giggles and nuzzled into the big cushions. I encouraged him to go to sleep by gently patting his head. *Works for cats.*

I kept a safe distance to avoid getting sweated on,

43

and turned on the television.

Careful not to stir the creature, I reached into my pocket and checked my phone. There was a ton of missed texts from Tammy:

Tammy:

> Party is lame. Ur not missing anything. Just the time of ur life ;)

> Miss you! Wish you were here. Please come. Address is 1603 Whitmore.

> OMG. Victor sighting!!! Your prince has arrived.

> Dressed as a pirate!!! ARR!

Tammy sent me a selfie of her making a funny face, with Victor talking to his friends in the background. He looked dreamy, even at an odd angle. Everyone in the picture was having the time of their lives on the coolest night of the year, and here I was, sitting on a couch with a doughy little troll.

It's finally happened, I thought. *My inevitable spiral into social obscurity. I've officially entered the black hole of babysitting.*

Jacob gently leaned his head onto my lap and closed

his eyes. His head was warm and cozy, like a hot-water bottle.

"You *are* kinda cute, little loaf," I said.

I brushed a strand of hair from his face and smiled down at him. Then I noticed the line of drool spilling out of the corner of his mouth, pooling onto my favorite jeans. *So gross!* I didn't want to wake him, but I had to get him off me—ASAP—so I slid my arms from under him and lifted him off the couch. I was surprised by how light he was.

Halfway to his bedroom, Jacob woke up in my arms.

"No!" Jacob begged. "No bed."

He wiggled to the floor and planted his feet on the ground in the hallway.

"Jacob. It's past your bedtime, and if you stay up any longer, I'm going to have a nervous breakdown."

Jacob looked down the long corridor leading to his room.

"I can't go to bed. Not without Liz here. Please . . ."

My phone vibrated in my pocket. I knew it was Tammy with more updates about the party, but I didn't dare check in case Jacob's sticky fingers swiped my phone again. He mumbled about the dark and swore he heard scratching under his bed. Monsters. I put on my best adult-sounding voice and explained to him that there are no such things as monsters.

"There's nothing to be afraid of, Jake," I said.

Boy, was I wrong.

Jacob stepped out of the bathroom. "Peed but I didn't poop."

"Thanks for sharing," I said.

Tammy:

WHERE R U!?? CALL ME! I HAVE TO SPILL!

I really wanted to know what Tammy had to tell me that was so urgent, but I had to put the little loaf to bed first.

That's the beauty of this job, I reminded myself. *Just put him to sleep, and you will be free and clear for the rest of the night.*

As we walked down the corridor toward his room, he

reached up and grabbed my hand. It was a sweet gesture, like we were about to cross a busy street together, except *gross.*

"You go first," he whispered.

In the darkness, his once overbearingly bright and poppy-colored room was gray and dim. The whites of his toys' big wide eyes stared back at me.

I groped for the light, but I couldn't find it. My blood rushed. Strange shadows crawled along the walls. My fingers finally found the switch, and I slapped it on.

The colorful toys were back to normal. I stood there a moment, surprised by how anxious I had gotten in the darkness. Jacob was rubbing off on me.

"It's okay, buddy," I said.

Jacob's little head peered around the doorframe.

"Did you check under the bed?"

I sighed. I knelt down to shine the bright bluish glow of my flashlight app across the empty, dusty space under his bed. There was a broken action figure covered in dust, its arms outstretched, as if it were a baby that wanted to be picked up. Creepy, but no monsters.

"Aaaaah!" I screamed.

Jacob cowered behind the doorframe.

"I see someone's dirty undies!" I laughed.

"Not funny," Jacob insisted. "Did you check the windows?"

Outside, a heavy fog was settling over the white

elms and well-groomed bushes. The window latches were locked. I pulled the curtains closed. "Nothing out there," I said.

"And the closet?" he said quietly, pointing.

Gimme a break. I walked to the closet and swung the door open.

"Empty."

Jacob nodded and slumped into uneasy relaxation. I patted the bed, and he jumped onto it.

"Bedtime story!"

"A quick one," I said, grabbing a book about an old lady and a sea turtle from a pile of picture books.

"Not that one!" Jacob shouted.

Horrific drawings spilled out of the book, fluttering onto the floor. They were jagged, scratchy crayon scribbles of disgusting creatures.

Jacob avoided my eyes and whispered, "I have scary dreams."

He pointed to a picture he had drawn of a human-sized rat. "Sometimes he comes out of my closet," he said.

Next, he pointed to a giant spider lurking over a stick figure family. "He lives in the trees . . . and they . . ."

I saw a drawing of four roly-poly things with long claws and wicked smiles on their beaks hiding under a bed.

"They live under my bed."

Lastly, he pointed to a drawing of a tall, slender man with a bald head and hooves for feet.

"And he comes to my window when I'm asleep."

The tall man in the drawing was wearing a black suit with long coattails, and his eyes were yellow. I'd seen this man before. Maybe it was on TV or online. I lingered on the drawing, and a chill rose up my spine.

"I used to have nightmares about a monster like this," I said, not meaning to say it aloud.

"You did?" Jacob's desperate eyes sent goose bumps across my forearms.

I nodded slowly. The memory of me waking and telling my mom about a tall man with goat legs played like a murky movie in my mind. I was crying. And I was Jacob's age.

News flash, Kelly. Kids have nightmares, and so did you.

I picked up the drawings and slipped them back in the picture book.

"But it wasn't real, Jacob," I said. "And do you know why? Because there are no such things as monsters."

"Yes. There are."

The ocean wind howled outside of the windows, and the lights in the room flickered.

"There's gargoyles and goblins and vampires and alligators that live in the sewers, and giant rats. And . . . broccoli."

Jacob's voice lowered into a foreboding tone. *"Broccoli is the worst."*

"Nice try," I said. "But they're just nightmares, little

loaf. They can't hurt you."

"Mine can."

Jacob pulled his knees close to his chest. He stared at the wall and then hid his haunted face. "I can make my nightmares come true."

Riiiiiight.

"Well, when I get scared . . . ," I said, trying to sound chipper. "I mean, when I *used* to get scared—I don't get scared anymore because I'm a grown-up—I would bring a teddy bear to bed."

I rummaged through a stack of discarded toys and held them up for his selection. Tank? No. Star Wars anything? No. Stuffed purple octopus? Nope. *Sheesh, this kid had a lot of toys.*

At the bottom of the pile, wedged between a toy chest and the wall, a brown teddy bear stared up at me.

Yes! Kids love teddy bears. Well done, Kelly. You are so getting the hang of this.

I took the teddy by the arm and liberated it from the bottom of the pile. The lower half of its fur had been burned off. Its legs were melted black nubs. Charred white stuffing bloomed from its side, and one of its plastic eyeballs had melted down its furry face, like wax dripping off a dying candle. Repulsed, I dropped it and stepped away.

"Dude! What is wrong with you?" I blurted out.

Jacob sighed heavily and wrapped his arms around

his shins. "I dreamed Teddy was on fire." He lowered his face to his knees, hiding his eyes. His voice was quiet and sad.

"When I woke up . . . he was burning."

Icicles slid down my back. This was way out of my league. I snatched the happiest-looking picture book in the pile.

"*Zambrini's Circus of Fantastic Fleas*! Yay, happy story!"

Jacob looked unsure as I sat on the edge of the bed and opened the book.

"Promise you won't leave me?" he asked.

"Yeah, totally."

"And hope to die?"

Even though his shining emerald-colored eyes were freaking me out, I nodded.

Bzzt. Bzzt.

"And that's how Miss Kensington's Fantastic Cake Shop was saved by a fifty-foot soufflé and an orphan named Sally."

Bzzt. Bzzt.

"The end."

I quietly closed the book as my phone rattled in my pocket. So many incredible things were happening out there that Tammy had to keep texting me every thirty seconds while I was trapped in here reading picture books just to get Jacob to doze off.

I slowly slid out from under Jacob's head and slipped off the bed, careful not to disturb him.

Victory! I reached for my phone.

"No. No," he whispered.

Beneath his eyelids, his eyeballs darted back and forth, like two beetles trapped under a napkin.

I dropped my phone back into my pocket.

"Hey, Jacob. You're having a nightmare, buddy," I said, gently approaching him.

"Dead . . . dead . . ."

I froze.

"The lighthouse is dead," he gasped. His arms thrashed under his sheets. His pillow was soaked.

"Jacob, wake up–"

The rattling windows flung open. A chilling blast of wind blew a blizzard of Jacob's drawings around the room as I lunged for the windows and locked them. A waft of seaweed and the stink of murky tide pools lingered in the air, as if the garbageman had just driven past.

Jacob's eyes remained shut.

Like the last leaf clinging to an October tree, a single piece of paper drifted down and settled beside Jacob as he twisted on the bed.

It was his drawing of the man with hooves for feet. The thick smudge-line smile on the tall man's face seemed to be leering right at me.

"No . . . ," Jacob mumbled in his sleep. "Not him."

My skill set is much better suited to bagging groceries at Foodtime, I thought.

Bzzt! Bzzt!

"It's okay, it's okay," I said, my eyes on the curtained windows.

I rubbed the sleeping pork pie's back, and he sank into his pillow. I cautioned a look out of the window. The street was dark and empty. The wind shook the bushes under Jacob's windowsill.

Bzzt! Bzzt!

I hate to admit it, but checking my phone makes me very happy. Some textasy was exactly what I needed at that moment.

I crept away, turned on Jacob's Iron Man night-light, and left the bedroom with the door open a crack; enough to let the warm light and soft sounds of the rest of the house inside.

I tiptoed into the living room and called Tammy.

"Tell me everything," I whispered into my phone.

"Why are you whispering?" Tammy shouted over the sound of music and laughing. "This party is awesome—obviously! Everyone is here!"

Everyone but me.

"Kell, there are high school kids here. High school! And one was like 'Hey, Frosh,' and I was like 'Yuck!' But he was wicked hot, not gonna lie."

"LIZ!" came the scream from Jacob's room.

Great. My source of pure joy and happiness was awake and screaming for his other babysitter.

"I gotta go, Tam."

"No, wait—I gotta tell you about Victor—"

"I gotta go!" I was already halfway down the hall when I saw that the door to Jacob's room had been shut.

I kicked it open. "Jacob!"

I gently peeled the covers away from his face. "You do realize my name's Kelly."

"Where were you?" he asked. "You promised."

A wet blanket of guilt weighed on my chest. He pulled his feet from the edge of the bed.

"Something's down there," he whispered.

"It's probably mice, Jake. Mice aren't that bad. They can't hurt you unless you're made of cheese. Are you made of cheese?"

He pointed across the room to the Iron Man night-light.

"They turned off the night-light," he said.

I cocked my head at the dark night-light bulb.

"Okay, buddy. Joke's over."

I snapped the night-light back on. A circle of golden light beamed onto the wall.

"Liz is the only one who knows how to stop them from getting into the house. Her number's on the fridge. Call her!"

"Okay," I said. "But you have to promise you'll stay here and try to go back to sleep."

He nodded emphatically.

"Deal." Maybe Liz knew some kind of lullaby or some secret handshake to calm him down.

I walked to the door and looked back at him. "Close your eyes."

He showed me that his eyes were closed.

"Head on pillow."

He rigidly placed his head on the pillow.

"Hurry, please," he whispered.

The fridge was plastered with magnetic frames filled with photographs of the Zellman family, all beaming from various destinations around the world. I riffled through lists of emergency numbers, notes, and take-out menus until I noticed a single business card among the papers.

LIZ LERUE
PROFESSIONAL BABYSITTER
(401) 555-4687
LizLeRue13@gmail.com

Who called themselves a *professional* babysitter?

Luckily, I got her voice mail.

"This is Liz LeRue, babysitter," said a serious voice.

"I'm sorry I can't get to the phone right now." I had an image of Liz as a stocky fifty-year-old linebacker and ex-nun, with gray hair, Reef sandals, and black socks pulled up to her knees. "If this is an emergency and you need to get a hold of me, please dial 912. But that number is for emergencies *only*."

Why would a babysitter need an emergency line?

"Hi, Liz LeRue? Sorry to bother you—I'm sure you're out with your friends at a cool party or something—"

KNOCK. KNOCK.

"Sorry, no candy!" I called out to the front door and then turned back to the phone. "This is Kelly Ferguson, I'm babysitting Jacob Zellman."

I paced around the house as I left the message. "Uh, and he would like to talk to you—"

I heard giggling from the living room. It sounded like Jacob. *Has that little squirt been playing games with me the whole time?* But when I walked into the living room, it was empty. I thought I heard raspy breathing, small and hurried, behind the couch. I remembered I was still leaving a voice mail.

"Uh. If you could please call me back, my number's—"

KNOCK. KNOCK.

This time the knocking was louder, demanding.

BANG. BANG.

The front door shook and bucked violently.

SCRATCH, SCRATCH, SCRATCH.

Maybe it was a squirrel. Or a rat. Please don't let it be a rat.

I dropped my phone as the banging crawled up the front door and clomped across the roof. I listened, frozen as heavy footsteps thundered overhead. My heart quickened and throbbed in my throat. The thumping stopped at the back of the house.

Above Jacob's room.

Silence filled the house. A shadow crossed over the warm glow of Jacob's night-light, and it clicked off.

"KELLY!" cried Jacob.

When I worked at Mulligan Pizza and Golf, part of my job was throwing out the trash into the dirty, dented green Dumpster that was home to a thousand moldy pepperoni slices and dozens of dead rats. Gallons of bleach had to be poured on top in an attempt to cover up the putrid smell. That acidic stench of bleach-soaked garbage as it roasted in the hot summer sun is what Jacob's room smelled like.

I gagged, eyes adjusting to the dark. Three small lumpy piles of rags and trash bags hunched on top of Jacob's bed. Their angry eyes beamed from slits made in their dirty plastic wrappings. Each fiend had a large beak and tiny leathery talons that held down Jacob's arms and legs. I froze in horror.

The tattered creatures stood two feet high, with round, fat bellies that hung low enough to touch the floor. Crudely made tools that looked like hammers and sickles clinked from belts made of soda can six-pack rings.

One of them produced a small crystal bottle and poured glittering green dust into Jacob's mouth as they all grumbled happy gibberish. Jacob tried to wrench himself from their grip, but his eyes grew slack. He yawned against his will and then went limp.

The creatures pulled a large burlap sack over him, like they were stuffing a ham into a pillowcase.

"Shoo! Get away from him!" I shouted.

Their heads snapped in my direction. Jacob was unconscious, knocked out from whatever stuff they had poured into his mouth. They cinched the burlap sack shut with a red ribbon, and hissed at me with rabid force. My stomach surged with electric terror.

This is happening. This is real.

Their little claws lifted the sack with Jacob inside over their heads and then dropped it onto the floor with a heavy thump.

"No!" I managed to scream as I lunged toward them. That's when I heard the growling from behind me, and I realized there were more than *three* terrors in the room. The fourth nasty sprang out from the toy pile like a cannonball. It bashed me aside and somersaulted into the others, knocking them aside like bowling pins.

Its buddies snarled and slapped it.

The four terrors dove into a small opening, wide enough for a child, cut out from the floor underneath Jacob's bed. A tunnel stretched down into the darkness.

"Weeee-aaah!" the little monsters howled.

"NO!"

I lunged, grabbing the top of the burlap bag. They pulled back in a toddler version of tug-of-war.

"You will not! I won't let you—" I commanded.

Jagged claws shot out and scratched me. "Ow!"

I instinctively let go and held my bleeding hand. The beasties and the sack with Jacob still in it vanished down into the darkness.

WHAM! The circle of wood flooring was shoved back into its original place, followed by hammering from below. A gooey, gloppy-like substance oozed up through the cracks and melted into the wood. In an instant, the ragged edges of the opening were gone, and the wooden boards looked like they had never been touched.

I pounded on the floor, but it didn't budge.

"No, no, no. Jacob, you are not gone. No. No!"

The sound of claws scuttled beneath the floorboards. The terrors' victorious gibberish grew distant as I tried to follow the sound. . . .

Across the room. *Thumpa-thumpa.*

Into the living room. *Thumpa-thumpa.*

Out of the back door. *Thumpa-thumpa.*

I scrambled on my hands and knees, following the sounds outside to the backyard, where I crawled across the cold grass. As their ghoulish noises grew fainter and fainter, I ran in the direction it sounded like they were heading, down a set of rickety wooden stairs that led to the rocky beach below and beyond that, the black Narragansett Bay.

I scanned the shoreline to see if they popped out from anywhere. Nothing. Just waves sloshing against the rocky sand.

Jacob was gone.

"This can't be happening," I told myself as I wandered back toward the house. "I did not just see four little trolls, dressed in tattered plastic, steal the little loaf."

No, my bleeding hand was proof something terrible had happened. This was all my fault. He tried to warn me.

But really, who pays attention to a five-year-old who is scared of the dark?

How was I going to explain this to his parents? To the police? How would I explain this to the thousands of news crews that were going to surround the house in an hour, or to the warden at the insane asylum they were going to send me to?

And, I know this is going to sound selfish but, *was I still going to get paid*?

As I walked back to the house, I noticed a nearby bed of flowers had been trampled. I stepped closer to investigate. Muddy clumps had been stamped into the ground.

Hoofprints?

I followed them around the perimeter of the house, all the way to a spot underneath one of Jacob's windows.

A gnashing engine roared toward the house, startling me.

The lone headlight of a moped shined onto the driveway.

A boot slammed down the noisy red motorbike's kickstand. A girl's silhouette slid off the saddle, pulled off her helmet, and strode toward the porch. I ducked back into the house and peered out of the window to get a better, safer look.

"Open up, Ferguson." The girl banged on the front door. "OPEN UP!"

"Who are you?" I asked.

She slammed her business card against the window.

LIZ LERUE
PROFESSIONAL BABYSITTER
(401) 555-4687
LizLeRue13@gmail.com

A set of big dark eyes locked on me from under a tussle of choppy, blue-and-black hair that looked like the girl had cut it herself. Her nose was small, dotted with freckles. A tiny diamond stud winked on her left nostril. She was older than me—by at least a couple of years—and she looked like she belonged in detention for punching someone in the stomach.

"You're Liz? The babysitter?"

"*Professional* babysitter," she said. "You called. Open up."

I unlocked the front door, and she rushed inside. That was when I noticed she had something lumpy tied to the front of her: a BabyBjörn. Inside of it was what looked to be a happy ten-month-old baby, its chubby little legs dangling from the saddle.

"You're Liz?" Stupid question, I know, but I just wanted to confirm. I'd had enough strange visitors tonight.

"Yeah," Liz grunted.

The baby giggled. Liz shoved her scuffed-up helmet in my arms and stalked through the house. She was wearing an Eastman backpack covered with graffiti, punk band buttons, and air force patches over her shoulders, the straps pulled tight.

"How did you—"

"You left me a very long voice mail," she said. "Heard every word you screamed."

"My phone!"

I patted my pockets. Gone.

Life was over. Probably so was poor Jacob's. My mom would be fired for sure. My dream of Camp Miskatonic definitely squashed.

I followed Liz down the hallway into Jacob's room, where she threw her backpack onto the bed and knelt down to inspect the dusty space beneath it. She gently cradled the baby's head to make sure it didn't bump against the floor. She sniffed the air.

"Toadies," she grumbled.

Liz ran her fingers over the wood. She knocked. It made a hollow sound. Liz let out an angry sigh and glared up at me. She unzipped her backpack. I thought she was going to dump out books or science home-work, but instead, the inside of the bag was filled with an amulet, two baby bottles filled with formula, a long loop of wire, an antique brass tube engraved with a dragon breathing fire, a high-powered microphone and headphones, a collapsible cattle prod, and who knows what else.

"Weapons. Sure," I muttered. "Because that's exactly what I carry around in my backpack. Right next to my Lunchables and Spanish II workbook."

Liz put on her headphones and plugged them into the high-powered microphone. Like a doctor listening for a heartbeat, she held the mic against the wooden floor.

"It sounded like they went that way," I said, pointing toward the backyard.

Liz shot me a "why didn't you say that in the first place" look and sprang to her feet.

"I . . . heard them go toward the back of the house. They went, um, northeast, I think?"

"You think or you *know*?"

"I was outside. The water was in front of me. The sounds vanished to my left and behind me. That's north." I squinted at the coastline. "And if not *totally* north, then definitely northeast."

Liz shoved the mic and headphones into her bag

and removed a UV flashlight.

"We'll catch up to them," she said. "Ditch the lights."

I didn't want to be standing in the dark after what just happened, but when she glowered at me, the stud in her flared nostril winked. Very intimidating.

She shined an eerie, blue light around the room and up onto the wall. Her jaw slackened. Illuminated in the glow and written in large, dripping slime-scrawl were the words:

THE TIME OF NIGHTMARES HAS BEGUN

My stomach filled with a cold, messy spaghetti feeling. I snapped on the lights and looked at Liz to see if she thought this kind of thing was normal. But she was staring off, pale and horrified.

She put her hand out for support, but her knees gave and she sat on the bed.

"What did that?" I asked.

She shook her head with a lost, gutted expression.

"Liz? Miss LeRue?"

Liz blinked and snapped out of her daydream. "What time are the Zellmans coming home?" she asked.

"One," I said.

She swung her backpack over her shoulders and marched out of Jacob's room.

I started to follow her when I saw the picture of the slender, creepy man Jacob had drawn. I snatched it, shoving it into my pocket.

We sped toward the front door. "What's a Toadie?" I asked. "Whose baby is that? Is it your baby? I'm not judging if it is."

"This is Carmella. I'm babysitting her," Liz said, never breaking stride.

"Uh. Okay. Those things . . . ?"

"Trash Toadies. Of the genus *Trollium,* subphylum Monsters."

I stopped so fast my sneakers squeaked across the marble.

"Like bad-guys-who-sell-drugs-to-kids monsters?"

"Like monsters-who-live-in-the-shadows-and-eat-you-in-one-bite monsters," she snorted, and growled under her breath. "I told them not to go out tonight. . . . I *told* them. . . ." She looked at her digital watch. "I have four hours and eleven minutes to find this kid. Thanks for nothing."

"I should come with. Jacob's my responsibility."

"Then why weren't you watching him?"

The sleeve of my sweater frayed in my mouth as I chewed on it. Something glowed on the floor under the couch.

"My phone!" I rejoiced, scooping it up.

I lovingly wiped it and checked for scratches. I was still leaving a voice mail to Liz. I hung up, dialed 9-1–

Liz's hand snatched my wrist. With a flick, my phone popped out of my grip and sailed into her other hand.

I blinked. Phone-fu?

"No cops," Liz snarled.

"The police are, like, our only option," I yelled.

"*I'm* our option," she said, stalking through to the kitchen. "We'll spend three hours explaining what happened, and they will not believe us. No one really will. Unless you've seen it with your own eyes. By the time we yak to the authorities, those Toadies could be all the way to Boston. We gotta move now."

She glanced at the bowl smeared with ice cream and candy bits that Jacob had devoured. "You're an idiot," said Liz. "You gave a kid like Jacob, a kid with *the Gift*, that much candy?"

"Gift?" I asked.

"Look. Just stay here; chew your hair; play with your phone; and if the Zellmans call, act like everything's normal. Can you handle that, rookie? Good girl."

She stepped outside, tossed my phone at me, and slammed the door in my face.

Wind rushed into my eyes, and tears welled up. Either Liz was insane or I was insane or . . .

This is real, Kelly.

I swallowed, wiped my eyes, and stared at the front door.

I was free. A professional was going to handle it.

I can call Tammy, and maybe even meet her at—

I stopped. Took a breath.

I lost him. I lost a kid. I have to get him back.

I twisted open the lock and chased after Liz.

"Excuse me," I called out, striding onto the driveway with my shoulders back in my best impersonation of my mom's power pose. "I'm not an idiot." I defiantly held her gaze, bracing myself under her stare. "My GPA is three point nine. And I'm on the school newspaper, which means I know how to, like, look for stuff. My algebra teacher says I'm a quick learner. And . . ."

"Hooray for you," Liz said, rolling her eyes.

She snuck up on a neighbor's antique Jaguar; looked left, right; grabbed the hood ornament; and twisted it off. I was about to tell her that it was very rude, not to mention against the law, to destroy other people's property, but her eyebrows were angrily fused together in a determined scowl, and I did not want her to punch me in the nose.

"Look. I've seen quick learners like you die as quick as you learn. You either get eaten, mauled, possessed, cursed, boiled, or turned into a toad."

"Sounds like a fun Friday night," I said, hoping to sound tough even though my insides were Jell-O. She grunted and got onto her clunky wanna-be motorcycle. "Wait!" I exclaimed. "There are prints below one of Jacob's windows. You've gotta see them. Come look!"

She narrowed her eyes. "You got one minute, noob," she said.

I ran to the spot underneath Jacob's window. Liz hopped after me, protecting the baby like a football.

I pointed at the muddy hoofprints in the broken bushes. "These don't match the claws those Toadie things had, and–" I said, trying to remember the night's events. "And . . . if the troll things came from below the ground, why did it sound like something was also on the roof? That means a different thingy–uh, monster–was here."

Liz swallowed a ragged breath.

"They match the ones in the room," she said quietly.

"I know!" I exclaimed, and unfolded Jacob's drawing. I shoved Jacob's crayon scribbles of the tall, terrifying man in her face. "And—and—" I stammered. "Jacob said this man was watching him from his window— It could be him. The thing that took him."

Liz glanced at the hideous drawing.

"No. No way . . . ," I heard her mutter, gently touching Carmella's head.

"What? Do you know this thing?"

She shook her head and ran back to her moped. Baby Carmella started to cry. Liz expertly removed a bottle from her pack and silenced her with it.

"Look," I said. "My mom works for Mrs. Zellman, which means she will get seriously fired, and my family cannot afford that right now. And . . ."

The words choked in my throat. I wanted to say it wasn't my fault, but I was the one who put Jacob in bed. I was the one who couldn't save him from the Toadies. Like it or not, I had to get Jacob back, and this odd, blue-haired girl seemed to know what she was doing.

"That little kid's life is in danger, and it's my fault. I'm helping you get him back," I said.

"Okay, *CSI: Rhode Island*," she said, throwing me a candy-apple-red helmet. "It's your funeral."

11

The moped rocketed out of Mercy Springs. "Where are we going?" I screamed.

"Backpack. Front pocket," Liz called out over her shoulder.

Clinging to my seat with one hand, I carefully unzipped the front pocket of her pack. I found a red spiral-bound notebook with a cracked, faded cover. Its edges were peeling over from years of use, and the pages were covered in ink splatters (at least I hope it was ink). A piece of duct tape and a rubber band kept it from falling apart.

"A BABYSITTER'S GUIDE TO MONSTER HUNTING" was scrawled on the front. The pages were crammed with drawings and facts about ghouls and creatures and

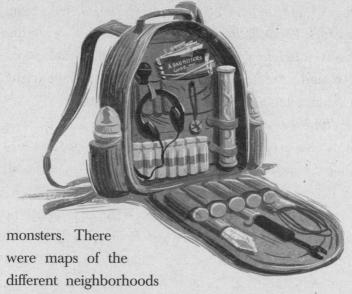

monsters. There
were maps of the
different neighborhoods
in Rhode Island. A few printed-out, blurry pictures of
ghoulish faces were stapled to the pages with Hates high-
pitched noises, hastily written underneath Caution: Third claw
venomous.

"Look under *M* for 'Mercy Springs,'" Liz said, swerving through the streets.

I struggled to hang on while flipping to the color-
coded tab labeled "M." Liz might not have had the best
social skills in the world, but she certainly knew how to
organize a notebook.

Under "Mercy Springs," I found a Google Maps
printout taped to the page. Red lines were drawn over
the map, with the occasional huge red circle.

"That's how they get around with no one seeing

them," Liz said. "Like ants. Playgrounds. Ice cream parlors. Kindergartens. And bedrooms, always under bedrooms. They've been building a whole tunnel system under the neighborhood for years. We keep trying to shut them down. They keep digging more."

"Oh" was all I could say.

It's not every day you learn monsters are real and running around under the bedrooms in your neighborhood.

I flipped through the guide. There were elaborate tracings and markings of Toadie tunnels throughout Mercy Springs. A few of the circles had *X*s through them. The wind was blurring my vision, making it hard to see. I squinted at the map. A large red circle was drawn over

the corner of Vanderbilt and Sasqanet Lanes. I looked up and saw we were passing Sasqanet Lane.

"Right here!" I blurted out. Liz swung the moped, squeezing the brakes. The back of the bike whipped around so hard I was flung into the air.

OOMF! OW!

I smashed into some bushes and skidded onto the grass, face-first, still clutching the red notebook.

Liz's boot flipped down the kickstand as she shut off the engine. I spit grass and groaned, like I had been punched in the stomach by a truck. Carmella kicked and whined. Liz pulled a squeaking giraffe teether out of her pack and popped it into Baby Carmella's mouth, expertly drawing her away from the edge of frustration and back to calmness.

We were in a moonlit, eerily quiet playground with a giant plastic pirate ship–jungle gym thing in the center. Liz stepped over me and walked up to the rubber safety mats. "This is the next stop along the Toadies' main route," she said, now holding a bottle for Carmella to chug. "Since they're lugging a forty-pound kid, we're probably right in front of them."

I nodded absently, too engrossed in the pages of the babysitter's guide.

"'Toadies love shiny objects and collect any trinket they can get their claws on,'" I read out loud while Liz poked the ground under a swing set. "'Toadies savor the taste of trash. Stinkier the better.' *What is this?*"

Liz called back over her shoulder, "The guide is a collection of thousands of years' worth of monster-hunting wisdom passed down through the Order of the Babysitters."

Either someone was pulling the world's greatest prank and had gone to great, detailed lengths just to film my surprised face or . . .

Or I was holding something more powerful and amazing than anything I had ever seen.

By the plastic pirate ship slide, Liz peeled back a rubber mat to reveal a circle of fresh dirt that looked like it had been dug up and replanted.

"Found it!" she crowed. "Tricky little buggers. They put one right at the end of the slide so when a little kid comes shooting down—*WHOOSH!* Right into their trap. It's been pretty mellow, though, since the neighborhood put in these stupid rubber safety mats. They thought they were protecting their kids from falling off the jungle gym when actually they were covering up a much bigger threat. Oh, the irony."

"So. These—these things—they're Toadies?" I asked.

She took a deep breath, tired of my questions. "Check the guide. Under *T.*"

From Liz LeRue's copy of
A Babysitter's Guide to Monster Hunting

NAME: Toadie
(toe-DEE)
HEIGHT: 2'—2 1/2'
WEIGHT: 50—100 lbs
TYPE: Troll Level 3
ORIGIN: Marshlands of the northeast. Some believe neighborhood dump.

LIKES: Garbage! Shiny objects THE SMELL OF NEWBORNS
DISLIKES: Daylight
STRENGTHS: Sharp claws, mouthful of daggerlike teeth, always travel in packs
WEAKNESSES: Intelligence (not much upstairs)
SMELL: Acidic whiff of garbage as it roasts in a Dumpster in the hot summer sun, plus bleach GAG WORTHY
SIGHTINGS: Playgrounds, ice creams parlors, kindergartens, bed-rooms—anyplace they can access through their tunnel system
ALLIES: Toadies are subservient to larger monsters such as Goraxes or Neeches.

My mind spun. As a young woman of thirteen, I pride myself on getting straight As in science and math. Equations make sense. Sure, when I was a kid, I believed magical, scary things lived in the woods and under rocks, but I also believed Santa's big butt slid down the chimney every year. I never actually saw them. I just believed. Then I went to school. I studied, got good grades, and I forgot all about the unseen mysteries and the monsters.

Apparently, they had not forgotten about me.

12

Liz sprinkled baby powder on the dirt patch and uncoiled a long wire to form a snare. It looked like something animal control would use to collar a rabid dog.

"What are you doing?" I shuddered.

Liz unhooked her BabyBjörn and laid Baby Carmella on a fluffy pink blanket on top of the dirt patch, just out of reach of the snare.

"Check the guide."

BEWARE! TOADIES LOVE THE SMELL OF
NEWBORNS. CANNOT RESIST A TASTE.

Liz kissed Carmella's forehead. "It's okay, honey," she said in a sweet voice.

Then she ran into the bushes and waited anxiously, wire in hand, as tiny Carmella suckled on her milk bottle.

"One of them pops out looking for a snack– ZIP! Got 'em!" Liz said with a wicked smile on her face. "Then we'll force it to give Jacob back."

Liz was using the baby as bait? *Not* logical! I moved to grab Carmella, but Liz yanked me back down by the arm. Hard.

"Not my first rodeo, Red."

I watched poor, helpless Baby Carmella's feet wiggle in her thick, woolly socks while Liz jammed her microphone into the ground and listened with her headphones.

The merry-go-round, pushed by the cold wind, slowly creaked in circles, making a rusty shriek.

"How do you know all this stuff?" I whispered, gnawing on the end of my sleeve so hard, it threatened to unravel.

"I'm a babysitter. It's what I do." Liz cracked open a fluorescent green can of Monster energy drink and downed it in a few heaving gulps. She never took her eyes away from the baby.

"I mean like . . . is every sitter like you?"

"Like what? A butt-kickin' UFC warrior?" She crushed the can in her fist.

"A deranged psychopath," I said.

Liz smirked. "Most people go their whole lives

having no idea what kind of cosmic horrors lurk in the shadows. But the horrors are out there." She nodded. "That's where we come in. We protect kids so they can grow up and change the world. We protect children from monsters."

"Like a secret society?"

"Yep."

"Holy cowbells. I was joking. That's a thing?"

"Most sitters are just regular kids trying to earn a buck," she whispered. "But if you're lucky—or unlucky—enough to encounter a monster and live through it . . . that's when you'll find the real sitters. Or we'll find you . . ."

I laughed nervously.

"The Art of Babysitting has been passed down through the ages, going as far back as . . . well, the ages," said Liz.

Cold mud soaked through the knees of my jeans, but I was too amazed to wipe it off.

"I mean, someone had to protect King Arthur when he was a baby. If a dragon ate Baby Arthur, there would be no Camelot. No Camelot, no Great Britain. Throughout history, babysitters have been the guardians of good. Y'know, like the Knights of the Round Table. Or Navy SEALs. But for kids.

"Just like a babysitter protected Baby Abe Lincoln, Baby Martin Luther King Jr., and Baby Obama, it's our duty to watch over the Baby Jacobs of the world. Babysitters make sure kids get through the night safe and sound, so they can grow up and change the world for the better."

All of a sudden, I realized just how very unqualified I was to be in this situation. I was just looking to make enough money to ride horses next summer. The last thing I wanted was to join some Almighty Order of the Chosen Sitter Clan.

"Don't worry. You won't be asked to join," Liz said.

Even though my heart was doing an impression of a jackrabbit, what Liz did sounded really brave and insane and fascinating. The only other time I'd felt this mix of curiosity and wonder was when I first heard about Camp Miskatonic.

"She's a really cute baby, by the way," I whispered.

Liz nodded. It was the first thing we'd agreed on all night.

"I always thought babies screamed and cried all the time." I tried continuing the small talk to work out my nervous energy, but Liz tensed and touched her headphones.

"They're coming!" she whispered.

I gulped and leaned close, trying to hear what she was listening to: static-filled warbling, the chilling sound of grumbling, scrapping, digging, sniffing.

The patch of ground sprinkled with baby powder

trembled. I tried to swallow, but my tightening throat refused.

"When I say, you run and grab Carmella," Liz said, planting her boot heels firmly into the ground. She looked like a prize fisherman.

I ducked into a runner's crouch as the muddy patch bulged from below. Blood throbbed in my jugular vein, making everything brighter and sharper.

A webbed Toadie talon shot up from the ground.

Wearing cracked safety goggles, a Toadie peered up from inside its little tunnel, shaking the sand from its garbage bag–covered head. It wiped the dirt from its glasses.

I felt like I was going to faint. Liz narrowed her eyes and wrapped the wire around her gloved fist. Carmella started to cry and roll around on the ground. I went to run, but Liz grabbed my arm.

"Wait for my signal," she hissed.

The Toadie sniffed the night air with its sharp beak. Its breath made the trash bag covering its face undulate in and out.

"Gerba derrrrrr," Goggles said in a hungry tone.

"Der, der?" called the other Toadies below him.

I could hear what sounded like five or six Toadies happily jumping and panting inside the tunnel. Goggles was yanked down, and another Toadie–this one with a snagglefang poking out of its mask–planted its webbed talons on the edges of the tunnel. It pulled its pudgy frame up out of the hole, like an acrobat.

Carmella was only two feet away from the creature. The long fang curled under the Toadie's smile. I imagined that snaggletooth sinking into Carmella, and before I knew it, I had jumped to my feet and was charging for the child.

"NOT YET, IDIOT!" screamed Liz.

I raced forward. *They're going to eat the baby. They're going to eat me. Don't let them eat her. Don't let them eat me. Will Victor speak at my funeral?*

Y'know, real life-affirming stuff that your brain thinks is superimportant when you need to be totally focused on the task at hand. Thanks, brain.

Without stopping, I reached down, scooped up Carmella, cradled her in my arms, and kept sprinting. Snaggle the Toadie hissed and clawed as it chased after me.

The swing set wasn't something I was planning on running into, but these things happen.

I fell, protecting Carmella, as if she were a golden egg. I slammed onto the rubber safety flooring and twisted around, almost breaking a rib.

OOOF!

Snaggle lunged at us, arms spread, twisted mouth wide open in hungry victory. I closed my eyes and held Carmella close to my chest.

*Z*ZZZZWIP!
    The lasso closed around Snaggle's feet, snapping them together. The Toadie slammed to the ground but still scrambled toward me. Liz reeled in the creature, and it turned on her with the speed of a rattlesnake.

Liz booted Snaggle in its lumpy stomach. It made a gulping, keening wail and somersaulted onto the ground, removing the wire from its feet. The Toadie coiled into attack stance. Liz snapped into her own fighting stance and faced the monster, fists clenched, feet dancing. The Toadie sprang at her, and she unleashed a series of swift kicks and hard-core punches that shocked the Toadie into submission.

I hung back with the baby, watching with growing

admiration as Liz battled the creature. She spun in circles and threw her elbow back, cracking Snaggle in the jaw. She was like a panther mixed with a ballerina.

"Whoa," I said, bouncing Carmella in my arms. "You're good."

Liz smirked—like "Of course I am"—and then climbed onto the highest part of the jungle gym and did a flying elbow drop onto Snaggle. I almost felt bad for the poor thing.

Bzzt! Bzzt! My phone had fallen out of my pocket and way too close to the Toadie tunnel. "It's Jacob's mom!" I announced fearfully.

Liz pulled the Toadie into a vicious headlock.

"Don't answer it!" she yelled as the monster wiggled in her grasp.

"She'll get suspicious if I don't."

I juggled Carmella in my left arm while reaching for my phone with my right. The tops of three Toadie heads bobbled in their hole, waiting to snap at me. Keeping Carmella close, I grabbed my phone away from the gaping black hole.

"Mrs. Zellman?" I tried to sound normal, but my voice cracked. The sound of the company Halloween party boomed behind her. My mother and father were at that party, completely unaware I had totally destroyed all of our futures.

"Kelly? Is everything all right?" Mrs. Zellman's voice

was sharp with concern.

I watched Liz slam Snaggle headfirst into the asphalt. It made a whimpering grunt.

"Yep! Everything's great," I said, bobbing Carmella up and down in my arms. "Jacob's, uh, already asleep."

"Well, that's a first," marveled Mrs. Zellman.

"Oh, it is a night of firsts, that's for sure," I said, resisting the urge to say more.

Liz howled as she hog-tied the Toadie's arms and feet together.

"What's that sound?" Mrs. Zellman barked.

"TV?" I sounded like a confused contestant on *Jeopardy!*

Carmella squirmed in my arms. I struggled to keep my concentration while I kept an eye on the dark Toadie tunnel.

"Sweet dreams, garbage breath," Liz snarled, dragging the Toadie toward her moped.

"Sounds like a scary movie," Mrs. Zellman said. "Check the list, Kelly. No scary movies."

"No. It's a fun movie. It's fun!"

"Fran, Phil—great to see you, darling. Thank you for coming," Mrs. Zellman crooned away from the phone. "See you at one. Call if there are any problems," she snapped at me. "And turn off that movie."

"Done and done!" I said, and hung up with a deep exhale.

Liz stuffed the snaggletoothed Toadie into a thick, canvas mailbag and removed a small crystal bottle with a batch of glowing green liquid inside from her pack. The container looked exactly like the junk the Toadies had poured into Jacob's mouth.

"What is that stuff?"

"Grit of the Sandman," she said, uncapping the vial. "Nicked it off a not-so-nice tooth fairy a year ago. A few grains knock you out for an hour."

Liz squeezed an eyedropperful of the powder into the canvas bag. The shifting Toadie sneezed, shook its head, and fell silent.

"Comes in handy when you need a monster to shut up. Or a hyper kid to go to sleep."

She zipped the canvas bag tight, clipping a small lock on the end, and swung it over her shoulder and marched to the edge of the Toadie tunnel. I cautiously stepped farther back, clutching Carmella.

"Hey, down there, you trash-eating creeps," she growled into the hole. "We got your friend. You want him back, give us Jacob."

Sounds of conspiring and raspy arguments between Snaggle's buddies chattered down below.

"Mmmph!" came a muted cry.

"Jacob? That you, buddy?" Liz called out.

"MMMPHEE!" replied Jacob from the depths of the earth.

"JACOB!" I called out.

I wanted to jump down there and grab him, but I knew that would be like diving into a blender on high speed.

"Sorry your rookie sitter got you into this, buddy," Liz said, shooting me a look. "But I'm going to get you out of it."

The Toadies laughed and giggled. It made something inside of me really angry. How *dare* they steal that kid and laugh about it? He was probably freezing and was going to have even more terrible nightmares.

Liz removed the Jaguar hood ornament from her pack and waved it over the tunnel.

"Nice sparkly. You like sparkly," taunted Liz. "Trade? Yes?"

"Aaah. Parklee," they gurgled.

I looked at Liz. Maybe this crazy person wasn't as crazy as I thought.

A final raspy bark ended the muffled Toadie argument. "Ferda-flug!" The hole quickly filled up with dirt. Their clawed feet thumped underground as they raced off, dragging Jacob behind them.

"Where are they going? Where's Jacob?" I asked Liz.

Liz opened her mouth to speak, but nothing came out. This was clearly not part of her plan.

"We have to go after them!" I said, handing her Carmella and dropping to my knees.

93

I started digging up the tunnel. Liz grabbed my shoulder. "Stop it." I didn't listen. "Fine. Keep digging if you want your hand bitten off," she said as she slipped little Carmella into her BabyBjörn. I paused.

"No one's ever gone down to the tunnels and come back alive," she said, angrily tearing off her gloves. "I knew you'd screw this up."

"So did I!" I exclaimed. "I've never done this before! Jacob's gone, and I'm going to go to jail, my mom's going to get fired, and . . ."

Liz clenched her fist. "Stop freaking out." She breathed deeply, closing her eyes and repeating, "There's always a way."

"So what's the way? How are we going to find Jacob?"

"This cretin"—Liz kicked the lumpy canvas sack bulging with the Toadie trapped inside—"is going to lead us right to him."

We sped west toward Carmella's house with our captured creature tied to the side of the moped. I shuddered each time the canvas sack bumped against my leg. It felt like a pillowcase full of eels as we made our way up to a large house on the hillside. Liz cut the engine and flipped down the kickstand.

"Where'd you learn to fight like that?" I asked.

Liz tossed me the guide.

"Section five, page ninety-six," she said, carrying Carmella toward the house.

In the guide, I saw charts of elaborate kung-fu moves titled Whispering Nanny, Rock the Cradle, and the Nap Time Headlock.

"Can you teach me how to do these?" I asked.

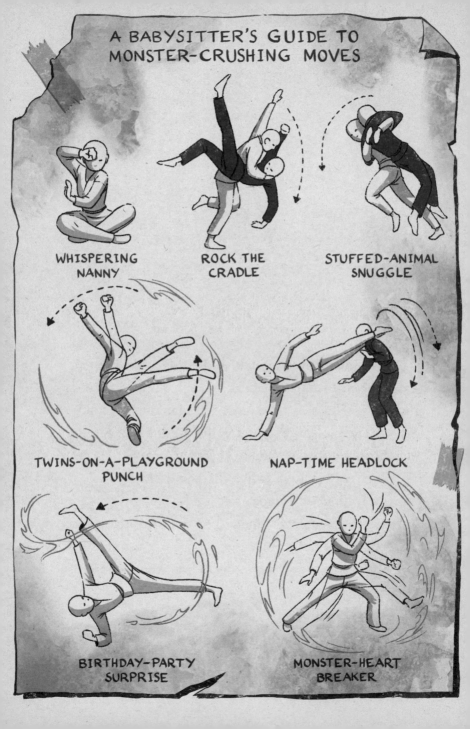

If I was going to dance with monsters, I wanted to have the right moves. Besides, I took ballet classes when I was three and totally confused every position. Then again, I was three.

"Those moves take years of training," she said over her shoulder.

"I'm a quick study," I reminded her. This was true about things in books. Things IRL might be stretching the truth. At the front door, Liz stopped.

"This ain't the SATs, Quick Study. Just wait here," she said, nodding at the canvas bag. "And make sure *that* doesn't get away."

Liz entered the front door, cradling Baby Carmella. I kept a watchful eye on the burlap sack. I imagined Snaggle coiled inside, pretending to sleep, waiting for me to poke it so it could snap my fingers into its mouth.

I looked in the guide at a diagram of a girl doing a high-flying punch.

I stood just like the picture, and then I swung my fist. I lost my balance, slipped onto the ground, and caught a faceful of grass.

Smooth, Kelly. Real smooth.

My phone vibrated in my pocket. It was Tammy again.

"Are you okay? Why haven't you picked up your phone?"

"Tammy! This has been the craziest night. I'm with

this girl, this babysitter named Liz, we caught this thing and . . ."

Since I was five, I had always slept over Tammy's house. We'd watch movies and eat endless bowls of popcorn and talk until three in the morning about things we didn't understand, like where heaven was, and why boys were so weird and yet so cool. She had this great SpongeBob sleeping bag that I would hop around in and do my best impression of the little yellow guy. Then she would yawn, and I would yawn too. I slept the soundest whenever I was at Tammy's house.

At that moment, I wanted nothing more than to curl up in her SpongeBob SquarePants sleeping bag, zip the top over my head, and sleep until I forgot this night ever happened. I looked up at the second-story window to see Liz gently dressing Baby Carmella for bed.

"I threw up," moaned Tammy.

"What?"

"All over. But I won the pizza-eating contest," she admitted, giggling and burping.

"I'm sorry to hear that, Tam, but listen to me—"

"I threw up in the back of my mom's car, too. Not good."

I laughed for a moment, imagining Tammy's uptight mother freaking out at all the puke covering her car seats.

"Seriously, though. I might need you to come and get me," I whispered.

"I'm in bed, Kell." Her voice sounded sleepy and thick. "I think the pepperoni was bad. It was definitely bad because I've been on the toilet a lot."

"Tam. Gross." While I felt bad for her, she *did* get sick trying to win a stupid pizza-eating contest. "Listen, Tammy—this is very serious."

"I gotta go," Tammy moaned again. I heard the sound of her puking, and then the phone went dead.

My jaw stiffened in frustration. Tammy was my best friend. I was up to my eyeballs in horrific, life-changing stuff. The least she could do was listen to me.

My anger sank into hopelessness. No one was coming to save me.

I was lost in the darkness with just a spiral-bound notebook in my hand and an unconscious troll at my side.

A black car parked in front of the house, and two adults that I guessed were Carmella's parents spilled out of the front seats. Carmella's mother held her high heels in her hand, swinging them around while the father danced the cha-cha around her. They didn't even notice me as they danced into the front doorway and greeted Liz. Liz sounded like a completely different person. Sweet and gentle and kind.

After a moment, Liz hopped down the front stairs,

popping two crisp hundred-dollar bills with a smile.

"Two hundred bucks?" I asked.

"Younger the kid, better the pay." Liz smiled. "Job's a nightmare, but it does have its perks."

Huh, I thought. *Not bad. Only a few nights like tonight, and I'll have enough to go to Camp Miskatonic. As long as I live through tonight.*

Liz sat on her moped, and I got on behind her. "Aren't you worried more monsters will come for Carmella?" I asked.

Liz shook her head. "They've already caught their big fish for the night. Besides, monsters are less likely to attack when a parent is home. Something special about the bond between a parent and child protects them."

The moped careened out of Mercy Springs, across the Blackstone River, past a slushing waterfall, and into the small town of Central Falls. Liz banged her fist on the handlebar and cursed.

"Toadies always trade," she said to herself. "This is worse than I thought."

What Was Happening
While I Was Flipping Out

Skulls with wings; sad-faced cherubs; and weeping, marble angels gathered silently in the graveyard. Slate tombstones leaned under a gnarled thornbush that stretched out like death's bony fingers. Layers of fallen leaves shuddered. The ground bulged. A human skull was thrust up from the ground. A tiny, trash bag–covered arm used the skeleton's head like a puppet.

"Nar, nar, nar," a Toadie said, using its other claw to open and close the head's mouth.

The other Toadies giggled and slapped the skull from its claws. They shoved the heavy burlap sack into its arms and snapped at it.

"Berker dur!" the one with the goggles snarled at its friend. This meant "I am tired of hauling this heavy kid while you mess around. It's your turn to lift him, jerk!"

They rolled the sack onto the graveyard's dead-leaf carpet, Jacob's muffled cry urging from inside. Goggles untied the top of the sack, and Jacob's dazed head poked out of the top, hair frizzed out. The little boy looked up at three vicious trash trolls surrounding him. He tried not to cry, but deep, painful sobs escaped from the lump in his throat.

"I . . . wan' go home." Jacob choked.

"Ah wagga ome. Waaah. Ha, ha, ha!" mocked the Toadies.

Jacob's head withered to the ground in defeat. His hands and feet were tied. The burlap sack scratched his neck like tiny needles. He was tired, and he had a belly-ache from all the candy he'd eaten that night. Candy, Jacob realized, he might never have again. Damp, dewy leaves fluttered under the boy's listless, sad breath.

Thump. Thump.

Through the crooked tombstones, Jacob saw the ebony hooves of his nightmares crunch across the weeds and thorns. A scraggly tail lashed into the air, keeping time with the song its owner was singing.

"'Ring-around-the-rosy. A pocketful of posies . . .'"

The Grand Guignol crossed the cemetery with the happy, upbeat attitude of a creature whose lifelong dream was about to come true.

"'Ashes, ashes. We all fall down,'" he sang, and danced.

Jacob's stomach twisted; his heart nearly stopped. This was the monster he had dreamed about. The pale man at his window. He was real. He was alive. And he was going to do terrible things.

"Ah. It's good to be back!" bellowed the Grand Guignol. He hunched down over Jacob and grinned. "Thanks for conjuring me back into this realm. You really are something."

The tall wretched man stretched his arms and legs like a yoga instructor. "I've been waiting quite some time for this opportunity. Big night ahead. Big night. Gotta limber up."

The Boogeyman bent down to touch his toes, and his pointed tail brushed Jacob's face. Jacob screamed at the top of his lungs, praying someone would hear him.

The three Toadies and the Grand Guignol laughed at Jacob's bloodcurdling cries.

"That's good," said the monstrous man. "Be afraid. Make those nightmares nice and juicy, Jacob. We'll need lots of them."

The Toadies dragged Jacob to the side of a shiny, black carriage helmed by four skeletal horses with black feathers adorning their heads. The Toadies unlocked a cage door at the back of the wagon and hoisted Jacob inside.

"Bergader guk!" said the goggle-wearing Toadie to its master.

"You're mumbling, darling," said the Grand Guignol. "Use your words."

"Bergader guk Snaggle," implored Goggles.

"Babysitters took Snaggle?"

The Grand Guignol's jolly demeanor darkened.

"*Babysitters.* I detest babysitters. With their back-packs and their pigtails and their faces."

"Bergader grabaa!" agreed Goggles.

"You're right, but you don't have to swear so much. This is a family operation. Babysitters have made our kind nearly extinct. They have no respect for beauty or perfection."

He dramatically tossed what little hair he had over his shoulders.

"Snaggle will be missed. But we cannot veer from the plan. Lots to do. So let us observe a moment of silence for the poor Toadie. Annnnd we're done with that."

He hopped onto the carriage, popped a plumed top hat onto his head, and cracked the reins. The ghostly horses galloped forward. Buckles and bridles jingled like wicked bells. With the hooves of the horses charging, the carriage launched into the sky and over the graves of forgotten Union soldiers.

The ground fell away beneath the wheels, and Jacob's stomach dropped into his feet. He wiggled out of the sack and, clutching the cage's bars, he cautioned a look down. Rooftops and treetops sailed past, growing farther and farther away until they were obscured by blankets of misty clouds and dancing snakes of lightning. The phantom carriage streaked across the full moon, trailing the sound of the Boogeyman's laughter.

Jacob stumbled back, wind ripping through the rocking cage. Spit and juice bubbled into his throat. He was going to throw up for sure.

"Yes, indeed. It's going to be a wonderful All Hallows Eve!" cackled the Grand Guignol.

15

Liz drove us past an old farmhouse with a cornfield and a scarecrow standing watch through the raggedy stalks.

"Meet at headquarters," Liz barked into her phone, steering the moped with one hand. "And don't tell Mama Vee." She pocketed her cell and gunned the engine.

"Who's Mama Vee?" I asked, squinting in the stinging wind.

"You don't need to know," said Liz.

I glanced back at the farm. I thought I saw the scarecrow's head turn ever so slightly to watch us go.

"Why did those things take Jacob?" I asked.

"Way I figure it is," Liz said, "if they were going to

eat him, they'd have done that by now."

The thought of Jacob being eaten stabbed at me worse than the cold cutting through my jacket.

"Because of some gift?" I asked.

"Yeah."

"Gift of what, eating ice cream?" I joked.

"The Gift of Dreams," Liz said with a low voice.

"Say what?"

A dark covered bridge swallowed us into its shadowy gullet. Shafts of moonlight flickered through the old wood. Our tires thump-thumped across the boards.

"Jacob can see the future when he sleeps," Liz said over the engine's echoing roar. "Lately, he can even manifest his dreams into reality."

"M-manifest?" I stuttered.

'Some kids are born with supernatural powers. One night this summer Jacob told me he dreamed it was snowing. That night, in the middle of the hottest August on record, it snowed."

"Supernatural powers?" I exclaimed. "Seriously. That's like unicorns or Deanna's nose. It's not real."

I caught Liz's amazed reflection in the rearview mirror on her handlebar. She was serious. That snowy day in August had rocked her world.

Very slowly, trying to accept the meaning of the words, I said, "Little loaf has psychic abilities?"

"Strongest we've ever seen," agreed Liz.

Liz and I ducked down as a flurry of squealing wings swished through our hair, sending icy shivers up my back. Liz cranked the gas, and we shot out of the bridge with a flock of bats arcing into the sky behind us.

I gasped for breath, worried I might topple off the moped.

"What is up with tonight?" I screamed.

"Halloween, man." Liz shook her head. "Freaks come out," Liz said, flicking a fleck of bat guano from her shoulder. "Since his fifth birthday, Jacob's only gotten more powerful. Been meaning to have the talk with his parents, but Mrs. Z. would poop a duck."

My worldview was shifting like quicksand. What Liz was talking about was impossible. But I said the same thing about monsters, and they were now as real to me as the bloody scratch they left on the back of my hand. And if monsters were real, then maybe, just *maybe*, a little boy with supernatural powers was also real.

I thought about the burned teddy bear, the creepy drawings, his nightmares . . . Jacob had been telling me the truth all along.

Black wings scattered into the night sky behind us, and heavy globs of guilt poured into my heart like wet concrete. Jacob wasn't just a hyper kid. He was unique. He was powerful. He could change the world.

And I let him get caught.

* * *

Multiple "Road Ends Here" signs crossed our paths before we approached a marsh where water hushed and gurgled over the rocks. The quick pulse of frog croaks filled the air. Like ruins from another time, there was a broken path hidden among the cattail reeds.

We bumped across the crumbling bridge, tires splashing through a shallow brook. Across the watery path, Liz stopped the moped at a dead end. I was pretty sure we were lost.

Liz held out a pendant on her necklace. It was a small tin flute that looked like it had been handmade, though I have no idea who had hands small enough to make something so delicate. The flute made a bubbly, warbling harmony when Liz played it, like a blue jay's whistle. Leaves rustled around us. Branches coiled back, twisting open to reveal a dirt driveway that led up to a rustic ivy-covered cottage. A series of scientific-looking TV antennae jutted out of its thatched and patched roof.

"Huh?"

"Welcome to the Rhode Island head-quarters for the Order

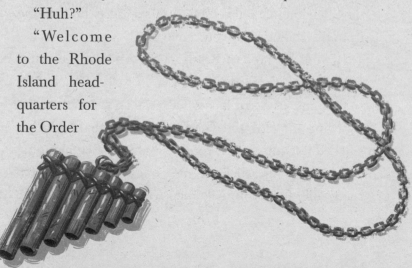

of the Babysitters," Liz said proudly, swerving us up the path and parking the moped at the front door. Three BMX bikes were leaned against the front of the cottage. A weathered stone statue of a lion, its mane covered in moss, stood at attention as Liz approached the door.

"Grab the Toadie," she said, ducking inside.

I hoisted the canvas bag with the Toadie inside of it off the moped's carrier and dragged it along the ground. For something so small, the troll was surprisingly heavy and dense, like a bowling ball.

"Your friends live here?" I asked nervously.

"I don't have friends," Liz said with a sarcastic smile, leaving me to heft the creature inside.

"Wonder why," I mumbled.

Liz twisted a two-pronged key into a double lock. There was a click and snap from inside. The heavy oak door opened to reveal a fanged, skeletal smile leering down at me. I gasped. Liz laughed and walked under the skeleton of a three-headed sea serpent hanging from the ceiling in the entrance hall.

"If you're scared of Bessie, then you better just turn around now, Ferguson," said Liz.

Portraits of stern-faced babysitters seemed to be watching me slog the Toadie down the hall. The air smelled like musky firewood and a hint of cinnamon.

Bag squeaking behind me, I followed Liz past a room full of aquariums loaded with snails and worms.

Beyond that room there was an oval-shaped library with a ladder on a track that circled the haphazard stacks of books of all kinds: used books, library books, books with covers made of bark, books with pages made of velvet, books made of scrolls, books made from pressed butterflies, half-open books, half-eaten books, and books covered in cobwebs.

"Do your parents know you do this?" I huffed.

"Yeah. They're cool." She shrugged. "They know I can handle myself."

That explains it. Whole family's crazy.

Farther into the house, Liz stopped at a large glass window looking into a padded room lined with mechanical dummies and rusty, swinging claw-gauntlets. It looked like gym class for creatures. A girl wearing athletic gear was running across a tightrope stretched over a pool of mud.

Whoa, that girl is good, I thought. *Why does she look so familiar . . . ?*

Liz banged on the window and shouted, "Berna, let's go!"

Oh my GOSH.

Berna vaulted off the final jump in the training room and landed before my totally dumbstruck face. She wiped the sweat off her forehead and adjusted a big pink headband over her thick hair.

"You . . . go to my school," I managed to say.

Berna nodded, plucked a wad of pink gum stuck to the wall, and popped it back into her mouth. "Bernadette. After the saint." She looked me up and down and blew a huge pink bubble. She inhaled it sharply, cracking it, chewing it. "But you can call me Berna or Bern. Kelly, right?"

"Yep. Just Kelly."

She giggled. "Lemme give you a hand, just Kelly."

Berna bent down to help me lift the heavy sack into another room lined with white, discolored tiles, lit by sickly green fluorescent lights. The smell of medicine hung around bizarre instrument panels. Shelves were crammed with all kinds of jarred things pickled in formaldehyde.

In the center of the room, a girl and a boy—who looked to be my age—were hoisting a rusty-looking cage onto a metal slab. They stood around a circle of moonlight that streamed down from the skylight above them. A large lamp sent their shadows arcing across the wall.

The boy pushed his thick glasses up his nose and looked at me with a crooked left eye. The girl with sharp black bangs glared at me and shoved her fists onto her hips. She pinched her entire face into a sour expression.

Cassie and Curtis. The misfit sitters.

"Are you sherioush right now?" Cassie said through her wiry braces.

NAME: Bernadette Vincent
RANK: Babysitter
AGE: 12

NAME: Curtis
RANK: Babysitter
AGE: 13

NAME: Cassie
RANK: Babysitter
AGE: 13

"You know her?" asked Liz.

Cassie made a high-pitched "hmph" through her nose and turned back to the cage. Curtis caught sight of the bag that Berna and I were lugging and his eyes widened.

"What'd you bring me?" he asked.

"Toadie," said Liz.

"You caught one? I can't believe you caught one!" Curtis giggled, and with great excitement rushed up and cradled the bag full of Toadie in his arms. "Come to me, my little Toadie."

"Chill out, Curtis," Liz said sternly. "Cassie, open the cage. Berna, Curtis, open that bag on three. Everyone, watch your fingers."

114

I stood back as Curtis removed the lock from the top of the bag, Berna unzipped it, and Liz helped them dump out the sleeping 'loadie inside the rattling, rusted pen. Berna slammed the cage door shut, and Liz locked it.

"Search it. See if it's carrying anything that can lead us to Jacob."

They snapped on yellow cleaning gloves and went to work.

I finally understood just why they seemed so strange to everyone at our school (including me). They weren't just babysitters.

"You guys . . . You're the monster hunters," I said awestruck.

"Don't you mean weirdosh? Total rando trifecta? Freak show?" lisped Cassie.

I cringed, remembering my shameless attempt to be cool in front of Deanna and the Princess Pack.

"We fight monsters for a living," said Berna. "We hear *everything*."

Liz's eyes bored into me. "You really said that stuff about them?"

"I . . . didn't mean it," I said.

"Then why'd you say it?"

I shifted and bit the inside of my cheek. Why did I say it?

Because I wanted to be cool, I was about to tell them.

115

"It's okay." Berna smiled. "We are weird. 'Specially this one." She nodded toward Curtis, who gave a backward salute. Berna's warm energy made everything feel okay.

"Did you call Mama Vee?" Cassie asked Liz.

"No. I got this," Liz said impatiently.

"Mama Vee'sh chapter president, Lish," Cassie continued. "She should be here."

"Well, in her absence, I'm commanding sitter on duty," Liz snapped. "So we do what I say. And I say I got this. End of discussion. Curtis? You bring it?" Liz asked.

Curtis bolted off and returned carrying a black, stinking bag full of trash. "Fresh from the Dumpster behind Wang's Chinese." He took a huge whiff of the trash bag. "Smells like . . . victory," Curtis crooned.

Berna and Cassie gagged and turned away from him.

"Keep it downwind," Liz said, pointing to the other side of the room.

"Copy that, sir." Curtis nodded and hauled the garbage away.

"And don't call me 'sir,'" Liz groaned.

Chewing gum in deep thought, Berna peered through a magnifying glass and studied the Toadie while Cassie quietly lisped into a microcassette recorder, like she was the host of her own National Geographic show. "Shubject ish roughly two and a half feet tall. . . ."

I leaned over Berna's shoulder. "So, are you guys

like the Order of the Babysitters?"

"Not the whole order," Liz said, shaking her head. "They're just SITs."

"Zits?" I asked.

"Shtupid rubber bandsh get wrapped around my tongue," growled Cassie, tugging at her metal mouth.

Berna laughed. "SITs. Sitters in training. One day we'll graduate to full-time babysitters," she said, like she had just eaten a bowl of sugar. "Then we'll move up to au pairs. Then part-time nannies." She raised her hand higher and higher. "Full-time nannies. Live-in nannies, chapter presidents. And who knows? Maybe even chief child minders and then maybe one of us will be Queen governess!"

"Wow," I said. "You love babysitting."

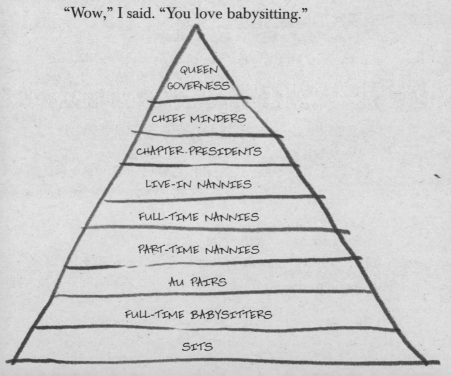

QUEEN GOVERNESS

CHIEF MINDERS

CHAPTER PRESIDENTS

LIVE-IN NANNIES

FULL-TIME NANNIES

PART-TIME NANNIES

AU PAIRS

FULL-TIME BABYSITTERS

SITS

"Yeah," she said, and shrugged. "But I hate injustice even more."

Cassie prodded the sleeping Toadie's mouth open with long sticks and searched under its tongue. "So, Lish," Cassie asked. "Why weren't you with Jacob tonight?"

"All the signs pointed to Carmella being taken," Liz mumbled.

"So you losht Jacob?"

"I didn't. *She* did." Liz jerked her thumb at me.

All their eyes shot at me. I smiled sheepishly, like I was posing for a yearbook picture with a giant pimple on my forehead.

"I . . . I'm just trying to save up enough money to go to camp," I muttered.

This was totally the wrong thing to say.

"Total soup sandwich, man," Curtis said, shaking his head.

Cassie snorted and smiled, as if she knew all along I was a terrible person, and my stupid remark had just confirmed it.

"Oooh, Lish," Cassie chuckled, wiping spittle from her lower lip. "You're going to get kicked out of the order for shure."

Liz's hand coiled into a fist.

"Liz, don't—" Berna started to say before Liz tackled Cassie to the floor.

"Stand down, sir!" Curtis kept shouting.

Cassie cowered in the corner and defiantly straightened her bangs, mumbling something about rules and regulations and fines under her breath.

Berna saw my jolted expression and smiled. "They do this all the time," she said with a wink. "You got hardware?"

I made a confused noise and shook my head.

"New girl needs hardware." Curtis saluted Liz. "Permission to leave the lab, sir? I mean, ma'am?"

Liz nodded. Curtis grabbed my wrist and pulled me into the hallway. He twisted the head of a statue of Joan of Arc, and the sound of gears gnashing and turning thumped from deep inside of the house. A wall across from us shook and then slowly slid down into the floor, leading to a dark, hidden staircase.

"Ladies first!" Curtis beamed.

I looked at him strangely. "You first," I said.

He clucked and jumped inside.

We descended the stairs into a room full of frightening weaponry. Ivory saws, the Grim Reaper's sickle, iron spears, a pitchfork with one bent prong, and a grappling hook attached to a chain.

Curtis grabbed a backpack from the top shelf and tossed it to me.

"Let's get you started," he squawked.

A BABYSITTER'S ARSENAL

NAME: Silver daggers
DESCRIPTION: Ancient daggers with green jewels embedded in the hilt
GOOD AGAINST: Werewolves
WEAK AGAINST: Boogeymen, Shadow Monsters

NAME: Grit of the Sandman
DESCRIPTION: Great sleeping powder—a few grains knock you out for an hour
GOOD AGAINST: Annoying Kids (sparingly), Toadies
WEAK AGAINST: Anything larger than six feet tall

NAME: Chimera Dragon Breath
DESCRIPTION: A brass tube that releases a spinning ball of explosive purple sparks. Smells like sulfur
GOOD AGAINST: Big monsters and some Boogeymen. USE IN EMERGENCIES ONLY!
WEAK AGAINST: The Grand Guignol

NAME: Angel Fire
DESCRIPTION: Flammable blue powder. Creates a supercool vortex.
GOOD AGAINST: ~~Grand Guignol~~ READ THE ENTRY ON GRAND GUIGNOL.
WEAK AGAINST: Shadow Monsters

16

Curtis snatched a fuzzy teddy bear from a shelf and carefully handed it to me.

"It's actually a grenade," Curtis said, grinning. "You pull this ear, throw, and–booyah! Frag city! Scorched earth, baby!"

Curtis mimicked pulling the teddy bear's ear, hurling it, and then ducking from an enormous mushroom cloud. I held the teddy away from me and slowly, gently set it back on the shelf with its other plush, flammable friends.

"We paint one ear red so we don't get it mixed up with a kid's real teddy bear," Curtis said, wandering down a row of shelves filled with jars of baby food, diapers, and toys. "We make our weapons look like kid stuff so parents don't freak out if they look in our packs and see a bunch of monster-hunting gear."

He held up a colorful tube of finger paint.

"Chupacabra venom. Highly acidic."

Curtis squeezed a glistening emerald drop onto the floor. The goo sizzled through the concrete, eating a large hole in the floor. *Definitely not finger paint.* I swallowed and moved away from the hissing puddle.

With growing excitement, Curtis grabbed an algebra textbook. He opened it, showing me that the pages had been neatly cut out in order to hold four twelve-bladed Chinese throwing stars.

"Fwing! Fwing!" Curtis pretended to hurl the stars at an unseen monster. "Splat! Glooooop, gloop, gloop." He made a gesture like blood was gushing from the middle of his forehead.

"Parents really let you look after their kids?" I asked.

"Yeah!" he said, shaking his head. "Can you believe it?"

I laughed and realized that though I had gone to kindergarten with this crazy kid, I had never actually *spoken* to him. Yeah, he was really weird, but he didn't hide it. Curtis was one of the good guys.

Liz darted into the room and saw the burned mark in the floor.

"This stuff is way too advanced for her, Critter," Liz said to Curtis.

"I can handle it," I shot back. I grabbed a long jousty-looking thing from a rack, and the entire row of weapons smashed to the ground.

"I'll pick that up," I said, cringing.

Liz growled, grabbed my hand, and slapped a flashlight into my palm.

"Is it some kind of laser?" I asked, aiming the bulb away from my face.

"It's a revolutionary piece of technology that helps you see in the dark," Liz said, shoving Curtis and me out of the weapons room. "Don't hurt yourself." Liz smiled.

I saw Liz slyly pluck something from the shelf that looked like a tiny, white metallic disk. She shoved it into her pocket and slammed the door behind her.

We crossed the hallway of looming, ever-watchful portraits of babysitters from the 1700s and went back into the laboratory, where Berna and Cassie were hunched over the snoring Toadie, carefully cutting open its trash bag outfit with a scissors.

"Stand over there and play the quiet game," Liz said to me.

I stood in the corner, hating myself. *This is all my fault. I lost Jacob.* I had to find him. I remembered the folded paper in my pocket. I fished it out and unfolded

Jacob's drawing of the scary, tall man.

"Have you guys ever seen a monster that looks like this?" I asked them.

Berna squinted at Jacob's hideous, scratchy drawing of the man's hooves.

"Could be a Minotaur, but they like warmer climates. And we're too far north for the Jersey Devil. Check the guide."

"Check the guide!" they all called out in unison.

Berna opened her backpack and tossed me her green spiral-bound notebook covered in unicorns and smiling sun stickers. "A Babysitter's Guide to Monster Hunting" looked strange next to all the happy stickers and doodles. I flipped through the notebook's scraps of information on demons, familiars, and witches.

I didn't find a match on the monstrous figure. But . . .

As I looked at Jacob's drawing, that faint memory pulled at the back of my skull.

"When I was a kid," I said absently, "I had a nightmare about a monster that looked exactly like this guy. . . . It felt so real."

"Maybe it was real," Berna said quietly while she snipped away the Toadie's trash bag.

I stiffened, thinking of Jacob's nightmares. No wonder he didn't want to go to sleep. Seeing my childhood nightmare come alive would send me screaming for the nuthouse. I swallowed a fearful gulp and shook the horrific idea out of my head.

His nightmare . . . Jacob's nightmare . . .

What was it about? By the ocean. A lighthouse.

"Jacob was having a bad dream about a lighthouse," I said, trying to piece things together. "A dead lighthouse. If he has this Gift . . . then, I dunno, maybe he was dreaming about where the Toadies were taking him?"

Cassie looked up from the Toadie. She sniffed and wiped her nose with the back of her gloved hand. "That'sh actually a good point," she said.

Liz thought a moment. "There are, like, fifty lighthouses on the coast. Jacob say which one?"

"No, but—"

"So it would be a monumental waste of time to search each one, wouldn't it?" Liz snapped.

"You guys," Berna whispered, signaling us to come look. Berna's prodding tongs lifted the Toadie's arm, showing a small, old leathery bag made from some kind of animal hide, with shiny jewels and bottle caps stitched onto its side. It had been tucked into its armpit, and now it reeked like satanic BO.

126

"Something's inside it." Berna gasped for breath as she fished it from under the Toadie's reptilian arm.

She reached out to unbuckle the bag.

The Toadie's eyeball was staring right at her. Snaggle was wide-awake.

Everyone jumped. Cassie's foot accidentally smashed down on my toes, and I yipped.

Clutching its bejeweled satchel to its chest, the snaggletoothed Toadie hissed at us.

"Trash time," said Liz. "Curtis, you're up."

Curtis wheeled over his glorious, reeking bag of trash, and the Toadie grew very still. Its tiny eyes locked on the black plastic sack full of rotted goodies.

"Nerm, nerm," grumbled Snaggle.

The squashy troll panted and bounced around the cage, stretching his chubby, lizard-skinned claws through the bars, reaching out desperately for the trash. He was starving.

Liz cautiously stepped toward the hungry monster. "And it's all yours if you just tell us where Jacob is," she said calmly.

"JAAAAA-COOOOOB," snarled the Toadie in a raspy, terrifying voice.

While everyone else was focused on the drooling monster, I caught sight of Liz turning her back to the Toadie, removing a piece of gray mystery meat crawling with maggots from the trash. She took out the small, white metallic disk she'd pocketed earlier and squished it into the disgusting flesh, which she then tossed back into the bag of garbage.

"Talk, you miserable troll!" Liz screamed at the Toadie. "Where's Jacob?"

The Toadie snarled angrily and violently shook the cage. In a hunger-fueled rage, its snaggled beak clamped down on the bars. *PING! SNAP!* The metal broke in its spiny maw, and it squirmed out of its prison. It dove through the air, sank its face into the garbage bag, and proceeded to suck down all the greasy, nasty trash.

I screamed and ran into the hallway while the babysitters circled the beast like a group of snake wranglers. I forced myself to step back into the lab. If they weren't running, I wasn't running.

"Get it!" Curtis cried, and rushed forward.

Liz held out her arm and stopped Curtis. She kept her eyes on the feasting troll.

"Wait," she whispered.

With sloppy, wet splashes, the Toadie wildly shook its head, like a puppy gnawing a bone. Fish guts and trash sweat flew in my hair. A carton of old, slimy pad Thai noodles (or were they worms?) slopped into Cassie's braces. She spat and howled, wiping her mouth.

The ill-mannered troll guzzled the last bit of garbage before inhaling the entire black bag, tucked his fancy leather knapsack under his armpit, and leaped across the laboratory, sending a microscope crashing to the ground. We scrambled after Snaggle. Well, *they* scrambled; I mostly made large and important-looking hand gestures while they tried to snare it.

The Toadie sank its sharp talons into the wall. Tiles cracked and broke as Snaggle climbed up and away from us toward the towering skylight overhead.

"Don't let him get away!" screamed Cassie.

Snaggle kicked through the skylight and scaled out of the jagged hole on its clicking nails. Glass shards rained down on us. It stood on the edge of the roof for a moment.

"Runk, runk!" cursed the Toadie as he grunted down at us from the roof.

We ran from the laboratory and down the long hall, and Cassie swung open the back door into the garden. Liz was calmly following after us. Berna pointed to a long, dark hole in the herb garden and a shower of dirt fountaining up from deep inside it.

Gerf, gerf, gerf. The sound of the angry creature digging deeper and deeper underground faded away, along with our hope of finding Jacob.

"You guysh let him get away!" Cassie spat.

"Y'know, Cass," said Liz, coolly removing her phone from her jacket, "you've got a way of making a bad situation feel worse."

Liz tapped on her cell and showed us the pet tracker app she had opened. A tiny blue paw symbol was racing along a map toward the edge of the screen.

"That's what you hid inside the mystery meat," I said.

Liz winked at me. Cassie wiped her lower lip with a dumbfounded expression. Berna watched Liz, quietly impressed.

"Ferguson and me will follow the Toadie," commanded Liz. "You three check the monster hot spots. See what you can find. We'll meet up in an hour."

"Yes, sir—ma'am—Liz." Curtis smiled as he saluted.

Cassie, Berna, and Curtis dashed to grab their BMX bikes by the statue of the stone lion. As Liz pulled on her helmet, Berna grabbed me by the arm and took me aside.

"FYI, working with Liz can be dangerous to your health," she whispered, handing me her business card. "Call me if things get hairy."

I nodded and zipped her card into my puffy green jacket pocket. Black smoke banged from the moped as Liz kicked on her engine.

"She's . . . intense." I nodded to Liz.

"Can't say I blame her," Berna whispered again, keeping her eyes on Liz. "Her mom ran off when she was just a kid. She lives with her dad, but . . . Mama Vee said he's really mean to her. Drinks a lot. So Liz mostly lives here."

"But . . . Liz said her parents were cool with her being in the order."

Berna pursed her lips and shook her head with regret.

Liz's life at home must have been pretty rough for her to lie to me about it. I couldn't imagine not having my mom and dad around. Yes, they had a tendency to smother, but they were always there for me. I watched as Liz checked the tracker with laser focus. If she was sad or living with any kind of heavy pain, her dark exterior hid it very well.

"Let's rock, Ferguson," Liz said, revving the engine. "Moonlight's wasting."

Meanwhile, Things Were Going from Bad to Worse

There was an enchanted connection among the people who lived on Edgehill Avenue. They loved the holidays, but they especially loved Halloween. That night, the street was alive with trick-or-treaters, apple-bobbing contests, homemade haunted houses, and a parade of jack-o'-lanterns. Mothers became far-off fortune-tellers, and fathers transformed into werewolves. So much candy was given out that the air was dusted with sugar, and the breeze tasted sweet. Days after inhaling so much candy, a trick-or-treater could pick his nose, eat it, and swear he was eating a grape-flavored jelly bean.

Among the costumes, floppy clown feet, and marching superhero boots, a pair of hooves and a swishing tail sauntered through the festivities. The Boogeyman went unnoticed in the sea of fantastical trick-or-treaters. A Toadie, wearing a cheap Frankenstein's monster mask and costume it had stolen from a child's closet, waddled at its master's side with eager hunger, clutching a large, empty burlap sack. To the average passerby, the man and troll looked like a father and son out for a Halloween stroll.

"Look at this disgrace," the Grand Guignol said to the Toadie. "All Hallows Eve used to be a night of demons running wild, monsters feasting on the souls of the innocent. Now what is it?"

"Ferger derp." The troll glowered at the crowd of children.

"Precisely, my darling," said the Grand Guignol, waving his hands across the street. "Kids dressed up in things they bought from a bloody pharmacy, begging for candy. *'Oooh, look at me, I'm a comic book hero.'* " He spat and stomped his hoof into the ground. "They've missed the entire point of the holiday. Fear. Horror. The good stuff—I mean, would you *look* at this one."

A little girl dressed as a sparkly angel-ghost skipped happily down the sidewalk. Her big blue eyes stared out from the holes she had cut into a white sheet that had been covered in rhinestones and other fake jewels. She wore a halo made from pipe cleaners. The Grand Guignol took one look at her and threw up his hands in defeat.

"And they say I'm repulsive," he said with a sigh.

The Grand Guignol's wiry tail snaked out and sliced open her candy bag. Luscious treats spilled quietly from the corner of the bag as the oblivious child rushed off to meet her friends. The Toadie swept up the trail of candy and shoved it under its Frankenstein's monster mask. *Gormph, gormph, gormph!*

The Grand Guignol sniffed the air, long scraggily nostril hairs quivering. Following the scent, he removed a brown scroll. His hooves scraped and grinded over the asphalt as he stalked toward the house at the end of the block.

"We've been hunted by those wretched babysitters so long we're almost extinct. I mean, they took poor Snaggle. Curse his heart," said the Grand Guignol as he marched with renewed purpose, Toadie scuttling alongside. "But now that we have Jacob, a child with a gift that comes along once in a thousand years—the ability to turn dreams into reality . . . that's money in the bank!"

He looked around the colorful street. Speakers on a nearby front lawn blasted audiotapes of spooky screaming, clanging castle dungeons, and moaning ghosts. Children's laughter filled the sugary winds.

"At midnight, the world will be crawling with millions of Jacob's Nightmares, and these pathetic humans will know the true meaning of All Hallows Eve."

The Grand Guignol unrolled the cracked-parchment scroll. The names of boys and girls crossed the page along with their addresses. His fingernail scratched out "Jacob" and then poked into another boy's name: "Timothy." The Boogeyman read Timothy's address and rolled up the scroll.

A pair of little girls dressed like fairies skipped past the cloven-hooved man and his strange, small partner. The reek of a dead petting zoo wafted from the Grand Guignol's fly-encircled tail.

"Ewwwwwoooo!" the little girls said.

"If you think I'm scary, you should see the monsters

under my bed," he said to them, raising his eyebrows.

The two girls swallowed and darted away. He sighed with a light pang of loneliness in his heart. Yes, he was a monster, but it also hurt when little girls screamed in his face and ran away when he was just trying to make a joke.

He shook his head and pressed forward. There was much to be done tonight. Emotions could not get in the way. "The nightmares will devour mankind. And finally, after all this time, it'll be Halloween forever," he said in a hushed tone, and slowly hunched down to the Toadie's eye level.

"Goo na, na, na."

The Grand Guignol sneered at his little friend. "Yes. And then maybe my sister will finally speak to me. You didn't have to bring that up," fretted the Boogeyman.

The Toadie apologized. A swift hoof knocked it off its feet. The Grand Guignol's tail shot to his mouth and dabbed a bit of foam from the corners.

The Grand Guignol stretched out his arms and inhaled deeply, savoring the smells of autumn trailing across the neighborhood. He cherished the toxic air pollution, the dead squirrel stuck in a power line, and the salty tears of a woman with a broken heart serving candy to children. But most of all, the Boogeyman savored the scent of a fearful child that wafted from within a house. To him, it was like standing in front of a bakery making fresh bread.

"I do love this time of year," he sang.

The Grand Guignol pinched his coattails, and his nimble hooves danced up the walkway to his final destination: the house at the end of the block. The Toadie bounced after him, singing along with his master's song.

"Here we go 'round the mulberry bush, the mulberry bush . . ."

Knock! Knock!

A mother dressed like a vampire answered the door with a bowl of candy and her third glass of wine. The Grand Guignol and the Toadie smiled at her.

"Ick-o-eeet!" growled the Toadie, thrusting out his empty burlap sack.

"Aren't you cute?" Vampire Mom said, and then looked up and down at the Grand Guignol. "And what a scary daddy," she purred. "Can you guess what I am, Mr. Scary Man?"

"A sad panda?" he replied, already weary of her sunshine smile.

"A vampire, silly! Watch out! Hiss!" she snorted, clawing the air.

The Grand Guignol drummed his fingers on the doorframe and exhaled heavily. Sometimes it was just too easy. "Madame, have you ever met a real vampire?" he said, peering down his skeletal nose at her.

"Can't say I have." She guzzled her drink and then said into the cup, "But if they're single, send 'em my way."

The Boogeyman and his troll stood there, staring blankly at her pathetic snickering. He leaned forward and whispered darkly, "Come midnight you will meet one. And you won't like them one bit. The vampire, however, will love you to pieces, Francine."

Vampire Mom's plastic fangs drooped as her smile slowly dipped. She took a step back.

"How . . . do you know my name?" she asked with a sudden chill.

The Grand Guignol looked over his shoulder at the festive street outside. No one was coming up the path, but they would be soon.

"Puis-je entrer?" he asked, gesturing to the inside of her house.

She nodded, transfixed by his eyes. The Grand Guignol stepped across the threshold, followed by his Toadie sidekick, and onto the well-vacuumed pink shag carpet. His tail gently closed the door and locked it. The Toadie instantly started shoving porcelain dogs, ashtrays, and an heirloom silver tea set into its burlap sack.

"Timothy?" The Grand Guignol's nose twitched as he carefully walked around the house. "We've been shopping for the most frightened children we can find," he called out, savoring every pungent odor of fear in the air like it was a delicious block of old cheese. "And I could smell your fear a mile away. So where are you, Tim? I want us to go on an *adventure*."

Timothy's mother stepped forward in an attempt to stop the tall creature, but he simply waved his hand. Her wide, spellbound eyes locked on the Boogeyman's alluring stare, and her shoulders slumped forward, as if his gaze were a string holding her up. The side of her mouth cracked open, and drool spilled down her chin.

Thump. Thump. Thump. Thump.

The sound of a rapid and frightened heartbeat was like a symphony to the Grand Guignol.

A door handle clicked open. A little boy named Timothy, wearing a pumpkin sweater, peered from his bedroom. Timothy squinted, rubbing sleep out of his eyes.

The tall man with strange legs at the end of the hall was calling and waving to him.

"Timothy! Oh Tim," called the man.

The door handle rattled in the boy's shaking hand. Something short and stocky joined the man. It was holding a large burlap sack with knickknacks clanking inside. The crooked Frankenstein's monster mask slung across its face steamed up from the small thing's hot breath.

The creature's hiss was muffled behind the moist plastic mask.

"Teemozeeeee."

"It's moving again!" I yelled to Liz.

"Where?" she shouted back at me.

I held on tight while gripping Liz's cell phone. The blue dot on the pet tracker app zipped left, right, wound in circles, and then shot off to the left.

"Left down Edgecliff!" I blurted out.

We shot down a busy street filled with pirates and pixies and devils. *HONK! HONK!* Liz swerved the moped through the crowd, barely missing a Dorothy, a Tin Man, a Cowardly Lion, and a Wicked Witch.

"Move it, Toto!" barked Liz, waving her hand for everyone to get out of the way.

"Sorry!" I yelled to the angry mob quickly receding from our view.

"Where now?" Liz said, unfazed.

I checked the tracker. "Looks like it's straight ahead, but there's no road there, so . . ."

Liz fiercely drove the moped off the road and up the sidewalk, and barreled straight for a large hedge.

"HEDGE! HEDGE!" I shouted.

A rush of leaves. Snapping branches. We crashed through the bushes and bumped through backyards, whipped around sandboxes, and ducked under clotheslines. I held on, screaming.

A shocked family rushed to their window to watch us shoot past as Liz smashed through an old wooden fence, launching us off a steep hillside and into the air. I grabbed on to Liz and buried my face in her shoulder.

We slammed down in a burst of sparks. My bones crunched. I bit my tongue hard. Liz skid-stopped the moped, the tires burning a black mark onto the street. She grabbed back her cell phone from my trembling hand and checked it. I touched my stinging tongue to see if it was still there.

"We're here." She smiled.

The pet tracker paw had stopped us in front of a two-level house with white wood paneling. All the lights in the windows were on, and the rumble of hip-hop thrummed from inside.

"Is this where it lives?" I asked. Call me crazy,

but I was expecting the Toadies' hideout to be a little spookier.

"Don't think so," grunted Liz as she parked the moped behind a nearby car.

As we snuck toward the house, I studied the address painted in cheery, red cursive on the mailbox. *Why did I know this address?*

Liz yanked me down below a window, where she was crouching in the dirt behind a thorny rosebush. "You want to give away our position?" she whispered angrily.

She carefully switched her cell phone to video camera mode. She slowly raised it like a periscope to the window.

"You play a lot of Call of Duty, don't you?" I whispered. Liz didn't laugh. I didn't expect her to; at this point, I was just trying to amuse myself.

Now that we were closer to the house, the music was louder. There was roaring laughter and the sound of a stereo blasting inside. The *thump-thump* of the bass radiated through the walls.

At least the Toadies have good taste in music, I thought.

Liz checked the video she had just recorded. She looked confused.

"What is it?" I asked. "Some kind of Toadie rave?"

"You sure you read the tracker right?" Liz said.

"You saw it for yourself," I said. "Toadie's right here. Why, what's wrong?"

She tossed me her phone. The video showed a living room cluttered with Coke cans and pizza boxes and a couch packed with boys jumping up and down while kids danced in the background. Not exactly the den of monsters I expected.

Then I recognized one of the boys.

"Jesper?" I exclaimed.

"Shhh!" said Liz.

"This is Jesper's house," I said.

"Well, the tracker says the Toadie's right here. So we have to check it out," said Liz as she waddled low around the house to get a better view from another window.

I froze with a sudden realization.

Victor might be here.

I looked down at my clothes. My puffy green jacket was caked with trash juice, leaves were stuck in my frizzed-out hair, my sneakers were soggy, and the knees on my jeans were soaked with mud.

Suddenly, I wasn't afraid of monsters. I was afraid of being seen by my crush, covered in dirt and sweat, with some deranged blue-haired teenager. Liz was already at the kitchen window, poking her head up to have a look inside.

"You don't understand," I said, crouching behind Liz. "Jesper goes to my school. Everyone here goes to my school."

"I care," she said flatly. Then she perked up and asked, "Are his parents home?"

"No," I said, realizing with horror. "That's why he's having a party."

A kid alone is a kid in danger.

I gnawed on the cuff of my brown sweater while Liz slipped around the back of the house and began to open the screen door.

"Wait!" I begged, closing the door. "Look. There's a ninety to a hundred percent chance my crush might be in there, and I'm covered in dirt and leaves, and I wore this exact same stupid brown sweater to school today."

I gave Liz my best "I know you understand this"

look. She crossed her arms and hawked a loogie.

"You're not one of those annoying wanna-be popular types are you?" she asked, wiping her chin.

"No. Actually, I'm an Invisible," I said, stepping away from her gross spittle. "Y'know." I shrugged. "I don't stand out, no one notices me. Invisible."

"You willingly call yourself that?" she asked.

I was about to answer yes when I stopped. I had never actually called myself an Invisible *out loud*. It felt awful.

"That is sad," she said, pushing past me.

I can't say I didn't agree with her.

Liz pointed to a large princess play set in the dark corner of the backyard. "What do you make of that?"

"Jesper has weird taste in toys?" I guessed.

"Or?" she said, circling her hand at me.

"Or he has a little sister," I said, snapping my fingers.

"Bingo," Liz said. "And where there's kids, there's monsters."

Liz boldly walked to the screen door. I followed so closely that I was hiding behind her. Her hand held the doorknob.

"Look, I get it," she said. "You're a huge dork."

"I wouldn't say that."

"You're afraid. It happens. Not to me, but it happens. But if we're going to get through this, you gotta grab your fear by the horns and punch it in the face until you own it."

"I've never punched anything in my life," I said quietly.

"It's easy. Watch."

Liz sprang into the middle of the backyard and snapped into a tense fighting stance. I jumped back, worried she was going to demonstrate how to kill a monster on me. Fists coiled, elbows raised, she hopped from one foot to the other.

"Feet shoulder width apart. Left fist blocks your face, right fist pulls back. Use your whole body to create the power behind the punch. Find your center, step, spin, duck, weave, twist, and KEEEYIII!"

Her arms and legs waved and exploded into a mixture of what I can only guess was jujitsu and kung fu. Her right fist hurled through the air so fast that the zipper on the end of her sleeve *whistled*.

Then she bowed. "That's called the Monster Heart Breaker. Most powerful move a babysitter can do."

A whirl of excitement and curiosity detonated inside me.

Liz laughed. "Kelly, I'm messing with you. It took me three years just to learn the first three steps."

I shrugged her off and spread my feet shoulder width apart, balling up my fists. A vision of Liz doing the punch played in my mind. Sneakers bobbing up and down, like there was a movie in superslow motion. I saw my arms and legs moving in sync with Liz's arms and legs. Suddenly, the night sky brightened, like I was wearing night-vision goggles.

I guess it was the nerves of possibly seeing Victor combined with the horror of losing Jacob, but I felt everything in me wind up, coiling like a rubber band about to snap.

My whole body shot forward with my fist leading the charge. My knuckles crashed into the princess play set.

BOOM, BABY!

The pink kingdom shattered across the lawn.

"Ow!" I cried, holding my fist and rubbing it.

I kissed my swollen, scratched knuckles and saw that Liz's jaw was hanging open in shock at the supreme damage I had done to the play set. She made a confused face and spun around to the party, tightening the straps on her backpack.

I rubbed my hand. What the pasta primavera was going on with me? The mind-moves? The night vision? And that punch? What is up, K-Ferg?

Ignoring the throbbing pain in my hand, I threw back my shoulders, lifted my head up, and marched into the craziest party in eighth-grade history.

19

The dark kitchen walls were streaked with splotches of cupcake frosting and pizza sauce. The trash can was overflowing with soda cans. The sink, clogged by a Barbie doll, was filled with murky water that was dripping onto the floor.

In the jam-packed living room, a gathering of cackling boys stood around a yellow Slip'N Slide covered in what appeared to be olive oil. Jesper Tanaka, wearing ski goggles, a grass skirt, a Hawaiian shirt, and the wild look of a boy from *Lord of the Flies*, ran and dove onto the Slip'N Slide at full speed.

WHOOSH, THUMP!

His buddies gave Jesper's run seven thumbs-up, one thumbs-down. Jesper bowed, slicked oil from his hair, and caught sight of Liz.

"Aloha, Shorty. Aaaaw, yeah," said Jesper in a raspy voice that sounded like he had been screaming at the top of his lungs for the past five hours. He danced up to Liz and removed his ski goggles. I saw the muscles in Liz's jaw flexing in growing anger. I gave Jesper a little hello wave. He stared at me, perplexed at the flushed redhead. "Oh, it's–it's you," he said. "Hey, you."

I sighed. "Hey, you" is code for "Hey, person whose name I don't remember."

Jesper's friends rushed up to his side. I recognized them as the soccer team guys who all sat together in the cafeteria during lunch. Victor's friends. But there was no Victor. I was relieved he wasn't with them, but I was also a little let down. As much as I didn't want to see him, well, *I wanted to see him.*

The boys' eyes were focused intently on us. Liz, specifically. They were clearly in awe of seeing a high schooler in their midst, especially one who looked like her.

"Who are you?" Kent said, flipping his preppy bangs out of his eyes.

"Friend of Kelly's," Liz said, looking through them. Her head was swiveling around the house, scoping for the Toadie.

"Who?" said Kent.

I tried to melt into the shadows, but Liz snatched me

by my brown sweater and pulled me to her side.

"Oh, right. Yeah. Kelly. You go to our school?"

I nodded and died a little on the inside. It was true. I was an Invisible. The thought made me stare down at the scuffs on my sneakers.

"Ooooh. Yeah. Kelly. Hey!" all the boys said in unison, hoping to impress Liz.

"You guys see anything weird tonight?" I managed.

"I saw Jesper's mom's underwear drawer," giggled one of the Soccer Buddies.

"Dude, I told you not to go in there!" Jesper said, shoving the laughing boys.

"Middle schoolers," Liz groaned, and pushed her way beyond them, farther into the darkened house. I followed after her, making sure to keep my distance from Deanna, who was dressed like a really pretty but kind of confusing mix of a devil, a cat, an angel, and a pixie. She was holding court with the Princess Pack and three guys who were all dressed like the Incredible Hulk.

"Great abs trump *everything*," I heard Deanna inform the group. "I mean, it's sad that our society has such a superficial standard of beauty, but it's true." Deanna jabbed her index finger into the palm of her hand to show she really and truly believed this. "Abs are the most important thing in the world; I mean, you guys get it."

Everyone around her nodded in total agreement.

Abs were indeed everything. "Surprise, surprise, bucket of fries!" Deanna purred, turning her full attention on me. "Kelly Ferguson came to a party." She looked me up and down and then cocked her head to the side. "And she's wearing the exact same brown sweater she wore to school," she announced to the cool kids.

"Buh-rave," confirmed one of her pack.

"Yeah, I figured I'd go meta for Halloween and be me," I mumbled.

"But like the bedraggled version?" Deanna laughed. "Are you like one of those survival guys who climbs mountains and drinks their own pee?"

I forced a laugh. Bursts of blinding light erupted around the living room. Kids' camera flashes cast twitching shadows on the wall. The music switched to a crazy-making pop song.

"Aren't you supposed to be babysitting?" Deanna asked.

"Actually, I am," I said, with a little grit in my voice.

"That would explain the general sadness," Deanna said snarkily, waving her hand around me. "So where's your baby?"

Liz came to my side. "Monsters took him," she growled.

"Oh! Two sitters for the price of one." Deanna

chuckled to the Princess Pack. "So you're like a goth-punk-rock-sad-person-at-the-end-of-the-world kind of thing, am I right?"

I saw the veins bulge and throb on the side of Liz's neck. Her fingers coiled into a fist. Having Liz beside me felt like I had an eight-hundred-pound gorilla with me. I stood up a little straighter and smiled at Deanna. Some dark part of me would love to have watched Liz pummel Deanna, but we had work to do.

Liz kept her eyes locked on Deanna as we walked away down a hall kaleidoscoped with shadows. A handwritten "Keep Out" sign was taped on a closed door.

Liz grabbed Jesper, who was following us—specifically Liz. "What's in there?"

Jesper hopped to Liz's side, happy to help. "That is the basement," he said. "The deal with my parents going away is I can have some peeps over as long as I look after my little sister. She's four, but she's super whack," Jesper said, leaning against the wall with his elbow. "Kids. What are you going to do?"

"She have any friends down there?" Liz asked.

"No. Just her bestie, the TV."

I shot Liz a knowing look. She nodded. *A kid alone is a kid in danger.*

We made our way toward the door, but someone

slammed into me, spilling a wave of soda onto my jacket.

"¡*Estúpido!*" Victor said, wiping Dr Pepper off his jeans.

My feet glued to the floor. My knees turned to water.

"Victor!" I shouted louder than I should have.

"¡*Voseo!* Kelly!" Victor exclaimed. He was wearing a black vest and a T-shirt and a fake parrot on his shoulder. He had a curly mustache drawn over his top lip. He was a pirate; a really handsome pirate with a shocked smile on his face.

"*Lo siento.* I did not see you," he said, digging into his pockets for a napkin. He began furiously swiping the napkin across my slime-green jacket. I stopped breathing. I just stood there with a million thoughts rushing through my head.

There may or may not be a goblin devouring your friend's little sister at the moment, but your eyes are so dark and dreamy that I seemed to have lost sight of my objective for coming here.

"Uh. It's okay," I said, waving my hand at my jacket. "My jacket's not only hideous, it's also waterproof."

He looked at me for a confused moment and then laughed. My cheeks burned. I flattened the spirals of red curls leaping from my forehead.

"Ferguson," said Liz, opening up the basement door. "We gotta go."

With a huge, goofy smile on my face, I looked at Liz. "Liz. This is Victor. Vic*tor*," I said, trying to gesture with my face that this was the future love of my life.

"Basement. Now," Liz demanded.

I looked at the stairs and imagined all the horrors happening down there. One of the soccer guys flickered the lights on and off, making a distracting strobe-light effect around the party.

"Everything okay?" Victor asked.

"Oh, yeah!" I sang nervously. "Everything is awesoooome!"

I danced in place and pointed to the ceiling, as if I were raising the roof. Victor's forehead crinkled in confusion. Liz shot me a "what are you doing?" expression. I took a deep breath and steadied myself.

"Be right back," I said, sighing.

Resigned to my fate, I ducked down the dark stairs behind Liz. I wanted to reach out for Victor, like we were saying good-bye in a train station in an old black-and-white movie, but Liz shut the door closed behind us.

"That was my crush!" I whispered. "I totally blew it."

"I've seen worse," said Liz, flicking her hand. "And

by 'worse,' I mean zombies eating people's brains. Now focus."

Liz showed me the pet tracker. "Toadie's here."

As we descended the carpeted stairs, I heard the faint sound of chewing and crunching coming from the depths of the basement.

The chilly, vast basement was decorated like a pink palace. Unicorns dangled from the ceiling. A regiment of Barbie dolls leered at us from their dollhouse.

In the center of the room sat Penny Tanaka, wearing pink striped pajamas and a crooked, broken tiara that had been fixed with duct tape. She was noisily eating a bowl of cereal, lying on a bed of tassel-edged pillows, singing along with *Frozen* for what must have been the zillionth time.

We perched on the last step and looked around at the toys and plastic furniture, tea set and bookshelves.

"Where is it?" I whispered.

"Hiding," she whispered, showing me the tracker. "But it's here."

"Shh!" said little Penny, without looking away from the TV.

"Ohmygosh!" said Liz in a bright, cheerful voice. "We looooove this movie. Can we watch with you, pleeeeease?"

Penny studied us a moment. She nodded with a quick smile.

"Super doo! Thanks. I'm Liz, that's Kelly," said Liz as she sat on a pillow and gestured for me to sit down beside her.

"I'm Penny," said the little girl.

Liz held out her hand, the little girl shook it, and Liz sang along to the movie with giddy glee. She rocked back and forth on the pillow, holding her ankles and keeping time with the song. I glanced down at the tracker and saw the paw dot was right where we were sitting.

The large wooden bookshelf rocked slightly. A book tumbled off the shelf, pages flapping. The hairs on my arms prickled.

A round lump rose under the blue carpet, like a swell in the ocean. It was the Toadie. It had come up from a tunnel under the basement and found itself sealed under the carpet, searching for a way out. I wanted to step on it like a bug, but if it knew where Jacob was, then we needed it alive.

158

The bump in the rug knocked into tea table chairs, tipping them aside. Little teacups and plastic dishes rattled as the table leg was knocked from below.

The bump shook with the distinct, angry, muffled grumble of Snaggle, the Toadie we'd let get away.

I watched in quiet horror as the little monster scuttled toward the laundry room in the far corner of the basement. The Toadie scurried out from under the carpet onto the floor of the laundry room.

Liz leaned over to me and whispered, "Get the Toadie. I'll protect the kid."

"What?!" I tried to whisper but it came out like a shout.

In her most bright and excited voice (with a hint of nerves), Liz chirped, "Hey, Penny! Let's go play upstairs."

"No thanks," replied Penny, eyes glued to the TV.

I stared at the dark laundry room and shook my head back and forth.

No. No way. Nooooo-hooooo way.

"You can do this," Liz whispered.

She nudged me in the ribs, and I stood up. I looked back at Liz and Penny, and a strange sense of protectiveness washed over me. There was a monster in this little girl's basement, and if I didn't do something about it, she might get taken. Just like they took Jacob.

Not again. Not on Kelly Ferguson's watch.

The sickening smell of detergent and bleach greeted me. The air was wet and moldy. The party sounds grew fainter, as if I were walking into a soundproof bunker.

As I quietly stepped past the washer and dryer, my foot kicked a forgotten Baby Laugh A-Lot doll. The toy giggled and rocked back and forth, looking up at me with its giant, egg-white eyes.

Ehee-hee-hee!

I kicked it into the TV room and tried to block its demonic gaze from my mind.

An empty laundry basket rolled across the floor and then stopped at my feet. Sour dread sloshed around in my guts. I saw a pile of dirty clothes next to a closet door at the very back of the laundry room. Suddenly, a red sweater was sucked under the door. My knees locked at the gobbling sound.

I looked around for anything I could use as a weapon. Bleach and soap would sting it, but unless I forced the Toadie to drink a few spoonfuls, I needed something stronger.

The only other thing I found in the laundry room was a toilet plunger. Wooden handle, orange rubber stopper. Not exactly a chain saw.

Crouching down, I held the plunger in my right hand while I slowly reached for the closet handle with my shaking left. I had to time this perfectly.

160

The door joggled open, and I jabbed the plunger into a box of Tide on a shelf. The Toadie wasn't in the closet. I spun around, gripping the plunger like a sword, expecting the Toadie to spring out from behind me. My feet danced in circles as I flailed the plunger in the air.

Other than cleaning products, there was just an old, dark fur coat scattered on the closet floor, covered with pieces of a half-eaten tube sock and a drool-covered sweater. Something was writhing under the fur coat.

I thrust out my plunger to knock it aside, and two large green eyes snapped open from under the coat's woolly folds. An enormous mouth widened, a red sleeve stuck in its silver fangs flapping as it let out a raspy roar.

I made a kind of quiet squeak.

This was no fur coat.

The beast lunged. Snapped the plunger handle off in its mouth.

I slammed the closet door (as if that would make it go away). Hands shaking, I ran. I looked back to see if it was following me. Black mist slowly crawled out from under the door.

CLANG! The washing machine's metal lid flew open. The Toadie popped out, claws full of fresh laundry. It hissed at me. I threw the broken plunger handle at the creep and bolted.

I dove to Liz's and Penny's side. They were watching

161

TV and eating cereal from the box.

"New m-monster," I stuttered, trying to hold back my fear. "New monster. Furry. Black. In. Closet."

I pointed. Liz remained seated, calm and cool in front of Penny. She swung her backpack onto her lap and slowly undid the zipper with the poise and focus of a samurai. The sound of a happy musical number boomed as I kept my wide eyes on the dark laundry room.

A gurgling roar shook the shadows. Inky paws and ethereal tendrils of long fur oozed out from the blackness. The noise of the party and the sound of the TV fell away as we stared at a lumbering, monstrous form. Wisps of dark mist wafted from the creature's fur and pooled into the darkness, camouflaging the four-foot-tall monster among the shadows.

As the mutant bearlike beast stepped into the light, its green eyes snapped shut, and it shrieked, recoiling from the bright room. It slithered back into the darkness.

Penny adjusted the tiara on the top of her head while her mouth made confused puttering noises.

"It's okay, Penny," Liz tried to assure her. "We got this."

Then the power died, the basement went black, and Penny's high-pitched scream pierced my eardrums.

If I had to guess, I would say that the Toadie peed on the fuse box or something because the TV, the music upstairs, and the basement lights all shut down, and we were plunged into pitch blackness. Empowered by the darkness, the monster howled and seemed to grow taller. Long, midnight-black fur floated around the rising creature, as if it were made of a hundred long wigs.

The beast lurched toward us, but Liz scooped Penny under one arm and swung her out of the way. The monster rammed into the TV, creating an explosion of sparks and shattered glass. The creature's head poofed into mist.

Penny blinked in utter disbelief. Her fingers felt for

the sparkly tiara on her head. Her lower lip shook like the first tremors of a five-megaton earthquake. An ear-shattering siren exploded from her mouth. I plugged my ears with my fingers.

"TEEEEE VEEEEE!" Penny wailed.

I heard Snaggle the Toadie scrambling out of the laundry room, up the wall, and into the air-conditioning vent.

"Toadie's getting away!" I called out.

Behind us, spirals of black living smoke re-formed into the Shadow Monster's head. It was growing with each moment it spent in the shadows. I stared at the beast, my legs turning to mush.

WHAM, POOF!

Liz kicked over a bookshelf, slamming it down onto the creature. The Shadow Monster groaned underneath the heavy weight.

Liz hoisted Penny up the stairs like a screaming sack of potatoes. I quickly followed after her. She swung open the door and then spun around and locked her hand on my shoulder. Her arm was really strong. I mean, she must work out *a lot.*

"I'll handle the Toadie. You handle *that*," Liz said, pointing into the semidark basement.

Me? Handle "it"? Exactly how was that going to happen?

With a flutter of pages, Liz tossed her red notebook into my face.

"Check the guide," she said, and swung out of the basement door.

"Liz, wait!!!" I said, scrambling up after her.

Liz poked her face through a crack in the door. "Kelly. Have faith in yourself," she said. "Or die a hideous death. Your choice."

She slammed the door and locked it from the other side. I tugged at the handle, but it stayed shut.

"Liz! While I appreciate what you're trying to do," I called out, banging on the door, "this is not how you treat friends or associates!"

I kicked the door furiously, but the sound was drowned out by the party music on the other side. The darkness crept up the stairs, and I swung around, back pressed against the door. My breath was all jittery, like I had just sucked down a venti-sized iced caramel mocha with an extra shot.

I heard a throaty gurgle and carefully peered down into the basement until my eyes readjusted to the darkness. Near the dead TV, mist was blossoming from the fallen shelf, forming into tufts of floating fur.

Tucking my legs up to my chest to keep from being seen, I huddled against the basement door. The babysitter's guide crinkled in my sweaty palm.

You can do this, Kelly. It's just like algebra. Only not.

I quickly flipped through *A Babysitter's Guide to Monster Hunting*, looking for creepy monsters with bad hairdos. Liz's scratchy writing was hard to read.

"Closet monster, closet monster . . . ," I mumbled to myself, tearing past monster entries.

There were fifty entries under "Closet Monster," but they all looked like fuzzy splotches in the darkness. I opened my book bag and removed the flashlight Liz had given me in the weapons room back at headquarters. Cradling the notebook on my knees, I shined the light onto the pages.

Does your closet monster have a dorsal fin?
   No.
Horns?
   No.
Scales?
   No!
Tentacles?
   No!
Fur?
   Yes!
Long, swirling fur?
   Yes! Yes!
See "Shadow Monster."

Oh, come on! That's all the way under S! I'll be dead by the time I flip to that!

A chilling roar shook the basement. I dared to look

down from my hiding spot. The dark, magical creature had re-formed and was sniffing its woolly nose around the basement, searching for fresh meat.

A hand reached out from the darkness. Fingers grasped my shoulder, and lightning shocked down my spine.

"Kelly?"

Victor was leaning over me. "I heard a crash?" he said.

I shot to my feet so fast that the top of my head smacked into his chin. He lost his balance and stumbled forward. I caught him, and together we fell back, thumping down the steps.

We landed on the basement carpet in a pathetic heap.

"Ow," we groaned.

I heard the basement door slam and the lock click.

"Yeah! Seven minutes in heaven," Jesper crowed from behind the door.

This was followed by "Ooooohs" from the other soccer guys.

Boys are so dumb.

"You okay?" Victor asked, pulling his head out from under my back with a dazed look.

His face was so close to mine that it was blurry and out of focus. His eyes were fuzzy, dark pools. I smelled the Mountain Dew Code Red on his breath, a soda that normally would make my heart feel like it was trying to burst out of my ribs. I had never been this close to any boy before. Things were, like, really warm between us. I am pretty sure this is known as "kissing distance."

Victor quietly laughed and then pulled away, checking me for scrapes or bruises. I wanted to stand on my tiptoes and lean in. But I didn't. I just stood there, holding my freshly bruised ribs.

The chilling sound of a muffled growl brought me back to reality.

Victor saw the thick, ten-foot-tall mound of matted black fur dragging along the basement floor. He screamed, high-pitched. I clamped my hand over his mouth.

"I'll explain later," I said. "But right now, I need you to help me get rid of it."

"MMPPHHMMM?!" Victor asked.

"Quietly," I said, removing my fingers from his warm lips.

"How?" he asked, catching his breath.

Read the guide.

I hurled the creepy Baby Laugh A-Lot toy at the monster. It gulped it down its mouth. If I were playing basketball in gym class, I would have scored major points. I never score points.

The beast's huge paws stepped out from under the hem of the ragged fur train swishing around its body. The muffled laughter of the spine-chilling baby toy giggled in the monster's belly.

Hee-hee-hee-hee-hee!

I really hated that toy.

I kicked a pillow in the monster's face, but it slashed it, feathers raining down on us. The creature batted bits of white fluff from the air, like a puzzled cat.

I grabbed Victor and pulled him into the small space under the foot of the stairs.

"We need to run," he whispered.

I held up my finger for a second as I flicked through the guide. If Liz said I could do this, then I could do this. The answer had to be in the guide.

And it was.

NAME: Shadow Monster, goes by the name Oleg (OH-leg)
HEIGHT: Changes to fit any dark space or closet
WEIGHT: Essentially weightless
TYPE: Closet monster, Class 2 spectral mass
ORIGIN: Mephistopheles (wherever that is)
DISTINGUISHING CHARACTERISTICS: Long, smokelike fur that grows the more you feed it. This explains why your socks always go missing.
LIKES: LOVES the dark
DISLIKES: HATES bright light

STRENGTHS: Can transform, dissolve, and re-form into any shape
WEAKNESSES: Light. Not very strong.
SMELL: Mothballs, like an old sweater in a closet
SIGHTINGS: Neighborhood closets
ALLIES: Grand Guignol

"It hates light!" I said to Victor, like he should have known exactly what I was talking about. DUH! I reached up and flickered the basement light off and on. And . . . nothing happened because the power was dead.

Victor was looking at me like I had two heads. He was about to run when—

The flashlight.

Where the heck was it? It fell when Victor and I tumbled down the stairs. I scanned the basement and saw a puddle of light on the other side of the room.

If (a) Shadow Monster is charging at you at thirty miles an hour and (b) flashlight is over twenty feet across the room, how fast does (c) Kelly have to run in order to grab b before being eaten by a?

Answer: Faster than I've ever run before.

I took a huge breath and launched off the carpet, elbows swinging. The room went bright white, and I saw everything like it was the middle of the day.

MY EYES! IT'S HAPPENING AGAIN!

Rushing for the flashlight, I saw the Shadow Monster turn toward me. I dove into the dollhouse wreckage and snatched the light. I rolled over onto my back and aimed the flashlight upward as a mountain of spiky, smelly fur descended on me.

It threw back its shaggy head and shrieked in a wash of black tendrils. It stumbled, pawing the smoking hole in its shoulder.

A surge of power lifted me to my feet.

I gripped the flashlight in my hand.

"Let there be light!" I said.

I know it's supercheesy, but it felt great to say in the moment.

The Shadow Monster was remarkably fast for something so huge and hairy. Victor jumped out of the way as the beast climbed the basement steps like an escaping octopus.

Flashlight beaming in my grasp, I charged after it.

Floating tendrils slid down the locked basement door, like a runny egg, and squeezed painfully out under the door.

"It's out!" I yelled to Victor.

He looked at me. His face was slack and serious. The pirate's mustache had been smeared across his top lip in a sweaty streak. His fake parrot was gone. He looked scared. Like a kid who had just seen a Mephistophelean Shadow Monster named Oleg for the first time.

I wanted to hug him, but there was work to do. That dark beast was out in the party with kids I went to school with.

I slipped Liz's babysitter's guide into my backpack and zipped it up, tightened my grip on the flashlight, and turned the brass door handle.

Yup. Still locked.

Brushing his damp hair out of his eyes, Victor followed me up the stairs, muttering in Spanish. He was pale and deep within himself, eyes narrowed. His brain was overwhelmed with processing everything.

I knew the feeling.

I gently reached out and touched him on the shoulder. His mumbling stopped.

"You play soccer, right?" I asked.

"Yes," he said.

"So can you kick the door down?" I asked him.

"The door?" he said in return, pointing to it.

"Can you kick it down, please?"

Victor made the sign of the cross and straightened up, as if he were about to run onto the field. His face darkened into what I can only describe as Victor's game time face.

Victor's knee shot up. His pirate boot heel smashed into the door, and we spilled into the pitch-black house party.

"Game time," Victor shouted.

I squinted around the shadowy living room. Glow sticks danced in the dark. Kids didn't care that the power was out; it only added fuel to the fire. They were playing music from their phones. A clash of electronic, country, pop, and hip-hop swirled around us. A line of shaving cream shot across the living room, spraying Melissa Beasely in the hair, covering her curls in thick tufts of foam.

Hee-hee-hee-hee-hee!

The syrupy, sickening laughter of the Baby Laugh A-Lot darted behind a cluster of kids on the couch. I fired the flashlight at it, catching the boys' eyes.

"Get that light outta my face!" threatened a kid dressed like the Grim Reaper.

A dark wind shot past the boy, blasting his hair and his robe aside.

I saw the Shadow Monster zip along the wall, snaking its hairy mass through the party. With the almighty flashlight I charged forward, elbowing past Deanna and the Princess Pack.

"Kelly!" I heard Victor call out to me.

My sneakers hit something slippery on the rug. I whooshed across the Slip'N Slide like a pro surfer.

"Whoaaa-OOOOOH!"

At the end, I tumbled into a somersault and landed on my feet in a wobbly finish. That was when I heard the party roar. Everyone was applauding.

How did I just do that? Where the heck is Liz? She should be seeing this!

"Ten points for Kelly What's-Her-Name!" cackled Jesper.

Camera flashes exploded in my face.

The Shadow Monster scaled the ceiling and scuttled away from the light above the party, its fur hanging down. I saw that Deanna was about to take a selfie.

"Deanna!" I warned.

"Please don't interrupt," she sneered, and then made a kissy face at her phone.

The beast dropped beside her; its shiny, almost aluminum jaws screamed in her face, blasting her hair back.

Deanna went limp and collapsed on the ground just as she took her selfie.

Flash! *THUMP.*

"Deanna, what's wrong?" the Princess Pack asked, looking up from their phones. Deanna's head lolled back and forth as she gurgled. She was going to be okay. Or as okay as she could be.

"Stairs!" Victor shouted, pointing up the stairs.

We bolted into the second-floor hallway. It was dark and empty. My heart whumped in my chest, veins pumping blood.

"That thing is the devil!" Victor said, crossing himself.

"Not exactly," I said. "He's only a class two."

"Class what?" Victor whispered.

I held up my finger and tipped my ear to the shadows. From the dark end of the hall came a muffled, mechanical giggle.

Hee-hee-hee-hee-hee.

Goose pimples rose across my arms. I beamed the flashlight into the darkness. The Shadow Monster screeched, trailing smoke as it vaulted back up onto the ceiling. My light flickered and died. I banged on the handle and toggled the switch off and on.

"Stupid batteries," I grumbled as we stood in the darkness.

The Shadow Monster lunged toward us. I screamed and ducked.

A pale-blue light beamed into the creature's eyes, stopping it in its tracks. Victor stood strong, holding out his phone with the flashlight app turned on. The roar of the party masked the wailing agony of the withering Shadow Monster.

Victor boldly stepped toward the beast, phone light blasting.

Then *his* phone died.

"Stupid batteries!" he cried at his phone.

The beast's thundering paw swiped Victor, bashing him backward. Victor buckled. I gasped.

"VICTOR!"

His head fell forward. His shirt was shredded. My hurt turned to rage. I threw my flashlight at the Shadow Monster, its stinking plumes of fur swishing like dryers at a car wash.

"You—you—thing! You terrible, mean thing!" was all I could say.

I pulled back my shoulders and inhaled. Fire shot from my belly and turned into a scream that sent the hair on the Shadow Monster's snout blowing back. The beast paused. Blinked. Then it bellowed at me, exhaling a reeking wind of sweet laundry detergent and sour belly juice into my face.

Checkmate, Oleg.

I darted toward the stairs.

THUMP, THUMP.

Meaty, hairy paws galloped behind me.

I was almost at the banister that overlooked the party.

I knew what to do to save the lives of everyone here. I had to scream. I had to roar. I had to become Visible.

I slammed into the railing on the balcony and screamed down to the party.

"Hey, you guys!" I shouted. "Take a picture of this!"

The party got quiet. Kids looked up at me as I waved my arms back and forth. From the corner, Victor weakly looked up at me like "What are you doing?"

"Happy Halloween!" I screamed.

I threw my legs over the banister and jumped, aiming for the couch, hoping the boys sitting on it would run away in time for my landing. The Shadow Monster roared and sprang after me.

Phones were aimed high and flashes exploded, filling the living room with a burst of nuclear light. Under the strobing lights, the monster howled and dissolved into wisps of smoke. Blinded momentarily, I plunged into the couch as the soccer guys spilled out of the way.

"Meh. I'd give that a five," Jesper said, putting his phone away. "Ken's been doing that all night."

I looked up. Oleg had vanished into thin air. I laughed to myself and rolled off the sofa.

"Someone's desperate for attention," I heard Deanna

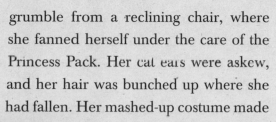

grumble from a reclining chair, where she fanned herself under the care of the Princess Pack. Her cat ears were askew, and her hair was bunched up where she had fallen. Her mashed-up costume made me giggle to myself.

Deanna's comments didn't sting as much this time.

Victor was clinging to the banister, gazing down at me, shaking his head in wonderment. His sideways smile was back.

I charged up the stairs and crouched down beside him, gently touching the tatters of his pirate shirt. Even though the claw marks scratched across his chest looked like they really stung, he held my hand with appreciation. All the fear that filled me moments ago was replaced by a flight of giddy helium balloons.

"AAAARRRGOTCHA!" came a scream from inside the walls.

A loud metallic thumping wound up toward the

ceiling. Victor and I braced ourselves for another monster attack. Then we both realized we were still holding hands. His fingers tensed in mine. I swallowed.

Stay focused, Kelly.

The air-conditioning vent in the middle of the hallway broke open, and Snaggle the Toadie spilled out, beakfirst. Victor and I recoiled, but then it jerked to a stop, midair. Snaggle was clinging to its little leather purse. Holding the other end of the Toadie's sacred satchel was a human hand with black nail polish.

"Liz?" I called out.

Liz jumped down from the air-conditioning vent, yanking the Toadie with her.

"Nurm! Nurm!" grumbled Snaggle, playing tug-of-war with Liz.

"Get the thing!" Liz shouted.

"I got this," Victor said, tucking in his pirate shirt.

He put out his arms in a "give me space" gesture and boldly stepped forward, like he was going to take a penalty kick. His leg swung with grace and ease, connecting sneaker toe to Toadiebeak. It was a perfect liftoff. The creature's whole body went flying across the hall and crashed into the fire alarm with a crack. The fire alarm shrieked, and emergency sprinklers shot water from the ceiling. I could hear the loud whoops and squeals of kids caught in the spray down below.

"Goal!" he shouted, and threw up his fists, water

streaming down his smile. We high-fived. It was awesome.

Snaggle grumbled, shook the fuzz out of its head, and clawed up the window curtains.

"No, no, no!" Liz said, running toward the Toadie. Her boots splashed across the wet carpet, but she was too late.

The trash troll broke through the window and dove outside.

We rushed to the ledge. The Toadie's rear legs kicked out of a hole it was rapidly digging. Liz crouched on the windowsill, about to jump two stories down, but Snaggle slipped into the depths of its tunnel system and vanished.

Liz scowled at Victor. "I said get it, not kick it."

Victor's arms withered at his sides. I pulled my puffy green waterproof jacket over our heads like an umbrella, and we huddled together. Victor was only trying to help, but he had just screwed things up for us, just like I had been doing the whole night. I was kind of glad it wasn't me for once.

Liz glowered at us, and she stalked off to inspect Snaggle's leather troll purse. There was a small bulge inside the bejeweled sack. She fished out a thick piece of round glass with spiraled ridges.

Liz made an unhappy growl. I tried to get a closer look, but she shoved the glass chunk and sack into her backpack. She was on the move.

181

Liz swung open the bathroom door.

"All clear, Penny," Liz said in a kind voice.

Penny, shivering in the falling water, poked her head out of the crack in the door.

"I wan' my mom," Penny mumbled.

Liz crouched down to Penny's eye level. "Why don't you call her and ask her to come home?"

"But my brother will get in trouble," Penny said.

Jesper rushed up the stairs, soaking wet. His ski goggles sloshed with water. I guess the cold sprinklers had snapped him out of his party trance, because his eyes were panicked and angry. "Penny! I'm gonna kill you!"

"Hold on, Jesper," I said. "You're the one who threw a big, stupid party and let it get out of control, and now you're blaming your harmless little sister for causing all this damage? Not cool, Jesper."

"Wh-what?" Jesper stuttered, surprised Kelly What's-Her-Name had just spoken up and called him out.

Speeding sirens wailed outside. Red-and-blue lights flooded the windows. Kids below screamed, "Police!"

Jesper cringed at the sound of furniture being bashed aside as kids stampeded around the house. He yelled for everyone to shut up, but his grass skirt caught around his ankles, and he fell down the stairs.

Liz flipped Penny her business card. "Next time your mom and dad go out, have them call me, and this will never, ever happen again."

I felt a little hand tug on my wrist. Penny gently pulled me to my knees.

She removed the sparkly tiara from her wet tangle of hair. It twinkled in her hands as she lifted it up to my head. The sprinklers stopped. The air around us was filled with mist that smelled like garden hose water.

"Thank you for getting rid of the monster in my closet," whispered Penny as she crowned me. The broken tiara fit on my head perfectly. My throat closed up. This little girl must have been tormented by that Shadow Monster for so long, and now she was finally *free*.

Liz's mouth was pinched into a frown, eyes red and withdrawn. Tears smeared her dark mascara into black smudges. She swallowed and then marched down the stairs without looking back. Fire engines wailed close to the house.

Headlights spilled into the windows, sending shadows skittering like roaches as Liz and I bolted out to her moped. She showed me the pet tracker. The blue dot was on the run again, veering away from the house.

"Why was the Toadie guarding that piece of glass?"

"We'll ask it when we catch it."

Victor kept pace with us. He had his strength back, and he looked ready to kick some butt. I was glad he was there—not just as my crush, but as my friend and fellow monster hunter.

"What have youuuu two been up to?" laughed one of the soccer guys who had gathered outside on the lawn. "No. Seriously. What have you two been up to? The basement's trashed."

"It was a raccoon," said Liz. "Went wild. Must have been rabid."

"Yeah. Raccoon. Totally," I said, glancing at Victor.

Was he going to play along, or would he rat us out to his friends?

"Yeah," Victor said, shaking his head. "Raccoon. It was crazy."

I beamed. *He was on my side.*

The soccer guys groaned and walked off, but Victor stayed with us.

"Is this . . . You do this?" he asked me.

I shrugged and was about to tell him it was my first night and that I'm not really a joiner, but if he wanted to join us, he was more than welcome to, y'know, join. And then I was going to tell him that I ramble and make stupid jokes when I'm nervous, but Victor squinted and shook his head in wonder.

"It is so . . . weird."

My smile deflated. His accent suddenly sounded sharp and mean.

I plucked Penny's tiara from my head and threw my wet hair to the side, accidentally whipping a line of water into his face.

Angry neighbors had emerged and were screaming at Jesper and the kids on the front lawn. Shaving cream and Silly String smeared the front of the house, giving it a foamy frown. A crushed pumpkin burned on the porch, candle wax oozing from its eyes. Parents were arriving, yelling at their kids.

"It's not what I do," I said, shifting my weight, hand on my hip. "I'm just trying to save up to go to Camp Miskatonic."

"Camp. Very cool," Victor said, brightening.

I smiled and zipped the tiara up in my jacket pocket. Liz growled and shook her helmeted head.

"I'm telling you, I saw something!" screamed Deanna. She clomped across the asphalt in a sopping wet mess of pink taffeta and runny makeup that stretched her face like Silly Putty. She pressed her cold hands into Victor's face for him to "feel how frightened" she was.

"Gotta go, Ferguson," Liz said over her shoulder.

Deanna wilted into Victor's side. "You're leaving? Aaaaw. Don't worry, my mom's coming. I'll give him a ride home."

Deanna's hands were now holding Victor's.

In a flash, I saw our story unfolding like an episode of *Tears of Flowers and Fish.* After the opening credits (sung by K-pop legend Na Feng), Liz and I would leave, and Deanna would seek comfort in Victor's arms. He would tell her about the monster we defeated, and she would call him a cool monster hunter, and Victor would like that kind of compliment, and pretty soon, they would be within kissing distance. All in subtitles, of course.

BANG!

The moped engine shot black smoke.

Liz's boot flicked down the kickstand. She took a Sharpie from her bag, marched over to Victor, snatched his hand away from Deanna, and wrote my number on his palm.

"This is Kelly's number," she said. "Don't text her. Call her. But—and let me be clear—if you go home with Spray Tan here, don't do either."

Victor nodded, speechless.

BEST MONSTER COVER-UPS

• Racoons
• Floods
• Nosy Neighbors
• Feral Girl Scouts
• Electrical Malfunctions
• Sudden Onset Diarrhea

(ew...)

As we followed the little paw on the pet tracker, rocketing through dark neighborhoods in pursuit of the Toadie, I felt alive and kind of light-headed. My wet hair was tucked under my helmet, getting crispy in the rush of autumn air. I was going to get sick tomorrow for sure, but right now I was thriving on adrenaline.

Did I just jump off a banister and onto a couch? Did I blast a Shadow Monster to pieces? I did that! Me! Kelly Ferguson! Yes!

"You think he likes me, or do you think he thinks I'm weird?" I blurted out.

"I think you sound pathetic."

"Right. But for the sake of argument, what's your opinion on the matter?"

"Of?"

"Victor and me."

"My opinion is that if you keep talking, I'm going to elbow you in the face."

"Right. But what if Victor calls? My phone's dead."

"Will you shut up?" she screamed.

I closed my mouth.

"Backpack. Third pocket," Liz mumbled.

As Liz kept steady on the handles, I dug out a portable cell phone battery pack from her bag. I plugged it into my phone.

"And I swear," Liz said, "if you're checking Instagram or sending some stupid emoji, I will end every last piece of you. We gotta focus on the mission, and that's you and me saving Jake. Got it?"

I nodded and tucked away my phone.

It grew quiet except for the echo of the moped's engine.

"Are you psychic or something?" I asked.

"What?"

"How'd you know I'd need a flashlight?"

Liz shrugged. "A babysitter's always ready."

"You're a good associate, Liz," I said, hugging her from behind.

Liz threw back her helmet and head butted me. *CLUNK!*

"I said 'associate,' not 'friend'!" I said, rubbing my forehead.

"I don't like people hugging me."

The road narrowed into a single treelined gravel lane, where there were no more streetlights to cast a glow on our way. The moped bucked and crunched as the tracker led us to a stretch of black forest path with the pavement consumed by dirt and weeds.

In the shadows, a house with a sagging garage door and a sign covered in scratches and muddy kitten prints that read "No Trespassing" waited for us. We rolled to a stop among the long weeds and bushes sprouting up from the stone walkway leading to the house. The screen door was torn. The windows were blacked out with garbage bags. There was the strong scent of you-know-what steaming off the house.

Something swished in the tall grass. I tensed against Liz. It was only a gray cat.

But then that cat joined fifty other cats that were perched on the branches of a dead tree nearby. Cats were crawling all over this house. And we're not talking cute and cuddly. These were deranged, crazy-eyed cats.

I chewed the inside of my cheek.

"The Cat Lady," she said.

Before I could ask who that was, Liz nodded to her backpack.

"Check the guide?" I asked.

"Check the guide," she said with a nod.

NAME: Cat Lady, aka Peggy Drood, aka the Cat Lady and her cats
HEIGHT: 5'4"
WEIGHT: 128 lbs
TYPE: Human, Class 3 apparition
ORIGIN: American suburbia; Peggy Drood loves cats. Over time, she collected over 200 felines in her house. However, when she couldn't afford to feed them all, she gave them one final meal: herself.

LIKES: Cats, milk, tuna, yarn, eating.

BRING FOOD. OTHERWISE, HER CATS WILL EAT YOU!

DISLIKES: Everything not listed above, especially swimming

STRENGTHS: Small, deadly feline army.

IF YOU ARE ALLERGIC TO CATS, STAY AWAY.

WEAKNESSES: Hair balls, being confined to her home, catnip, laser pointers, frail human body; cats are easily distracted by the possibility of food.

SMELL: Constant faint whiff of tuna

SIGHTINGS: Peggy was last seen in her condemned home forty years ago. Rumored to have been eaten by her cats, who still live there.

ALLIES: Cats are too self-centered for allies but will mildly tolerate people who feed them.

I closed the notebook and then looked up at the decrepit house.

"Are you kidding me?" I yelled.

Liz's phone rang.

"Berna. Hey. We're at Peggy Drood's. Yeah. Pretty gnarly. I'll drop you a pin now."

Liz hung up. I assumed we would wait for them to show up, but Liz marched up the weedy path. I stared, dumbstruck. Liz wanted to go in *there*? "What if this is another trap? Like Jesper's house?"

"This is different. A monster doesn't just stop off at another monster's house."

"You think they might be in—whadayacallit—*cahoots*?"

Liz nodded.

"So we wait for backup, right?" I said hopefully. "Oh! I know. We passed a Starbucks about two miles back; we could wait there. I'll get a pumpkin spice latte, you get a decaf anything–"

I trailed after Liz, begging her to reconsider going into a house with cats that had been raised with a taste for human meat. Sure, I owned that shadow beastie back at Jesper's, but I was crashing from eating nothing but candy all night.

We checked the tracker. The Toadie hadn't moved. Liz reached into her backpack and removed the long cattle prod. She flicked it on, and it hummed and crackled with electricity. She found a sandwich bag full of Cheerios and handed me some. "I always keep a bag of treats for the kids. You can feed the cats if they get too hungry."

I looked at the cereal in my palm.

"These things are used to eating human flesh. I don't think they'll be in the mood for breakfast cereal," I said.

"Did you bring catnip?" Liz asked.

"Uh. No."

"Then Cheerios are what we got."

Gray cats darted under the sagging porch boards. A flicking tail brushed against my cuff. I kicked my leg up and accidentally banged my knee into Liz's thigh. She elbowed me, told me to get control of myself, and climbed through the window. I followed her, but my foot caught on the sill, and I fell into a slippery pile of old magazines.

I gagged. The rancid stink of old books, mud, and cat pee, with a spray of lavender perfume, hung in the dead air. I covered my nose and mouth with my sleeve and caught up with Liz, who was crouching around the corner, wiping her nose.

"You okay?" I whispered.

"I'm allergic to cats." She sniffled, eyes red and bloodshot.

"WHAT?"

"I'll be fine," she mumbled, swallowing hard.

My mouth hung open as she ducked through the reeking must. Her threshold for pain and fear amazed me, but I was scared for her. She coughed fiercely even though she tried to hold it back. She hawked a loogie, then swallowed it.

Our only flashlight illuminated tattered chairs and an overturned table with the legs chewed off. *BZZT! BZZT!* My phone was vibrating. It was a text from a number I had never seen before.

That was crazy.

This is Victor, BTW.

"Oh. My. God!" I gasped.

"Are you hurt?" Liz whispered, scrambling to my side.

"He *texted* me," I said, showing her the phone.

Liz's angry eyes burned into me.

"Put it away," Liz hissed.

"I will," I said. "Just help me think of what to text back first."

Liz made a grab for the phone.

"Fine. Fine. I'll text him later! See? It's going away. Jeez," I said, making a big show of putting the phone away.

She snorted and held out the cattle prod, ducking behind stacks of old newspapers that were piled so high they formed a maze within the decrepit house.

"Boys are useless," she mumbled to herself as we moved through the newspaper maze and stood at the edge of what I was guessing was the basement door. "Trust me. You're just a kid."

"You're, like, two years older than me."

"I am a *lifetime* older than you."

"So that means I have to be as miserable as you?"

Liz made a sour face, and I backed off, realizing we were both hungry, frustrated, and terrified. We checked the tracker. The Toadie was here. Right beneath our feet.

My toe kicked something. I thought it was a rock, but it was too shiny and bright. It was the metallic pet tracker, wet and moist with bile. The Toadie had spit it up.

That's not a good sign.

Liz shivered.

We started to creep back toward the window we'd come through, but the entire floor was covered with cats. From the shadows, green and yellow eyes appeared. Cats were crawling out of the walls and from the broken floor. We were slowly being surrounded by them.

"Nice evil kitties," I whispered, trying to soothe them.

Flashes of light reflected off their jewel eyes. Their tails brushed against our legs.

The window was completely blocked by wriggling felines. They were scratching at the door, slicing long grooves. My heart flopped in my chest as I looked for another way out.

Click-clack. A tapping noise sounded behind us.

Liz sneezed and coughed. Her allergies were kicking in fierce. She wiped her nose with her shirtsleeve.

Click-clack. The sweet smell of lavender wafted through the air again. Through a hole clawed out of the wall, I saw into the living room. On a tattered, old couch sat a woman, watching us.

Click-clack.

One of her bony hands was stroking a cat in her lap, running her long, curled fingernails through its coat. The other hand was tapping against the gnawed wooden arm of the couch. Liz and I darted toward the window, but piles of cats blocked our path, as if they were furry bricks. Liz tripped and wheezed for breath. I held her hand, both of us shaking.

Click-clack.

Peggy Drood cocked her head. Long gray hair hung over her shoulders in brittle clumps. She slunk off the couch and slithered across the floor, blocking our exit.

The strange, old specter sat on her stumpy legs like a cheerful little kitten. The guide wasn't lying about Peggy Drood giving herself to her cats as a meal: her legs had been nibbled off.

She looked up at us with large, dark eyes. That's when I saw they weren't dark; they had been clawed out long ago.

"Yooooou . . . have come to feed my cats?" hissed Peggy Drood. The low, warbling growl of a hundred cats rose around us.

Liz and I exchanged glances. Liz shrugged.

"Y-y-yes. We have . . . ," I managed to whisper.

This made the Cat Lady smile.

"Feeeeeeed them . . . ," she said with a hush.

The cats were slowly circling us.

We began throwing Cheerios at the cats. The creatures sniffed our offerings and licked them, then . . .

Crunch, crunch.

"We have to keep feeding these cats or they are going to start feeding on us," I whispered to Liz as I threw down my last Cheerios.

Tears rimmed Liz's red eyes. She was squinting painfully as she cleared her throat.

I unzipped Liz's pack, removed a baby bottle, and squirted a puddle of milk onto the floor. The hungry cats slurped it up. This drew some of the attention away from us.

"Jacob . . . ," Liz rasped to the ghostly Cat Lady.

Peggy Drood stroked her sickly yellow fingernails through a mangy cat's fur. "The boy is *very* special to us. We . . . need him . . . ," she purred, and gestured her hand across the room. My stomach churned as I realized she was talking about more than just her and her cats. She was talking about the entire world of monsters.

"*He* said you'd come looking for the boy."

"The—the—Toadie?" I asked.

The Cat Lady gave a throaty chuckle.

"No, my dear. The Grand Guignol."

"The Grand Goo-who?" I said.

There was a loud clang. Liz had dropped the cattle prod. Her face turned white.

"That's impossible," Liz whispered.

Peggy smiled, satisfied with Liz's terror-stricken reaction. A fly buzzed out of her eye socket.

197

"Kevin . . . ," whispered Liz.

"You know the Grand Guignol?" she purred again.

I saw Liz clench her jaw and curl her fist. "He's dead."

The Cat Lady giggled wildly, her shoulders bouncing up and down, like a jack-in-the-box. "He's very much alive, sweetie." Liz stumbled, her hands shaking and swollen, cat hair dancing in her nose. Her sneeze threw her backward. "You lie. You lie."

"He asked me to do him a favor," creaked the ghostly woman. She thrust her arms out over her cats and gave a shrieking, chilling command, "EAT! EAT, MY DEARIES! EAT THEM UP!"

A cat tsunami descended on us. In a roar of hisses and hungry meows, we were buried in fur, fangs, and claws. Ducking under the feline ceiling, I heard a strange voice speak inside of my head.

Stand up, Kelly, said the voice.

This wasn't my voice doing an impression. This was someone else, speaking to me. A woman's voice. Strong, echoing. It was coming from deep within me. And I know this is going to sound crazy, but she sounded *a lot* like the poet Maya Angelou. (Mr. Gibbs, my honors English teacher, is a huge fan and is always showing us videos of her reading her poetry.)

"What?" I said back to the voice.

You heard me, Kelly, said the powerful voice. *Grab your*

199

weapon and stand up. You need to get Liz out of here before she chokes to death.

"That sounds really hard."

It is hard, but you can do this, Kelly.

"Am I going insane?"

Not at all. There's no time to explain. Go!

I reached down, grabbed Liz's cattle zapper, and felt its powerful hum in my hand.

I swung. Flashes of bright, blue light crackled. Cats howled.

MEEEEOOOOW!

I leveled the zapper at the scrawny black cat chewing on Liz's jeans. The prod crackled against the cat's fur. The nasty feline yelped and swiped its jagged claws at me. I lunged like an amateur Musketeer and hit it right in the whiskers.

ZZZT! MEEOOOOW!

Here's the thing: I love cats. Really, I do. I love all animals. I felt bad as electricity sparked from their tails. But their claws were tearing holes in the pockets of my jeans. A fang sank through the top of my sneaker and pierced the side of my big toe. Liz's hands were covered in scratches.

The cats' tails began interlocking with one another, twisting and curling like barbed wire. They were turning themselves into a wall of claws and teeth. A wall of cats? I screamed, grabbed Liz, and dragged her to the wall. We were trapped. The front door was a million miles away, and Peggy Drood was shrieking and hissing by the window. There was no other way out.

I screamed and unzipped Liz's backpack. My hands dashed across the weapons until I found a small tube of finger paint.

Please don't be real finger paint.

I uncapped the tube, and acid-smelling emerald goo splattered out. It struck the floorboards and sizzled, burning a hole clean through the wood.

YEAH, BABY!

I smeared the end of the tube on the wall, careful not to get any on me. The chupacabra venom ate through that brick wall like butter melting on pancakes. The fizzing, bubbling acid burned a three-foot hole into the wall.

"*NO!*" shrieked Peggy.

She made a hacking cough, her pointy shoulders shuddering. Something gurgled up from deep inside of her throat and swelled into her mouth. Peggy vomited up a writhing hair ball the size of a peach, full of twisted, gnarled dark hairs.

THWACK!

It splattered into the wall by my head, splashing kitty spittle into my eye. I screamed and shoved Liz out the hole and then pulled myself through.

Panting, I heaved Liz toward the moped as cats

flooded into the tall reeds. The pattering of thousands of paws rolled behind us. I flung Liz across the seat and dug around inside her pockets.

My eyes bulged at the immense tide of a thousand wild, hungry mouths and twisted tails descending on us. I found the keys to the moped and jammed one into the ignition, and the engine came to life. I twisted the throttle, and the moped shot off, taking Liz and me bouncing across rocks and tree roots. The handlebars wobbled, but I held tight, remembering how Liz's hands looked when she drove. Cats leaped onto the seat.

Claws swiped my hair. I drove faster. I heard Peggy, trapped in her house for eternity, screaming, "NO! NO! DON'T LEAVE ME, MY BABIES!"

I sped off down the weedy lane, clutching Liz's backpack. The cats ran to the very edge of the decayed pathway and stopped in strange obedience. Then the wall of cats untangled themselves, twisted up in the air, and tumbled onto the dirt.

Hundreds of them, in all colors and shapes, just stood at the edge of the street, licking their paws like nothing strange had ever happened. Slowly, they slithered back to their cursed house with their tails in the air and their nasty butts waving good-bye.

I smashed into a trash can outside of a 24-Hour Gas 'n' Guzzle on Warick Road. It was the only bright spot among the dark woods. The back tire kicked up, and Liz fell off. She groaned and rubbed the sweat and patches of cat hair from her face. Her breath crackled, as if hairs were still stuck in her throat. She wheezed like my great Auntie Charlotte, who smoked ten packs of cigarettes a day.

Rushing through the minimarket, I snatched allergy medicine, a Monster Energy drink, and a water. I threw down five dollars to the zombielike clerk. Liz drained the can, green fizz spilling down her chin. I dabbed her scratches with baby butt–wipes I found in her backpack. She inhaled loudly and belched, spitting up clumps of cat hair.

"Gross, dude," I said. "You okay?"

She grunted, shielding her eyes from the fluorescent lights beaming down on us. Her elbows were leaning on the torn knees of her jeans. The tenth time I asked if she was okay, Liz shoved me and nodded. I was happy she was pushing me around again; it meant her strength was coming back.

Wind blasted us, knifing through my jacket and jeans. I guzzled my water. It splashed in my empty belly and made me nauseated.

What was that voice I heard back there?

I was about to tell Liz about all the strange things that were happening to me when I saw her hands were trembling and blue. I reached out to warm them up, but she pulled away and walked to her moped.

"What happened back there, Liz?" I asked. "Who is the—"

Liz knelt down to inspect her twisted front tire. "You banged it up, dork," she said, jerking the fender into place. Her hands stopped. She took in a big breath while I nervously chewed the cuff on my brown sweater.

Liz stared up into the bright, buzzing lights and closed her eyes. Her skin was almost bluish in the harsh light, and I could make out small wrinkles around the corners of her mouth and eyes.

"I had a hunch it was him when you showed me the

drawing and the prints at Jacob's house," she said. "But I didn't want to believe it. No way. Not real. But it's him."

I unfolded Jacob's drawings of the hooved man and turned it over in my shaking hands. Liz looked at it and nodded.

"The Grand Guignol's the reason I became a babysitter," she said.

NAME: Grand Guignol (grahnd GEE-nyole)
HEIGHT: 6'3"
WEIGHT: 216 lbs
TYPE: Boogeyman
ORIGIN: Underworld? Realm of the Unknown and Unmeasured? Alabama?

DISTINGUISHING CHARACTERISTICS: Has the torso of a man, but furry legs and black hooves. His skin is very wrinkly (to be fair, he is SUPER old), and he has snakelike yellow eyes. He is always dressed as if he were going to the funeral of someone who has died for the second time: elegant black suit covered in soot and corpse-dust with a ragged, black bow tie, and sparkling black pearls.

LIKES: Fashion, the smell of fear, kidnapping children

DISLIKES: Being reminded that he's balding; humans ~ESPECIALLY BABYSITTERS

STRENGTHS: Superpowerful mind that can make you believe something you knew wasn't true or make you see something that isn't there. ~BEWARE: IT'S LIKE MIND CONTROL

WEAKNESSES: Angel Fire

SMELL: A combination of wet mud, a thousand belches, and a pile of rotten eggs

SIGHTINGS: Notoriously hard to track down. Current haunts uncertain—Western Hemisphere? Eastern Hemisphere?

ALLIES: Oleg, the Mephisthophelean Shadow Monster; the six other Boogeymen

FROM LIZ'S JOURNAL

July

We were at a carnival. It was night. Kev really wanted to go on the Gravitron, but we were too small. I was six, Kev was five. I wanted to get on that ride so bad. I snuck us in behind a group of extra-large people. The ride spun around so fast, I thought I was going to throw up . . . but Kev was laughing. . . .

That's when I saw him. He was peering up from under the operator's booth. He had on a black suit so dusty it looked like he had clawed his way out of a grave. And those hooves. He was watching Kev.

Next thing I remember, we were back home. There was a knock at our window. There was no reason for anyone to be knocking on our window that late. I drew back the curtains and saw him. That black suit . . . that evil, wicked smile.

I looked everywhere for Kev. My family and I talked to the police for a whole year. Nothing. They never found him.

My parents started to fight. It was too much for them to take. I tried to explain it was the Boogeyman, but they refused to listen. Dad stayed at work later and later. I hated myself for losing my brother, and I wanted to take it out on the world.

I started hanging out with older kids and did dumb stuff that got more and more dangerous. Funny, though—I didn't get grounded. My mom was too busy getting into her own trouble. I was the most depressed twelve-year-old I knew. I wouldn't talk to anyone. I would just break things and blast punk in the middle of the night.

My mom got fed up and called a babysitter named Mama Vee, who was, at the time, something like the cochair of the New England babysitters. So, Mama Vee would hang out with me. I told her about the Boogeyman. And she was the only person to believe me. My folks finally got a divorce. It was the worst time of my life, until Mama Vee told me that she had caught and killed the Boogeyman. And that was when I learned the name of the demon who took everything from me: the Grand Guignol. But we never found Kevin.

Mom left. Dad was sad and mean about it. I became invisible to him.

As the years passed, I spent more time with Mama Vee and our chapter president, Madame Leanne Moon, and less time at home. Vee and Moon forced me to go back to school, and I agreed as long as I could stay in the cottage and train to be a babysitter.

Every day I think about Kev.

I'll find what happened to him. I have to.

He was too young to fight for himself. So I'm fighting for him now.

"The Grand Guignol tore my family apart." Liz said, her face buried in her arms. "I lost Kev. I lost Jacob. The Grand Guignol won. *Again*. It's over."

Tears spilled down the sides of her face.

"Liz. It's not over," I said, slowly walking toward her. "You . . . you have to have hope."

"Oh, *please,*" she spat.

I dodged her goober and stiffened up. "Edith Cavell helped more than two hundred Allied soldiers escape from German-occupied Belgium and was shot to death by a German firing squad for it. If she can do that, we can do this," I said, pushing my shoulders back.

Liz screwed up her eyebrows at me, with no clue what I was saying.

She shook her head and scoffed, "You're just a kid."

I wanted to tell her she was wrong, but . . . I *was* just a kid. Even so, I had to keep trying.

"The thing you got from the Toadie," I said, reaching out my hand.

"It's junk," she groaned.

"I'll be the judge of that," I said, trying to show some sense of authority.

Liz tossed the thick glass lens at me. I fumbled to catch it. It was four inches around with smooth spirals spinning outward from the middle.

I was holding it up to inspect its thick ridge when it caught a beam of light and magnified it, sending the light glowing onto the black street. Liz and I both cocked our heads to the side, studying the glowing lens.

BZZT! BZZT! My phone buzzed. I looked at it, and my heart flipped.

"That Berna?" Liz asked.

I bit my lip and fought the urge to answer it.

Then I answered it.

"Victor?" I said.

"Hello, Kelly," said Victor.

"Unbelievable," growled Liz, and she jumped on her moped.

"Are you okay?" he asked.

"Uh, y'know," I said. "Could be better." I looked at Liz and pointed at the phone.

"Some of the guys are going to a midnight movie. Maybe . . . can you come?" he asked.

"A movie?" I said aloud so Liz could hear. I thought maybe Victor inviting me on a sort-of, kind-of date might cheer her up, give her hope, but she did not share my enthusiasm.

She sped off on her moped. Through the cloud of exhaust blasting in my face, I saw her red taillight streak into the dark road, stranding me in the middle of nowhere.

"Uh. Can I call you back?"

I hung up the phone and ran. The glass lens slipped out of my hand and fell into the grass. I rummaged through the brush, found the heavy disk, jammed it into my pocket, and ran after Liz's vanishing taillight, flailing my arms like a foolio.

Yep. Just a kid.

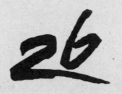

"Liz! Wait!" I felt the flashlight bobble around in my backpack as I darted after the moped.

I am going to be in so much trouble. My phone battery is going to die again, and my only hope of a ride is speeding away from me. Then I'll be lost in the middle of nowhere, surrounded by monsters.

"PLEASE!" I screamed out, my voice cracking.

My lungs were on fire. The whine of Liz's moped brakes bounced off a long fence made of rocks and slate ringing the edge of a field. Her red taillight illuminated the plume of exhaust rising before a large apple orchard. I hunched over to catch my breath.

"Dude, are you serious?" I shouted.

Liz clasped her hands, mockingly. "'I'm not weird, Victor. I'm just trying to go to Camp Cool Kids.' *Me, me, me*," Liz snapped, jabbing her finger at me. "The whole night that's you. You're just like everyone else. You don't care."

I swiped her hand away.

"I do too care," I said.

Liz leveled her eyes at me with laser-like intensity. "I've been sitting for Jacob ever since he was six months old. He's like my little brother. He's the only family I've got. But to you he's just a trip to Camp Miskatonic. So go to your movie, Kelly. Go suck up to the cool kids."

"I'm sorry about what happened to your brother. That must be the worst thing ever–"

"You have no idea–"

"What it feels like when no one cares about you?" I shot back, heart pouring into my mouth. "Like you're invisible? Yeah, I wouldn't have a clue how that feels, Liz." I made a sarcastic sneer at her, but in my mind, I was flooded with memories of walking alone in the halls of Willow Brook Middle School, feeling like a ghost.

She looked at me, a flicker of understanding and thankfulness softening her eyes, but then something in her reached up and dragged her back down into the darkness. "I don't need you," she retorted, scowling. "I don't need anyone."

"Yeah. You do."

Liz's upper lip curled into a cruel smirk. "Unlike you, I don't need people to tell me I'm awesome. I know I'm awesome."

I was in her face now, yelling. If she punched me in the nose, fine. I wasn't afraid of her anymore.

"Oh yeah? Well—well—you've been hanging out with monsters so long you turned into one!" I shouted.

Lightning crackled. It sounded like the sky was being ripped apart over our heads.

"You and me!" Liz shouted over the coming thunderstorm. "We're over." She sliced the air with her hand.

"You and me"—my voice cracked—"were never even a thing!"

In a flash of lightning, the wooden sign nailed among the apple trees glowed bright: "Dunwich Farms." Another flash of light revealed a dark figure on a distant branch, propped up on one elbow. Its long legs ticked back and forth. Its yellow eyes smiled at us. The sky faded to black.

"And don't even *think* about applying for the Order of the Babysitters." Liz was screaming at me. "I'll make sure you never get in."

"Liz," I said, keeping my eyes on the tall creature in the trees.

Hooves for feet.

A sick, runny feeling sliding down my guts.

213

"I'm not talking to you," she said, gunning the moped's engine.

My hand shot out, grabbed her, and turned her to face the orchard.

KRAKA-BAM!

I pointed at the branch where the Grand Guignol had been reclining. A fork of lightning sent the trees flickering with electric fire. The perch was empty.

Thunder marched. Wind reeled flecks of ice and hail, stinging my cheeks.

"'The two little kittens, they lost their mittens, /And they began to cry.'"

That voice. I knew that low, crooning voice. . . .

"'What! Lost your mittens, you naughty kittens! Then you shall have no pie.'"

A memory of hooves stepping from my closet. A tail snaking in the air.

Hooves. Clopping across the branches, cracking dead leaves and twigs.

My breath shuddered into cold plumes. The distant figure sprang off his haunches and scuttled up a tree trunk. He pranced across the branches with the poise of a dancer.

"Hello, little girls," said the goat-legged demon. "Or should I say, young ladies?"

I had seen this monster before. He had come for me once. And now he was back to collect.

"It's him," Liz said, stiffening.

My heart broke for her. The last time she saw this creature, it was stealing her little brother and destroying everything she loved. I stood beside Liz so this guy would know that we were a team.

"'Meow, meow, meow, We smell a rat close by!'"

THUMP. He dropped onto the dead grass and skipped toward us. I looked to Liz for her big brilliant plan of action. Her hand snaked into her backpack.

"Where's my zapper?" she whispered.

"I dropped it back at Peggy Drood's," I said out of the side of my mouth. "Sorry."

A frustrated breath shot from Liz's clenched teeth. From her pack she removed a brass tube engraved with dragons. There was a cap with a chain corked into the top.

"Grand Guignol!" Liz shouted.

"You got me, baby," he said, shaking his hips, holding out his arms.

Liz aimed the brass cylinder up at the Grand Guignol.

"As commanding babysitter of the Rhode Island chapter of babysitters, I—I—hereby demand you return

Jacob Zellman to our care immediately!" she yelled, voice wavering.

The slender monster paused. He sniffed the air and cocked his head at the brass object in Liz's hand.

"Is that you, little Lizzie?" he sneered.

Liz swallowed. She struggled to hold up the quaking tube.

"Couldn't be. Not this . . . dark, sad little creature I see before me," he said, the words oozing out of his mouth.

My fingers curled into fists. I hated his mocking tone and cruel smile. I wanted to grab him by his chicken wattles and punch his face, but I was too frightened to move.

"What did you do with Kevin?" Liz whispered.

"Kevin . . . Kevin . . . let's see . . . ," he said, putting his finger on his lip. "So many children, you see. Ah! Kev. How could I *forget*. Little Kev."

He stared at Liz, lingered on her sadness, and he laughed a meaty, deep chuckle that shook my spine.

"What did you do to him?" she screamed, aiming the dragon-covered weapon at the Grand Guignol.

With a wicked smile, he sprang back on his hands, arcing gracefully tail over head, vanishing deeper into the dark orchards. Liz gunned the moped past the stone wall. Holding the brass tube, she veered down the corridor of rotted apples.

I chased after her. "LIZ!"

Deep in the cathedral of trees, the Grand Guignol vaulted from branch to branch like a ballerina. Liz's moped stopped in a swish of mud. She aimed her strange cylinder up and yanked back on the chain. I was running to Liz's side when a loud flash of purple light exploded from the end of the tube. Everything went bright, and we were thrown backward by the blast.

A steady ringing filled my ears. Branches and rocks cascaded all around us. The air smelled like sulfur and roasted apples. Fire crackled through the trees. I choked in the smoke curling in the blazing orchard.

"What was that?" I gasped. My voice sounded small and far away.

"Chimera dragon breath," Liz mumbled. "Emergencies only. Where is he?"

Black shapes rose behind the wall of flames. The ground trembled with the thundering of hooves. Liz snatched me by the backpack and yanked me to my feet as skeletal horses crashed through the towering fire, dragging a black carriage. The Grand Guignol was clutching the reins, cracking a long whip.

"Holy shiitake mushrooms," I said.

The horses barreled toward us, trees cracking under their powerful steps. Liz cranked the gas on her moped. The back tire shot mud as it spun around.

"Hop on," Liz said.

The fire roared behind us. We launched away from the heat of ripping embers.

The Grand Guignol stood atop the carriage, snapping the reins. The horses' galloping hooves left the ground. In a rush of dark wind, the entire carriage flew over our heads.

The Grand Guignol leaned down from his soaring perch, caught Liz's backpack, and hauled her up into his clutches. Toadies clawed at her from inside the flying carriage, yanking her into a dark cage.

"Liz!" I screamed.

The moped, short a driver, veered sharply to the left, launching out of the orchard and toward the edge of a sea cliff.

I jumped off as the moped dove over the side, tumbling down and smashing into the jagged rocks and water. I hung from the side of the precipice, fingers and toes jammed into the dirt wall. Misty waves smashed two hundred feet below. Sea spray dampened the legs of my jeans.

Don't look down. Don't you dare look down.

My whole body shook as I dug my hands into the mud and began pulling myself up. I clamored over the dirt wall and flopped onto the weeds, chugging air. I lay on the cold ground and stared up into the stormy sky, watching helplessly as the phantom carriage vanished into the thick clouds above.

Over the roar of the waves and the crackling fire raging in the orchard, I heard the high-pitched laugh familiar from my nightmares: the stomach-turning cackle of the Boogeyman.

28

Ashes fluttered from the smoke-choked sky. Wind shrieked through the pines as I stumbled down a long, dark road, away from the ocean. I held Berna's business card in my trembling hands. Only 1 percent battery was left on my phone. I wanted to call Tammy and tell her everything that had happened, but she wouldn't understand. I wanted to tell my parents, but they would freak out.

An avalanche of texts shook my phone.

Victor:
That was crazy.

These were followed by more frantic texts from Victor throughout the night that I had missed while dragging Liz from the killer cats.

R U OK?

I'm worried

Kelly

U alive?

C U @ movies?

Wow, I thought. *His texting game is bad.*

I quickly opened Google Maps and texted my location to Berna right as my phone died. My reflection stared at me from the dark glass of my blank screen. Black circles hung under my eyes. My hair was in sad, hopeless tangles.

I was a million miles away from home. I never felt so alone and small before in my entire life. Every part of me wanted to scream and curl into a little ball by the side of the road. *Maybe a neighbor saw the fire and called the cops. Maybe they'll be here any minute with a nice loud fire truck.*

Neighbor? Look around, Kelly! The only thing that lives out here is probably some seven-headed cougar or a killer with an ax.

My feet stopped. I tried to walk, but they just wouldn't move.

Liz is gone. You lost her too.

Life seemed cruel and unfair. The bad guys won. The good guys never even stood a *chance*.

I clamped my eyelids shut and inhaled a shaking breath. Crickets and wind-whispers surrounded me. I listened for that voice within myself, the one that sounded like Mother Earth, the one that had helped me survive Peggy Drood's cats, but all I heard was my own frightened, tiny voice.

Liz is gone. Jacob is gone. And it's all your fault.

A roar blasted through the trees. I jumped off the side of the road and hid behind the stone fence as the howling and shrieking of what sounded like a parade of screaming goblins rumbled toward me.

When I peeked over the edge, I saw an old 1994 black Ford van with a large metal plow welded on the front bumper screech around the corner. There were cages around the windows, and iron racks on the roof.

The devilish screaming was old-school rock 'n' roll exploding from the van's speakers. And not the lame stuff my dad listened to. This was nasty and shrill. The music shrieked, *"Stayed awake all night! Stayed awake all night!"*

The driver slammed on the brakes. I held my breath and gathered dead leaves over me. Camouflage was my only hope. I heard the van's side door roll back with a bang.

I listened, waiting for heavy footsteps to crunch across the gravel.

Please, no, no, no.

Images of the fighting how-tos from the guide flashed in my brain. The Whispering Nanny. Rock the Cradle. Birthday Party Surprise.

My muscles coiled, ready to spring. Whoever was inside the creepy van was going to feel the full wrath of my anger in a serious knuckle sandwich.

"HIIIYAH!" I screamed, and vaulted myself up, throwing out my fist.

A woman in her midtwenties, with a long serpent's braid of hair, flung around to face me. Her hand caught my wrist and yanked me forward. I kicked, but she blocked me and stamped her palm into my chest, sending me stumbling back into the fence.

"Sit," said the woman. She wore a hooded robe over a pair of worn-out denim overalls.

I held my shaking fists up, slowly realizing that this woman looked familiar. Though she was in her twenties, her hair was silver and gray, like a wolf's coat. And she wasn't wearing any shoes. I made out heart and star tattoos on the tops of her feet. Her eyes were bright green and beautiful. She held out her empty hands in a gesture of peace.

224

"Nice moves, kiddo," she said, dimples flashing.

I blinked.

"Kiddo" . . .

"My old babysitter used to call me kiddo." I gasped for breath, lowering my fists.

She threw her three-foot-long braid of silvery white hair behind her shoulder. Crystals and amulets around her necklace clanked.

"Who you calling old?" she said, hands on her hips. She cartwheeled lazily back over the fence, where the giant black van purred like a wicked cat.

"Veronica . . . Preston?" I gasped. "You're Mama Vee?"

NAME: Veronica Preston, aka Mama Vee
RANK: Northeast professional babysitters chapter president
AGE: 25ish?

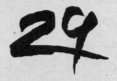

I let out a goofy, excited laugh and embraced her. I'd never been happier to see anyone ever, especially my old babysitter. "How?" I mumbled.

Veronica Preston, aka Mama Vee, glanced into the dark woods. "Where's Liz?"

My breath caught in my throat. "She's gone. Jacob's gone."

Mama Vee's eyes bulged. "Get in," she said.

I sat on a beanbag in the back of the van, which was surprisingly cozy compared to its military-grade outside. It was like a traveling gypsy den. Vee climbed in after me, rolled the side door shut, and the van rocketed forward. The sound of birds' wings rattled from the back of the vehicle as it shot off.

A throaty voice from the driver's seat mumbled, "Where's LeRue?"

We were not alone in the van.

Mama Vee peered out of a periscope in the back of the van wall. "Somewhere we gotta be, Wuggie," she replied. "Get the others and step on it."

I watched a leathery tail snake out from the driver's seat and wrap itself around the stick shift. The van kicked forward. I froze and stared at the back of the driver's seat as the nub end of the thick green tail pressed a button. Heavy metal exploded in the van, and I jolted in my seat.

"Turn it down!" Mama Vee shouted over the music.

I carefully leaned forward to see a squat hobgoblin with his scaly, three-fingered hands on the wheel. His nostrils flared, with a gold ring pierced in the center, like a bull. A gnarled horn poked out of his "We're #1" trucker hat.

My jaw hung open, and I pointed dumbly at the hobgoblin.

His head snapped around to face me so fast that the gold ring in his nose shook, like a door knocker.

"Check yer guide," he said in a ragged, gravelly voice. "Point a finger at a hobgoblin, and it might get bitten off." His crooked tusks snapped at me. I pulled away and Mama Vee laughed.

"He's kidding," she said, squeezing his chunky,

lizard-skin arm. "Been blood-free seven years, right, Wugnot?"

"Eight if you don't count that relapse," Wugnot muttered.

His tail pulled his hat down lower over his eyes. Mama Vee gave me an assuring nod. "Not all monsters are evil."

I nodded along with her, but inside I was freaking out.

NAME: Wugnot (WUG-not)
HEIGHT: 3'
WEIGHT: 184 lbs
TYPE: Hobgoblin
ORIGIN: Truck stop off Route 39
WEAKNESSES: TERRIBLE driver
SMELL: His feet smell like patchouli and stinky cheese.
SIGHTINGS: Usually with Mama Vee or in the basement of Sitter HQ
ALLIES: The other members of the Order of the Babysitters

The van pitched as we turned another corner. I heard an angry chirp come from a box covered in cloth. I tried to get a better look at it, but Mama Vee cleaned the dirt off my face with a baby butt–wipe. She removed a kettle bubbling in the kitchenette and poured me a cup of hot tea. My insides warmed with the flavor of cinnamon and honey.

"Talk to me," she said, tossing me a bag of home-made cookies.

Only when I crammed the cookies into my mouth did I realize just how hangry I was. I handed her Jacob's drawing of the cloven-hoofed Boogeyman.

"This is the monster that took Liz and Jacob," I said between bites. "I have the weirdest feeling I've met him before," I said.

Mama Vee's emerald eyes narrowed at me. "You have," she said.

I stopped eating. The cookies bunched in my stomach.

Images shined in my memory. My closet. The Grand Guignol's voice. Singing, hypnotizing. My hands clutching my teddy bear. The inside of a dark burlap sack. Veronica's face smiling down at me, dimples, long hair. Back then she said it was just a nightmare.

"That wasn't a nightmare. That was real," I said. "And you . . . saved my life?"

The silver-haired woman nodded and then stared off with a disappointed, faraway look. She clutched a crystal dangling from her necklace. "I thought I got rid of him. That's why he's not in any of the SIT guides. But . . . he's in mine. . . ."

She removed an old, dusty Trapper Keeper with a tattered blue notebook tucked inside. "Property of Veronica Preston." I thought back to teenage Veronica sitting on our couch, scribbling notes inside of it, claiming it was algebra homework. I smiled a little, remembering how cool I thought she was. She wore toe rings, and she talked on the phone to boys, and her braid was as long as I was tall.

Vee opened the guide. Sketches of monsters and demons were lit by the flicker of passing yellow streetlamps. She handed it to me and turned to a page taped with fluttering newspaper clippings: "Twins Missing, 1823." "Explosion in Kindergarten, 1900." "Baby Vanishes, 1900." "Drowning at Falls, 1923." "Kidnapping from Mall, 1975."

Old, blurry photographs and children's drawings from different eras crinkled in the guide. Each of them showed a man with hooves for feet, wearing a black suit and matching Jacob's drawing with chilling similarity.

THE GRAND GUIGNOL

ORIGIN: Underworld? Realm of the Unknown and Unmeasured? Alabama?

CURRENT HAUNTS: Western Hemisphere? Eastern Hemisphere? New England?

BEWARE! El Grande's mind is powerful. It's worse than any slithering tail or sharp claw, because he can make you believe something you knew was false—and he can make you see it, too. If he wants you to think the sky is green, well, when you look up, the sky will be green. Having a powerful mind doesn't make you a monster. It's how you use it that does.

The Grand Guignol is one of the Boogeymen.

He feeds on fear.

POSSIBLE WEAKNESS: Silver daggers. Angel Fire. Silver daggers NO BUENO. Angel Fire BIG WIN.

I looked up in panic.

"'One of the Boogeymen'?" I squeaked. "As in . . . more than one Boogey?"

Mama Vee gave me a grim look. "The council has identified a total of seven Boogeymen."

"Seven?" The cookie crumbs in my mouth felt like sawdust.

Mama Vee's face darkened. Her eyebrows knitted with sadness. "I thought I got rid of him. But . . . I failed. And now look what's happened. . . ." The sound of tiny wings angrily flapped from inside the tucked-away box. "Tonight's only the tip of the iceberg, kiddo," she said, biting the inside of her cheek.

The pages of the guide rustled in my shaking hands. There was a picture of a four-year-old preschool boy, with the name "Kevin" written below it, stapled to the page.

His shaggy hair, his missing front tooth.

Kev. Liz's little brother.

"I need you to focus, Kelly," Mama Vee said, touching my shoulder. "I checked where El Grande used to haunt, but he wasn't there. It's just a grocery store now. We don't know where he is, so it's very important that you remember where he took Liz."

"W-where—?" I stuttered, trying to remember the carriage vanishing into the cold fog.

Where did it go?

My mind was blank except for Liz's echoing scream. It all happened so fast. I didn't see where he went. I didn't even know the direction. I hit my forehead with my knuckles, as if my memory were a bottle of ketchup

I could get flowing. Still nothing.

Mama Vee's glum reaction made me hate myself for not paying more attention at the moment Liz was taken.

"Don't beat yourself up," she said, taking my fist away from my forehead. "I should have been there tonight, but I got held up." Her strong demeanor seemed to crumble. "Ten-foot-tall tarantula in Seekonk laid its eggs in a kid's attic. Don't ask," she sighed, then tensed the muscles in her jaw. "Now I realize, it was a distraction to keep me from the big show. I should've known better."

The van rattled as Wugnot downshifted, steering through a suburban street.

Come on, Kelly! Think.

I dug into my pocket and pulled out the lens. "Liz got that off a Toadie," I said, handing Mama Vee the odd piece of glass. "So maybe it's from wherever they're keeping Jacob. I dunno. Maybe it's a giant contact lens?"

"I'd hate to see that eye," Wugnot said, chuckling.

Mama Vee turned it over with her fingers, feeling the spiral ridges.

"Guide says Toadies like shiny stuff." I shrugged. "They probably stole that from the Grand Guignol's hideout." A puzzled yet amused smile spread across Vee's face as she stared at me. I blushed, self-conscious. "I mean, I could be wrong," I said into my sleeve.

"Doubt it," she said, looking through the glass, her magnified eye fixed on me, like she were reading a book printed on my forehead. "Always knew you'd be a babysitter." Her tone sounded strangely proud.

My eyebrows peaked. "Me? I'm . . . not really the warrior type of girl."

"Then what type of girl are you?" she said.

I shrugged and chewed the sleeve of my brown sweater.

I'm the type of girl who wants to live long enough to go to summer camp.

At least that was honest, but it didn't feel right to say it.

"What about all those random jobs you had? Don't you think they prepared you for this?" Vee asked.

Packing groceries *was* a good workout, but how did she even know about that?

"I keep track of all my kids," she added with a wink. "Especially the ones with . . . promise." Passing headlights flooded the van, illuminating Mama Vee's eyes like shining emeralds. "But you never stayed too long, did you?" she continued in a mysterious tone. "Because they weren't the right fit."

"I thought it was 'cause I hate working," I mumbled.

She smiled and shook her head. "Ever think maybe *this* might be your fit?"

I shifted under her piercing stare. The smell of

patchouli and stinky-cheese hobgoblin feet was gagging me. And the fluttering, shaking thing in the box at the back of the van was really freaking me out.

I rolled down the window. Icy wind shot inside, refreshing me as I breathed in deep. I stared at the houses streaking past and thought of all the people asleep in their beds, cozy and clueless. Mama Vee leaned closer to me.

"Why do you think the Grand Guignol came after you all those years ago, Kelly?"

I went completely still.

Mama Vee reached out to gently turn my chin so my eyes met hers. "We've been waiting a long time for you, kiddo."

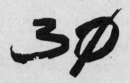

The van veered off the road and roared across the remains of the Enchanted Forest Amusement Park. Mud splattered the windshield as the van shot past a giant, cracked plastic unicorn with cartoony eyes.

I held on to the rocking cabin, thousands of questions whizzing through my head.

"We"? More babysitters, monster hunters? Waiting? For me? What did I do? Or what was I going to do? 'Cause I'm not planning on doing anything. The Grand Guignol came after me when I was a little kid, not because I was weak, but because I was . . . What was I?

Not to toot my own horn, but what if . . . what if this was like my truth or something?

A strange warmth fluttered through me. The thought

of one of the seven Boogeymen being afraid of me when I was four years old made me smile. Maybe I wasn't so helpless after all.

The van jolted to a stop, and I tumbled forward, bonking my head on a wood cabinet. The door rumbled open.

Moonlight beamed on the melted faces of fairy-tale statues in the failed theme park. Glints of light and metal swooped through the decaying figures of frog princes and knights in armor.

"Vee!" screamed Berna.

Cassie, Curtis, and Berna pedaled fiercely toward us. They bumped down a hill onto a fallen sign that read "Welcome to the Enchanted Forest." They launched off the makeshift ramp and flew toward the van.

WHOOSH, WHOOSH, WHOOSH.

They skidded their BMX bikes to a stop in line with one another, standing at attention before Mama Vee.

"President Preston," Curtis said, giving Mama Vee a crisp salute.

"KELLY!" Berna shouted happily at me. She sprang off her bike and into the back of the van. "Newbie's still alive." She hugged me, her gum snapping in my ear. "I got your location and I sent it to Vee."

I hugged Berna thankfully. She smelled like sugary, fruity candy.

"Way to be alive, Newbie." Curtis said, snapping his boots together with a crooked salute.

Cassie narrowed her eyes and crossed her arms. She seemed suspicious that I could have made it this far without getting killed. Wugnot scrambled out of the window to help them tie their bikes to the roof.

"Ooorah, Wugnot!" Curtis said, reaching up to high-five the hobgoblin. Wugnot snorted, his tail slapping Curtis's palm.

"I inshishted we call you, Preshident Preshton," Cassie sprayed to Mama Vee. "But I wash vetoed."

Berna groaned. Mama Vee cocked her head at Cassie. "No one likes a suck-up, Cassie." I giggled with Berna and Curtis.

Cassie blushed and then looked around the van. "Where ish Lish?" she asked.

The smile fell from my face. They all stared at me.

"She was taken by the Grand Guignol," I said quietly.

Berna stopped chewing her gum. Cassie mumbled, spit dripping from the end of her hanging lip. Curtis's crooked eyes darted around, as if he couldn't believe Liz wasn't here.

"This is a total"—his breath trembled to get the words out—"soup sandwich, man."

"We're going to get her back," Vee called out, breaking our sad silence. She clunked down in the passenger seat and pulled a lever. The seat unhinged and swiveled around to face us.

"Liz nicked that off the Toadie," she said, tossing the glass lens to Berna. "It's our only chance of finding her and Jacob and the four other kids that have gone missing tonight."

"Four other kids?" whispered Berna.

Mama Vee nodded regretfully.

"Do your thing, Bloodhound," Mama Vee said to Berna.

Cassie and Curtis huddled around Berna as she balanced the Toadie's glass on her fingertips and her gum chewing went into overdrive. Her eyes narrowed, and she blew a fantastic bubble. Everyone watched in silence, their eyes widening with the expanding swirls of purple and pink and green gum. Ever so slightly, her left hair puff twitched and trembled.

"Could've come off a chandelier, but I don't know where," I said.

Berna's bubble popped, but her eyes remained fixed on the spiral ridges winding around the glass. "Keep talking," she said.

"Uh. Or it could be like a lens for a lighthouse." I shrugged.

Berna blinked. She sucked in her gum and held up her finger for total silence. The only sounds were frogs croaking in the swampy, rundown park and Berna's teeth grinding into her gum.

"Last year, I wrote a history report that got a B plus," Berna began slowly. "The report was about an Italian shipbuilder slash whaler named Enrico Colleti who moved to Rhode Island in 1803." I glanced around the van. Everyone was leaning forward, drawn in by Berna's voice. "He had a method of making glass that left spirals in it that looked just like this," she said, pointing at the winding ridges. "He also built a lighthouse here and named it after his Native American wife. And it was called . . ."

Her chewing slowed. Berna reached into her mouth, removed the wad of gum, and stuck it to the wall of the van in defeat.

"I forget," she blurted out.

Cassie, Curtis, Wugnot, Vee, and I slumped back, the spell broken. I pulled at the frayed end of my brown sweater and wondered if I would be judged for chewing on it like a rabid bunny.

"THE QEEQONG LIGHTHOUSE!" Berna cried. She snatched her gum from the wall, popping it back into her mouth.

"Get us there, Wuggie!" Mama Vee commanded.

Wugnot's tail threw the van into gear. I tumbled off a gypsy fart pillow. Wugnot snorted. "Please keep your

241

arms and legs inside the ride at all times," he said, pulling the wheel violently to the left. He snatched a scroll from a box above the driver's seat. Driving with one hand, his tail unrolled a centuries'-old map of Rhode Island.

"Eyes on the road!" screamed Mama Vee.

Wugnot swerved around deer standing in the middle of the street. We screamed. The thing in the box let out a piercing shriek. Wugnot coolly tossed the map back to Curtis, who looked like the only one who enjoyed Wugnot's merciless driving.

"You navigate, I'll drive, soldier," Wugnot growled.

"Sir, yes, sir!" said Curtis. He stuck his nose an inch away from the map. "Qee-kong? Quong? Am I saying that right? It's two clicks due north and seven clicks east, sir."

"Just tell me left or right, kid," grumbled the ancient hobgoblin. He punched the gas while jamming the stereo on full blast—heavy metal insanity. I pressed my palms against my ears and saw Berna and Cassie and Mama Vee casually stuff cotton into theirs.

"Cool down, Wugnot," Vee warned him. "Remember what happened last time you got excited."

"Buckle up," Wugnot smirked as he reached for a switch on the dash marked "Ax Beak Boost."

BOOM! The engine wailed and screamed sparks, and we rocketed across the jagged, coastal road, clinging to the seats. Wugnot's chuckle went from raspy and

242

low to a shrieking, high-pitched cackle.

Curtis held on to Cassie for support while he read the old map. "Lighthouse! Dead ahead!"

Like a skeleton's finger jutting up from the earth, the lighthouse glowed bone white in the full moon. A fierce wind ripped across the ocean, smashing massive waves into the rocky shore below. Its dirt-caked windows were dark and cracked from years of neglect.

Wugnot's tail yanked up the emergency brake, sending the van into circles. The world blurred and my teeth rattled. Berna reached out and grabbed my hand. The van finally wobbled, stopping on its giant tires.

We piled out and stood before the dead lighthouse. Someone had spray-painted a huge smiley face with Xs for eyes on the front. The face's drippy, red-painted smile looked like it was grinning a mouth full of blood. There was a steel door at the base, welded to the frame with a thick metal scar and rivets. The handle had been torn off.

Mama Vee reached into the van and pulled up the old carpet on the floor to reveal a hidden compartment lined with swords, clubs, blades, potions, and a small wooden box. A large test tube of twinkling blue powder was nestled inside the box's velvet lining. She held it up, admiring its sparkling crystals.

"Angel Fire. Collected from the tears of angels by

ancient Irish babysitters. Grand Guignol, you're going down."

It felt good to know she was confident and ready to kick the Grand Guignol's twitchy tail—especially when my insides were nothing but a bowl of shuddering pudding.

She tucked the vial into her overall pocket and pulled her long, silvery braid into a bun, jamming a knitting needle in it to hold it in place. She snatched a hook and chain from the secret compartment and swung it around her midsection, and it wrapped around her like a snake, locking into place.

Next she pulled a large oak tube from underneath the passenger's seat and whirled it in her hands. Slammed it down. A thick steel barb shot from its end. *SHINK!*

"Be careful in there," she said. "The Grand Guignol can worm his way into your mind and make you believe things that aren't real." She warned us as she tapped her finger against her forehead. "So keep a clear head."

A terrible thought crept up on me. I raised my hand. "If the Grand Guignol can manipulate minds . . . what would happen if he got into Jacob's nightmares?"

Mama Vee slung her harpoon over her shoulder, and I was filled with an ominous feeling.

"If he seizes control of Jacob's nightmares," she said in a chilled hush, "he could turn the world into a living nightmare."

"That's why he took Jacob," I said. "He's going to turn his Gift into an atomic nightmare bomb."

Swirling black clouds boiled as crashing waves sprayed me with chilly salt water. I shivered, finally understanding. . . .

The Time of Nightmares has begun.

31

My hair whipped wildly into my eyes. Curtis smeared his face with camouflage makeup and offered me some. I thanked him and looked at the hardware Berna was sliding out of her backpack: a Louisville Slugger baseball bat with an iron skull fixed to the end. Cassie turned on a headlamp, reached behind her backpack, and removed a pair of machetes that she spun through the air like color guard flags.

She tucked her swords back into the holsters under her pack and straightened her collar. Curtis stroked a teddy bear in his hand.

"Um. Can—can I get, like, a sword or a cool crossbow?" I asked, feeling very empty-handed.

Mama Vee tossed me batteries for my flashlight.

"Keep the fire burning, kiddo." She winked.

"But. Um. I'd like some—some hardware, please."

Mama Vee turned her full attention on me. "A babysitter's greatest weapon isn't their fists or their ability to change a diaper with one hand. It's their brains. Their courage. Their love for those in need. That's why parents entrust us with their children. And that's what gives us the power to defeat evil."

The SITs nodded, listening to Vee. I shifted, pulling at my green jacket. "Totally. Yeah. I get that. But can I get a weapon?" I asked again.

Mama Vee sighed. "Fine."

She dug around the van and lifted a long, gnarly branch out of the secret compartment. Holding it delicately in her palms, she presented it to me, as if we were in some kind of ceremony.

"Behold. The most powerful weapon in the babysitter arsenal. The Staff of Destiny. Enchanted by the Ninth Circle of Shaolin Sitters on Shingow Mountain." She waved the branch around in front of me. "The staff gives whoever holds it utmost power to win any battle."

"Why doesh she get the Shtaff of Deshtiny?"

"Shut up, Cassie," said Berna.

"Are you serious?" I asked.

"I never kid a kiddo."

My hands hummed and tightened around the staff. It felt powerful, almost magical. My muscles tingled. It

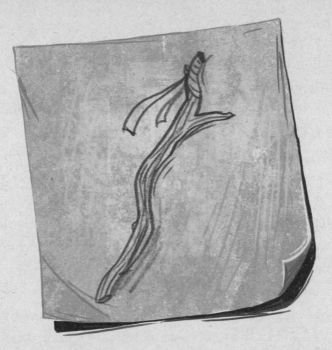

made a sharp whistle as I swung it through the air. It felt . . .

"Wow," I said.

Mama Vee whisked the black silk from the hidden box, revealing a small, Gothic birdcage with ornate carvings. She tapped three times on the birdhouse's front door.

"Neech, Katella, Malik," Mama Vee called out, opening the tiny gate. "Double-time."

The birdcage jumped, and shafts of light darted out between the wooden bars. Three balls of light with see-through hummingbird wings shot out. I stumbled back, mouth hanging open. The glowing orbs circled Mama

Vee, surrounding her in a rush of warm light.

"Recon pixies," Berna whispered to me. Her eyes were wide and locked on the flying wonders swooping around the white bricks of the lighthouse. "Vee rescued 'em. Pretty cool."

Mama Vee whispered something to the biggest, brightest creature and showed all three the circle of glass and Jacob's drawing of the Grand Guignol. With a loud ring and a rustle of invisible feathers, two golden fairies shot toward the lighthouse like shooting stars. The last one gave Mama Vee an affectionate nip on her nose before following the others.

The streaks of golden light shot higher and higher, illuminating the fog around the broken lighthouse lantern. Mama Vee watched them with a small pair of binoculars. One of the pixies found a crack in the window at the very top and rang out for the others to join it. A dumbstruck smile appeared on my face as I watched them vanish inside the lantern, which was momentarily set aglow by the passing pixies, making it look like it had been quickly turned on, then off. Over the sound of the crashing waves and hissing wind, a crystal-clear ringing, like a tiny Christmas bell, echoed in the tower.

"Yep. This is the place," Vee confirmed.

The faint halo of light vanished as the recon pixies went deeper into the lighthouse to check things out. I imagined them swooping down drainpipes, lighting up the shadows.

"Super blood moon's rising, Vee," Wugnot said, peering up. We all craned our necks to see that the moon overhead was tinted a bloody, pale red.

Mama Vee groaned. "This night just keeps getting better and better."

Berna threaded her arm with mine and whispered, "Super blood moon makes for a powerful surge in evil."

"Means we have twenty minutes before it reaches peak and the Grand Guignol's at his strongest power," Mama Vee said, checking her watch.

"Twenty minutes to save the world?" gulped Curtis as he set the timer on his digital watch. "Suh-weet." He popped a black beret on his head.

I looked at Berna like "Are you serious?" and she looked at me like "This is for real serious-serious."

Golden light flooded from under the steel door, and three musical knocks quickly followed.

"Clear," Mama Vee said.

I held my staff before me, and the Order of the Babysitters and I marched toward the looming metal door. I saw a lone twisting tree growing from the cracked mud ringing the lighthouse. Shiny black apples dangled from its branches. Some had large bites taken out of them. I felt a strange need to pick them.

"Don't touch thoshe!" hissed Cassie. "Could be poishon."

I looked to Mama Vee, who gave me a "go for it" nod. I plucked a few and zipped them into my backpack. Pulling my puffy green jacket tighter, I joined the others, who had lined up outside the steel door.

Mama Vee signaled Wugnot. The hobgoblin backed up. He stuffed his trucker hat into his pocket. He lowered his chunky horn at the door and charged with powerful speed. The door buckled and fell with a clang. Wugnot steadied himself against the empty doorframe and shook the fuzz out of his head as Vee and the others gave him a thankful pat on the shoulder.

I gripped my warrior's staff and followed everyone into the abandoned lighthouse.

"Follow my lead," Mama Vee said. "And no matter what, stay together."

Their flashlights swept a cramped chamber lined with grimy tiles oozing brown muck, streaked with giant tears of dirt. The sound of trickling water echoed from deep within the lighthouse. I stayed close to Berna and choked up on my staff, like I was ready to hit a fast-ball (or anything that moved).

The glowing pixies zipped down a drainage grate. Their twinkling bell-like ringing bounced off the pipes and grew faint as they descended deeper underground. Mama Vee peered through the bars. "Something's down there," she said.

A pukey smell, like a zombie's burp, rose from the drain, and I backed away. There was a fireplace in the corner, an old one, paved with slabs showing pictures of strange creatures with forked tongues. In the center of the creepy images was a brass horseshoe.

"Lookit!" Cassie shrieked, reaching for the shining horseshoe.

"Don't—" Mama Vee started, but Cassie touched it, anyway.

Click.

The floor dropped out underneath our feet.

32

Screaming, we rushed down an oily slide. Spongy, wet moss and ribbons of seaweed slushed under my fingers as I tried to stop myself from falling face-first down the world's stinkiest waterslide.

Spiraling out of control, I cried out for Berna and the others as they whooshed into a different tunnel.

"Kelly!" Berna screamed.

Her hand grabbed mine, but our fingers slipped apart.

I snatched on to a sewer grate on the side of the tunnel. Trembling, I clung to it with one hand and the Staff of Destiny with the other. Water gushed over me.

SPLASH! SPLASH! SPLASH!

Through the sewer grate, I could see into a sea cave

where a sludgy funnel spat Mama Vee, Wugnot, and the SITs into an icy pool of seawater. They each let out a shocked howl.

"Kelly?" Vee frantically swam around wrecked rowboats and the rotted wooden figurehead of a mermaid bobbing nearby.

"Up here!" I cried out.

Treading water, Berna and the other kids looked near the chute that barfed them out and saw me behind the grate. I tried to shake it lose, but it didn't budge.

"Hang on, kiddo!" Mama Vee cried out.

"I don't know how much longer I can!" My arm was shaking.

A long white stick floated past Berna. No. Not a stick. A bone. Most likely a leg bone. Human. Berna watched, transfixed with horror, as it floated along the waves and bumped into a towering pile of picked-clean skeletons.

The only way out for them was through the moss-stained mouth of a large, hideous face carved into a faraway cave wall. "Over there!" I said. Mama Vee nodded thankfully up at me.

"We're outta here, gang. Let's move," Vee said, desperately swimming toward their only hope of an exit.

Beneath the water, something flittered across Cassie's ankle. A fish? An eel? Cassie clenched her jaw and squinted into the depths. Panic rose inside me.

"What's wrong?" Curtis asked.

Cassie jolted suddenly and was pulled down below the surface.

"Cassie!" Curtis cried, diving down after her.

Mama Vee spun around and grabbed for them.

Behind the babysitters, the water's surface swelled.

"Look out!" I screamed.

An enormous, human-sized tentacle rose. In its grasp, Cassie hung upside down by her foot, gasping for breath. Curtis arced over them, swinging from another squid-limb the size of an oak tree. Berna hollered and swung her bat at the ten-foot-tall slithering shape, but her bat stuck in its thousands of little sucker mouths.

Wugnot and Mama Vee drew their weapons, but another tentacle shot from below and caught their arms with the speed and squeeze of an enormous boa constrictor. Vee and Wugnot were yanked upward, dangling over a fang-filled mouth the size of a doorway. I shrieked.

Berna looked up at the forest of tentacles writhing over her.

"Is this in the guide?" screamed Berna.

"No. But it should be!" said Mama Vee.

Berna's bat slipped from her grip. A rumble rolled from the dark depths of the water.

In an explosion of waves, six enormous tentacles lashed out, snatching Berna and thrusting her up in the air. An ancient-looking sea monster breached the surface, its slimy skin covered in hermit crabs and scuttling shrimp. The Leviathan's spiky fantail slapped the water, like a happy dog waiting to receive a treat.

Mama Vee was hanging by her ankle, trying to free her harpoon from the tentacle's vicious, leechy grip. A throaty gurgle of glee bellowed from the sea monster, shaking its fat, slimy belly. The creature blasted her in the face with its damp, rotten-sushi breath.

Vee gagged and turned away to see the upside-down, frightened faces of the children she had trained and the hobgoblin she called a friend swaying from the beast's unforgiving limbs. I thought Vee was going to say something inspiring, like "Don't give up" or "We'll make it," but the sea monster threw back its head, stretched its jaws wider, and released its grip on the babysitters, dropping them into its hungry, waiting mouth.

I cried out for them, but my fingers slipped from the grate, and I nosedived straight down the sewer-slide into misty darkness.

33

I shot out of the edge of the tunnel and plunged into a bank of damp fog.

WHAM!

I slammed onto a sandy floor and wheezed, like I had been punched in the stomach. My flashlight fell out of my backpack and clattered across the sand. It shined upon glistening rock walls dotted with spiky starfish, puckering mussels, and clusters of jagged barnacles. Seaweed had taken root in the ceiling, dangling in thick, rubbery clumps.

I waved my wooden stick through the hanging weeds.

"Berna? Vee?" I called out.

The sound of distant, crashing waves was all I heard.

Through curtains of algae, I could see a faint glow at the very end of the tunnel. I walked toward it, praying it was the recon pixies.

"You guys?" I cried.

At the end of the corridor was a monumental door with grotesque, gargoyle-like figures etched into it. *Monster chic.* It was half-open, like someone was waiting for me to enter. Beyond the bizarre door, I saw what looked like the inside of an underground palace.

He's in there. Waiting for you.

I walked through the arched passageway, carved out from the rock by ancient, expert hands. Behind me, the seaweed stirred down the tunnel's dark throat. Crashing waves echoed, as if I were standing inside a giant seashell.

I can't stay here. The blood moon thing. It's almost midnight.

You can do this, Ferguson. You have to do this.

My sweating palms gripped the staff tighter.

But he's in there.

I cautiously peeked around the stone door.

That's why you have to go in there, Kelly. Now be brave, move your butt.

I ducked through the giant doorway and into a massive cave where a great chandelier was suspended from the rocky ceiling. Hundreds of candles burned in its crystal holders, casting the cavern in a deep, golden glow. The lair was decorated like an old French castle, fit for the Prince of Darkness.

How charming.

Along the walls hung old paintings of people who looked like royalty. Not-so-human royalty. One portrait of a man with a stately expression on his face had a third eye in the center of his forehead. The third eye seemed to be following me as I crept around the room. There was also a painting of an elegant woman in a ball gown, posing with a fancy dog in her arms, but upon closer inspection, I saw that the woman had sharply pointed ears and the fancy dog in her arms was actually a furry serpent.

The seven Boogeymen, I realized, feeling like I had swallowed a snail. *Please don't let them be here, too.*

I scanned the cavernous lair for any sign of Jacob, Liz, or the others as I moved past a long dining table. Silver platters of skewered eels and bowls of broth with bobbing chunks of mystery meat were on the table.

So this is what Thanksgiving looks like in hell.

Seven empty dinner plates with neatly folded napkins and glimmering ivory-handled cutlery waited before their chairs.

Seven plates. The Grand Guignol was expecting company.

Past hell's kitchen, a dark, shadowy hole had been dug out of the ground, with rocky stairs spiraling into a hidden chamber. A pale, flickering light twitched from the base of the stairs.

Totally normal, I thought, trying to laugh my way out of my fear. Didn't work.

Footsteps shuffled along the sand-strewn floor. I held my staff before me and crouched behind the dining table. Someone was emerging from the farthest end of the underground palace. I felt dizzy and a little nauseous, like I had just eaten a multivitamin on an empty stomach.

A person stepped into the light. I gripped my staff even tighter as they walked toward me.

It was a boy.

"Victor?" I whispered.

Victor craned his head around the chair and gave me a warm, innocent smile. His big puppy-dog brown eyes made me feel less alone. "Hello, Kelly."

I could hardly speak. "What?"

"*Estoy aquí para ayudarte.* I'm here to help, silly," he whispered.

I nervously adjusted my ponytail and straightened my sweater.

"But . . ."

"I followed you," Victor said, flipping his dark hair away from his eyes. He gently took my hand and rubbed it, blowing warm air on my fingers. "So cold," he whispered.

My blood warmed, but my bones were still cold.

"If you're worried about the others, they're here."

"Jacob? Liz?"

Victor smiled at me. "Everyone. Come."

I lowered my staff to stand closer to him. He was still holding my hand. He stepped back, guiding me to step with him, and he placed his left hand on the small of my back.

A brass phonograph nearby whirled, playing an enchanting Spanish guitar song that echoed around the cave. Victor smiled bashfully and let my hand go.

"I'm sorry. I . . . cannot resist," he said, and bowed elegantly before me. "May I have this dance, *por favor*?"

I laughed. It felt good to laugh. Like everything was okay. Liz and Jacob were somewhere here, and they were fine. I laid my staff on the table, straightened up, and imitated a fancy-pants duchess.

"You may," I whispered, offering my hand.

He squeezed my fingers and took a step to the right. Before I knew it, we were waltzing.

My head was a helium balloon about to pop.

"You're a very good dancer," he said.

I felt like water gliding across glass.

Wait, I thought. *This is wrong. I am a terrible dancer.*

No, Kelly, you are a wonderful dancer, said a dark voice in my head.

No, I'm not! Remember Marissa Bergman's Bat Mitzvah? I was making wild, sparkly jazz hands to "Firework," and I hit a waiter who was carrying a tray of Cokes, and they all went flying down Marissa's dress? Marissa hasn't spoken to me since. I can't dance!

"Stop. This . . . this isn't right," I said, feeling like I was about to throw up.

Victor spun me past a giant mirror. My woozy, stretchy reflection was dancing with a tall slender man wearing furry brown socks.

Light-headed and dizzy, I looked past Victor's shoulder into the mirror and saw that the slender man holding me had black hooves for feet. I looked back at Victor, but in his place was the tall, wretched man from my nightmares.

"Hello, little girl."

35

I screamed and thrashed. The Grand Guignol's tail coiled around my ribs, and he held me tight as a noose. His nails dug into my wrists. I fought, kicked, bit, snarled, and spat, but he just calmly held me in a rigid, icy grip pulsing with impossible strength.

I felt like a cockroach was running through my brain, feeding on my thoughts.

"Where are my friends?" I screamed.

The Grand Guignol smirked and then twisted his wrinkled neck to check a grandfather clock leaning against the wall. Seven minutes to midnight.

"I'm afraid they didn't make it past my pet Leviathan."

I felt my heart slam to a complete stop.

He smiled like he knew this would destroy me. "That disgusting traitorous slob of a hobgoblin and those weird little kids." He scowled, waving his hand away. "Goldfish food."

"That—that's not possible," I said. "Veronica— She—"

"She's not here to protect you anymore, Kelly. It's just you and me."

My shoulders sagged. That couldn't be right. The chuckle gurgling from the demon's mouth confirmed my horrible feeling.

The fight began to drain from me, like an unplugged bathtub.

"And those little pixies. I saved those for myself. Deeelicious," he said, kissing his fingertips and rubbing his belly. "They do tickle going down, but I've worked up quite an appetite."

Mama Vee protected me. So did Berna, Curtis, and Cassie (in her own way). They were weird and strange, but they looked out for me. For one another. For the world. All they wanted was a safer place for kids to grow up, and this monster was laughing at their deaths.

"They were my friends," I whispered.

"Bit of an overstatement, isn't that? You only just met them tonight."

"Doesn't matter." My voice was still quavering.

The Grand Guignol cocked his head, studying me

with his sickly yellow eyes. "If they're your friends, then where are they? Where's Tammy, hmm?"

I gulped with growing fear.

"Where are Mom and Dad, hmm? Answer: They're not here, and you're all alone because they don't love you. No one does. But I'm here, Kelly. Because . . . I care."

I shook my head, fighting the muddy, dull feeling that pulled me down.

"Don't be sad. They had their chance. Now it's our turn." He handed me a lace hankie and circled me, like a great white shark. "In a few moments, it's going to be a whole new world, Kelly. What fun we'll have! What games we'll play! We can braid each other's hair and eat popcorn and talk about boys! Come see!"

He snatched my hand and pranced me around his lair. "Do you like my palace? Believe it or not, I found that chandelier on Craigslist. Amazing what steals you can find on there." He nodded at the enormous entrance door with its creepy gargoyle carvings far across the cave. What do you think? Scale of one to ten. Be honest. It's a ten, I know."

I swung like a helpless rag doll in his grip as he yanked me around. My focus stayed on the long table where I had laid my staff down, like an idiot. I needed to grab my weapon and end this monster.

"I don't haunt just anybody, Kelly," he said. "I like

you. Both of us can't stand children. We both love raw slugs. And we both have very large empty spots in our hearts."

I looked at him with disgust as he sniffed and dabbed fake tears from his eyes. "Banished to the shadow realm. No one to call. Alone. Invisible. When all people do is scream and run from you, it's very hard to make friends."

He scowled at the seven empty place settings at the table. "I invited the Others . . . ," he said mournfully. "Serena, Cleetus, Baron." He shook his head at the bizarre Boogeyman portraits on the wall. "Do you think they RSVP'd? No. Not a word. Not one of the six others! They're just jealous because I'm the only one who really counts."

I slipped my hand out of his and crept toward the table while he moaned on about his sad life.

"And so I hide in closets. Lurk under beds, choking on dust and broken toys. And I get called names like 'creepy evil, twitchy goat legs' or 'that scary man who keeps trying to eat me.'"

I was four steps away from the table.

"I might be a monster. But I have feelings, too."

My hand slowly reached for the staff.

A black blur shot before me. *WHAM!* The Grand Guignol snatched my staff and spun it in whirling, hypnotic circles.

267

"That's why I know what you really want . . . ," he hissed with a smile.

I wanted to run, but I was strangely drawn toward the spinning staff as it blurred around and around in circles.

Oh no. It's happening again. He's pulling you under his spell. . . . Resist, Kelly. Don't . . . resist, Kelly. Don't resist, Kelly.

He jammed the staff into the floor and reached into his tattered coat pocket. A brochure with a picture of a lake and forests on it sprang into his hand. He unfolded the shiny pages, and I saw pictures of beautiful teenagers around a campfire. Arts and Crafts. Happy horses. A warm breeze that smelled like pine needles, suntan lotion, and hamburgers on the grill blew my hair back. I tasted chocolate s'mores. I felt warm sunlight streaming through evergreen trees while I rode on the back of a horse.

No, Kelly, I thought. *Don't let him trick you. . . .*

The Grand Guignol was standing in a field, dressed in red running shorts and a yellow tank top, with white socks pulled up to his furry knees. He blew a whistle that was hanging around his neck and gave me a thumbs-up to dive off the wooden dock into the refreshing crystal-clear lake with all my friends.

Splash.

"It's everything you wanted, Kelly." His voice

slithered, hot against my ear. "Independence. Confidence. Your truth. And you'll never be invisible again." His finger tapped on the payment information page of the magical brochure. "And I'll give it all to you. Just come with me."

His foul, poo-smelling breath snapped me out of my daydream. My fists hardened into stones and rose, shaking, shivering.

"I want Jacob . . . and Liz . . . and Kevin . . . *now.*"

The wrinkled warts and moles on the Grand Guignol's face drooped as he frowned down at me, his tail angrily ticking back and forth. A hermit crab clicked along the sandy floor. His hoof stepped on it with a sickening crunch.

"Wrong answer, Kelly."

Talons grabbed me from behind. Toadie claws sank through my sweater, almost piercing my skin. "Ow!" The smell of rotting garbage gagged me as the Toadies pried off my backpack and tossed it onto the dining table. The more I shook in their grip, the deeper their claws dug into my skin.

"Keeeeeleeeee," cooed Snaggle.

"Jacob's just a kid! Let him go!" I demanded, kicking at the Toadies.

The Grand Guignol's smile widened. "That *kid* has the ability to turn dreams into reality . . . and nightmares into monsters. He's the most powerful force I've encountered since I first looked in the mirror. That boy is the first chime in the Time of Nightmares, the beginning of the Era of Monstrosity, the—the . . ."

He stared into space for a moment and then snapped his fingers at the Toadies. "What did I call it earlier?"

"Drumpf?" gurgled Snaggle.

"Ah, yes—bringer of a world of evil. That's the one," said the Grand Guignol.

I shot my heel into his shin, but he just jeered at me, as if to show me I had no power over him.

"And here I was, so worried about you, Kelly. But you're just a girl," he said, stroking the knotted tangles of my red hair with twisted pity. "You truly are invisible."

I bit my lip and refused to cry, even as tears blurred my eyes.

"Now, go do as you're told, little girl. And disappear into nothing," he said.

The Toadies dragged me back, and something within me snapped. My knee caught a Toadie in the face. My elbow crunched Snaggle's beak. They acrobatically climbed over me, collapsing me under their weight.

"No!" I kicked and wailed as the Toadies dragged me off. "By the Order of the Babysitters of Rhode Island, I demand you surrender!"

The Grand Guignol's eyebrows peaked, and he let out a snooty cough. "First night on the job, huh, Kell?"

"I know you're scared of me!" I screamed. "That's why you tried to get me all those years ago!"

The tall monster looked down his nose at me, a hint of concern in his snake eyes.

"Well, guess what?" I shrieked at the top of my lungs. "I found you this time. And I'm gonna get *you*!"

My voice echoed off the cave walls, and there was total silence. The Grand Guignol swallowed, adjusted his cuff links, and cleared his throat. Even the Toadies looked surprised by the crazy threat that had shot from my mouth.

"Douse her with extra rosemary and lemon," the Grand Guignol called over his shoulder as he walked away. "We need to sweeten her up. Horrible, bitter, *smelly* thing that she is." His hooves clicking across the floor sounded like my mother's high heels. He marched down the rock-hewn staircase and into the dark hole as the Toadies hoisted me over their heads and carried me away.

Riding atop their talons, a teeny-tiny feeling of victory passed through me.

I got to him. I got to the Grand Guignol.

That little thought, that flicker of hope, lit a small flame in my heart, and even though I was being carried away to my death, I smiled.

The Boogeyman is afraid of me.

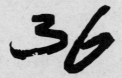

A crude cage the size of a car hung by a large chain at the end of the cavern. Snaggle unlocked it, and the others flung me inside.

"Merken der donugs!" mocked Snaggle from behind the thick iron bars. They drizzled olive oil and clumps of rosemary on me. They squeezed lemons in my face, stinging my eyes and blinding me.

"Gerf, gerf, gerf!" grunted Snaggle as he turned a crankshaft fixed to the wall.

My cage rose in jerky bounces up to the rocky ceiling. Rubbing my eyes, I saw the floor was littered with candy wrappers and moldy bits of Starburst and Tootsie Rolls. There was a bag ripped up near the candy with "Trick or Treat" written on it. A final clink, and the cage lurched to a swinging stop, high off the ground. Drifting back and forth, I could see that little pest Snaggle latch the crankshaft and scurry off with Goggles and the others.

I shook the bars, but the cage swayed uselessly, bumping into another hanging cage nearby. Someone was inside!

"Hey," I called out hopefully.

The figure, dressed in a fisherman's outfit, didn't turn around.

"Hey!" I called out again.

With a dusty creak, his head rolled back on his shoulders. A skeleton with a crooked jaw glared back at me. I gasped and turned away from my new neighbor. My guts twisted, and I was seasick in my rocking cage.

I picked a piece of rosemary out of my eyebrows and nervously bit the edge of my brown sweater, trying to think. Fifty feet below, I could see the crankshaft that held the chain to my cage in place. If I could reach that latch, I could lower this cage. . . .

I undid my shoelaces and tied them together, but that didn't reach nearly far enough.

I'm going to be cooked like a roasted chicken. My parents, Tammy, Victor, and the rest of the human race would have to live in a world of darkness, ruled by evil monsters and living nightmares. And it's kinda all my fault. Great movie! Bad night for Kelly.

I took a deep breath and searched within myself for that spark of greatness Mama Vee believed I had.

There's always a way, I remembered Liz saying.

I gnawed my sleeve, like a nervous mouse, and felt the clump of woven yarn unravel in my teeth. I pulled at the woolly string in amazement. The knitted sleeve slowly came undone in one single thread. I kept pulling it until I held a coil of thick yarn in my hand, my eyes widening.

I was wearing my way out.

"I love you, itchy brown sweater!" I cried as I threw off my jacket then quickly unraveled my entire sweater into a pile of woolly yarn onto my cage floor. I shivered in my green T-shirt as I knotted and braided the yarn into one long, fuzzy rope. Watching all those YouTube videos on how to weave friendship bracelets, like they do at summer camp, finally paid off.

Good ole Camp Miskatonic. I might just get there yet.

I tied a loop at the end and knelt down in my cage to lower the world's longest friendship bracelet toward the crankshaft's lever.

The rope swayed inches from the latch. I stretched out my arm. The loop brushed the release. "C'mon," I muttered.

I needed to get closer. If only I had the staff, I could tie the rope on the end. . . .

Think, Kelly.

I slumped against my prison's bars, and it wobbled. I narrowed my eyes and jumped to my feet. The cage shifted with my weight. . . . Yes! I grabbed the bars and pushed with my feet, like I was standing on a giant swing. The cage waved backward and forward, gaining distance each time.

When I swung closest to the wall, I dove, holding the rope out.

The loop brushed the crankshaft's lever. I drifted backward.

No, no! Push it, Kelly!

With all my might, I pressed my face against the rust-caked bars, squeezing forward, fingers barely holding the thick yarn.

My tiny lasso caught.

"Got it!" I crowed, pulling the sweater-rope.

The latch clicked, and I braced myself for the drop of a lifetime.

Gently, my cage creaked back and forth. I blinked and leaned my head against the bars to see if the latch had been pulled clear, but the rusty gears were not turning.

I sighed in defeat and looked at the limp brown rope of friendship in my hand.

Whoosh.

The cage suddenly dropped.

You know that feeling when you're on an elevator and it whooshes down so fast your stomach floats up a little? Multiply that by a hundred and then follow it with a shuddering, bone-shaking crash.

I was thrown into the other side of the cage. One of the bars had snapped and broken, pointing its jagged end an inch from my eye. I gulped.

"What the devil?" The Grand Guignol's voice boomed from below the chamber, followed by the sound of swishing trash bags.

Pulling back on the broken bar, I dragged myself out from the wreckage. Toadies launched from the depths, claws scratching against the rock walls.

"Gerba-dunk!" Snaggle snarled at me.

I backed up against the cave wall and held up my hands. "Wait! I've got something for you!"

I pulled Penny's sparkly tiara out of my back pocket. A glint of light hit it, sending sparkles into the greedy trash trolls' eyes.

"Parrrrrkllleeeee," they said, gurgling together.

I moved the tiara to the right, and the Toadies hungrily followed it. When I swung the tiara to the left, they lunged to the left, sniffing at it and rubbing their grubby claws together.

"Oh, yeah. It's from a real princess, too," I taunted them.

They stalked toward me. One troll's key ring jangled like cowboy boot spurs.

I tossed the tiara three feet away, and the trolls launched for it. They wrestled one another for a chance to hold it. I grabbed the lever on a second crankshaft, the one holding the skeleton's cage. I pulled. Gears spun out a fury of clanking chains. Huddled tightly around the gleaming tiara, the Toadies looked up at the massive falling cage.

"Nurm?" was Snaggle's last word.

Like four roaches meeting someone's heel, the Toadies burst into waves of goo. I shielded my face from the gloopy splatter. It was awesome and gross at the same time.

"Anyone for Toadie pancakes?" I smiled.

I glanced at the leaning grandfather clock. Only two minutes to midnight.

The Toadie's keys. I had a feeling I would need them.

"I can't even," I said, looking at the gooey mess that was formerly a Toadie quartet.

Yes, you can.

I looked away and jammed my hand under the cage into the juice and entrails. Feeling past slimy bones, I pulled out the key ring, slicked with a ribbon of slime. I wretched and wiped my hand on the wall.

"Nastiness!" I said.

No one said it would be pretty.

I grabbed my staff off the diabolical dining table and swung my backpack over my shoulders. I felt a surge of power. I forced my feet to walk to the edge of the dark staircase where the Boogeyman had gone.

Like a tiger wagging its paw at a mouse, the hole seemed to smile at me. *Step inside, little girl. I won't hurt you.*

My hands choked up on my gnarled, heavy staff, like it was a sword. I climbed down the stairs and into a ghostly, flickering light.

At the very least, I could stop this guy from hurting anyone else. Even if it meant I wasn't exactly around tomorrow, I had to do it for a chubby-faced boy; a crazy, blue-haired girl; and the whole stupid world.

38

The bottom of the stairs pulsed in a wash of colored lights. Something big and bright was beaming around the corner. Static electricity tickled the hairs on my neck. Clenching my staff to my chest, I stepped into a hallway of glimmering light.

Hundreds of televisions, flat-screens, big glassy TV tubes, and old computer monitors were stacked around the cave. Each screen was playing a horror movie or a creepy cartoon or a news broadcast about an environmental disaster. I squinted at freakish home movies of bugs, rattlesnakes, and explosions, playing on a loop.

"What is this?" I whispered in the bewildering light that was giving me a headache.

A snort in the shadows made me spin around. The

black carriage with the four towering skeletal horses was standing in the corridor. They were sniffing at something in my backpack, hooves hungrily stomping the ground.

Something else moved at the back of the carriage. Children. Four of them.

A little girl dressed like the Red Queen from *Alice in Wonderland*, a four-year-old boy in polka-dot pajamas, a six-year-old girl dressed like a cowgirl, and a boy wearing a pumpkin sweater. But no Jacob.

The children's eyes bulged like hard-boiled eggs. They were glued to the wall of televisions. I waved my hand in front of them, trying to break their trance, but they remained spellbound by the scary images pulsing around us.

The children had on leather skullcaps with straps buckled under their chins. Long glowing wires ran from the top of each cap and out of the carriage, deep into the cave.

Poor little guys. What is he doing to them?

I tried to open the cage door, but it was locked. The keys I dredged out of the Toadie puddle jangled in my pocket. I tried a few keys until one fit. As I unlocked the door, the skeletal horses whinnied and rose on their hind legs in protest.

"Shh. Quiet," I angrily whispered. "Shut up."

I quickly removed the strange black apples from my

pack and held them out. The horses bit them hungrily, bridles clacking in their bony jaws as they shook their ghostly manes. Bits of apple fell through their spectral throats, plopping onto the floor. I guess ghosts can't eat no matter how hungry they are.

A funny smile crept over my face.

Good thinking, Ferguson.

I made sure the phantom horses were all munching happily before I opened the cage door, unbuckled the straps beneath the little kids' chins, and ripped off the bizarre wired helmets.

One by one, the children blinked, their eyes shrinking back to normal size. Seeing they were in a very bad, very smelly place, they began to panic.

"Please, please, don't scream, you guys," I whispered. "My name's Kelly. I'm a babysitter. I'm here to help."

They looked at me, chins trembling.

"I have to pee," said the Red Queen.

"I want my daddy," said Polka-Dot Pajamas.

"I'm hungry. I want Doritos. Did you bring Doritos?" begged the cowgirl.

"Mommy?" wailed Pumpkin Sweater.

I clenched my jaw in frustration.

Kids.

"Shh!" I said, making a "zip it" move with my hand. "We have to be quiet or the bad guys will find us. Have you seen a boy named Jacob or a girl named Liz?"

Polka-Dot Pajamas pointed down the dark corridor. "Creepy, evil, twitchy goat legs took him in there."

A damp, cold wind howled from the shadows beyond the bright, sickly lights. The staff creaked in my fists. The horses' cobweb-colored tails swished as they finished their apples. I looked back at the kids' sad, lost faces as they huddled together. They were all staring up at me, waiting for me to tell them what to do. I was suddenly the adult in the situation, not the freaked-out kid.

What would Vee do? I thought. *What would Liz do?*

Pumpkin Sweater reached out his arms to me. I scooped him up, thinking he wanted to get down, but instead, he just hugged me, burying his face in my neck.

"My name's Timothy," whimpered the little boy. "I live at 555 Edgehill Avenue."

"It's going to be okay," I said, patting him on the back. It felt good to feel a heartbeat other than mine.

I carried him to the floor, and then I saw the other kids were reaching their arms out to me. I helped each of them out and got the warmest hugs I've had in a while.

"Okay. Now, uh, go upstairs and, uh, wait by the big front doors," I whispered, pointing up the craggy stairs. "If I'm not up in ten minutes, run and find the police."

"I can't," wailed Cowgirl.

"You can," I insisted. "Nothing's impossible. Even if you're little. Now stop being annoying and go hide." I spun her around, making her face the stairs.

That seemed to start a fire in the little girl. Her spine stiffened, and she jutted her chin forward. The other children quickly followed Cowgirl marching up the stairs. Cowgirl stopped at the top and glanced back at me with an anxious look. I waved for her to run and she finally did.

Leaving the sparkling, pulsing tunnel of evil screens, I followed the black wires snaking into the shadowy depths. I exhaled heavily and entered the chamber of nightmares.

39

I crouched behind a spiraling rock, staff braced against my heaving chest, stealing glances around the dark temple. An enormous fire burned at the other end. Silhouetted by its red glow, the Grand Guignol stared into a large glass box that hovered under his palms. Firelight beamed through the glass, creating prisms of incredible rainbows that crisscrossed around the dark chamber.

Someone was lying on a black satin pillow inside the box. It was Jacob.

LITTLE LOAF!

He was breathing, fast asleep. Good. Alive is good. But he was trapped in some kind of monster jewelry box. Not so good. Something was on his head. I squinted through the array of colorful shafts of light to see . . . wires running into a helmet strapped to his head. He looked like a supernatural science project. I could see his eyes rapidly darting under their lids. He was mumbling in his sleep.

Poor little guy, I thought. *He's having a nightmare and living one at the same time.*

"Dream, little one" I could hear the Grand Guignol coaxing. He held his palms over the floating glass box, like he was warming his hands over a campfire. "Feed on the children's fears and let the nightmares come."

I held my breath. Hugging the chamber wall, I quietly crept through the shadows, careful not to let the Boogeyman see me. I looked into the darkness for any passageways or weird holes where he might have stashed Liz. No such luck.

I really wish Liz were here.

I slid the staff between the straps of my backpack, keeping it tucked behind my shoulders. I was exploding with energy, and not in a good way.

"Grab Jacob and run. That's all you gotta do," I whispered.

GONG!

A deep, loud bell rang. It echoed off the temple walls. The clock struck midnight.

GONG!

It was now or never. I crouched into a sprinter's pose and tried to steady my breathing.

285

GONG!

I ran for Jacob. Sneakers pounding.

GONG!

A tremor rolled beneath the huge ancient temple, throwing me off balance.

GONG!

I wobbled and kept charging forward in a curvy line as the room shook.

GONG!

A crack shot through the ground, zigzagging from under Jacob, splitting the temple floor like an eggshell.

GONG!

Beneath my feet, chunks of the ground fell into a howling chasm. I jumped back from the fiery break. Hot winds shot from the divide that now separated me from Jacob and his captor.

The Grand Guignol's eyes were bewitched, crazy. He didn't see me through the curtain of swirling smoke. He was too enchanted by what was rising from below.

"'Mary, Mary, quite contrary, how does your garden grow?'" he whispered gleefully to himself.

Spirals of golden light rose from deep within the broken earth. A living cloud of twinkling glitter blew up into the monster cathedral.

"'With silver bells and cockleshells. And pretty maids all in a row.'"

Tingles prickled my skin as I watched the glitter,

this dream dust, swirl into hundreds of thick floating shapes.

Jacob screamed in his sleep and writhed in his glass chamber.

"No, no!" came Jacob's trapped, muffled cry.

I clamped my hands over my mouth to hold in my scream as I saw, with awe and terror, just why everyone said this five-year-old was so special.

Giant rats, goblins, snarling gargoyles, a fanged rabbit, foot-long centipedes, a dentist wearing a white jacket, and a hundred other unspeakable nightmares now filled the temple with throaty growls and haunting moans. It smelled like a sewer had exploded.

I clung to the wall, desperately trying to hide.

"Hello, darlings," the Grand Guignol called.

Oozing eyes and slimy mouths turned to face the Boogeyman. He held out his hands, welcoming his carnival of monsters.

"Happy All Hallows Eve. *Forever*," he said with a proud smile.

A gargoyle threw back its head and roared to the ceiling. The others joined him, crying their own freaky laughs or squeals.

The Boogeyman waved his hands higher and higher, rousing their vicious cheers.

I crouched down low behind a pile of fallen rocks and jammed my fingers into my ears, afraid I might go deaf or crazy from their blood-chilling shrieks. Squinting, I saw Jacob tossing his head back and forth, still trapped and asleep.

The hairs on the back of my neck rose, like an angry cat. I boiled with rage for the poor, helpless boy. Jacob had a gift, a remarkable power, and this jerk was twisting it for evil.

The monsters' attention was fixated on the Grand Guignol, who was giving them a motivational speech about taking over the world.

"In a few moments, we will be charging up the stairs and out into the world," said the Boogeyman. "This is our opportunity to feast and push humans to extinction, just like they pushed us to extinction."

He was all revenge this, devour that. *Blah, blah, blah.* Point is, their backs were to me. This was my only chance.

Fists clenched. My lips curled into a snarl. I was panting, like a wild dog. Maybe it was the magic nightmare dust in the air, but I felt myself becoming just a little bit of a monster. Scary part was, I liked it.

I shot from my hiding place, dodged a birthday clown, and sprang over the jaws of a horny bullfrog.

My mind raced faster than my legs. *Careful. Stay low! I don't think they see you—ZOMBIE! ZOMBIE!*

I slammed into a pack of undead businessmen. Their dry limbs exploded, and one of their heads rolled by me like a soccer ball, glaring at me.

"Braaaaaains," the businessman's head groaned.

This caught the attention of other nightmares nearby. I scrambled to my feet and ignored the sea of evil turning toward me.

I needed speed to make it across the fiery crack ahead. I ran, jammed my staff into the edge, and vaulted into the mist.

WHOOSH. WHAM!

I tumbled to the floor, skidding to a stop beside Jacob's glass prison. His eyeballs shook under his lids. I threw open the top of the glass box and tore the weird dream-helmet off Jacob's head.

Growls of confusion and disapproval rumbled around me. Through the wall of swampy gas, the monsters leered at me.

They've seen you, Kelly. No time. Just run.

I shook Jacob, screaming his name.

"You're too late." The Grand Guignol smiled, stepping toward me.

My blood raced, and I jabbed my staff at the cloven-hoofed monster. "Back off!" I screamed. "You have no idea what I'm capable of doing to you!"

The wretched monster put up his hands in mock surrender.

"You're too late, Kelly," he said, looking down at Jacob, who was stuck in a coma-like state. "I've been feeding him a steady dose of fear. He's petrified. My little goose is going to lay golden eggs for me until he's dead."

Tiny glitters of light rose from the depths of the cavern. More nightmares.

"The bigger the fear, the sweeter the nightmare! Aren't they just *gorgeous*?" he said, casting his hand across the twisted, hideous faces of his small army. "And these are just the beginning."

I clutched Jacob close to my heart. I made a wish. Not a wish to leave or run and hide. But a wish deeper and greater than myself. A wish to put an end to this nightmare and wake this poor, helpless child.

I felt Jacob stir in my arms. I looked down, and his eyes blinked open.

"Kelly?" Jacob said with groggy terror.

"I got you. I got you," I whispered as I held him.

The tiny glitters of light stopped rising and fell back down into the earth.

Hundreds of monsters still remained, but at least there would be no new ones.

The Grand Guignol's wrinkled mouth hung open in anger and amazement. If it was possible, his corpse-like skin grew even paler. His breath quivered. "That can't be. SLEEP! SLEEP, BOY!"

But Jacob was wide-awake.

I snarled, satisfied with the Boogeyman's shocked expression. There was no time to waste trading clever banter with this turd. I threw Jacob over my shoulders and looked back at him. "Piggyback?" I said.

He smiled. "Piggyback."

Jacob clung to my neck, wrapping his legs around my waist.

"Stop!" demanded the Boogeyman.

"Love to stay and chat, El Grande," I said, "but it's way past this little guy's bedtime."

Monsters leaped across the chasm, charging toward me. I held Jacob and ran, ran, ran.

Barks. Roars. Snapping jaws. Skeleton hands, ragged paws, and blobby messes grabbed at us. I swung my staff, knocking them aside.

With Jacob's arms wrapped around my neck, I clung to the boy's legs and hurdled across the growling sinkhole, barely making it over to the other edge due to the extra fifty pounds of ankle biter on my back. We spilled across the floor, heads clunking together. Through dizzy spots dotting my vision, I saw a sea of monster feet marching toward us.

I yanked Jacob off the ground and sprinted. Behind us, I heard the Grand Guignol scream, "Kill the girl and bring me the boy!"

I slung Jacob onto my back again as we ran into the screaming tunnel of TVs. The four ghastly horses raised their heads in the hopes I had returned with more apples.

I quickly undid their bridles and waved my hands furiously at them. The horses bucked and kicked, charging into the path of the monsters chasing us.

CRASH! The nightmares collided with the horses in a clatter of bones. They toppled to the ground, creating an epic monster pileup.

I rushed Jacob into the palace. My lungs burned worse than the time I tried (and failed) to run a seven-minute mile in gym class.

The four other children, who were huddled by the ancient gate on the other side of the cave, saw me and waved their arms in relief.

I held Jacob close and sprinted toward the towering doors.

Someone stepped in my path.

Liz.

"Liz! Oh, thank God, you're "

Her eyes were pure black. Her face was bloodless and her expression evil. Her lips looked like she had been drinking squid ink.

"Possessed," I finished with a gulp.

Liz snarled at me with wicked, spellbound intent.

"Liz!" exclaimed Jacob. Excited to see his favorite babysitter, he squirmed off my back.

"No!" I cried, grabbing for him.

Liz glared down at the boy with a dark expression. "Come to me, Jacob. I'm your favorite." Jacob slowly backed away from her, shaking his head.

"She looks scary," he whispered.

"Too much mascara," I said.

"Give him to me!" Liz snarled, stalking toward us.

Jacob hid behind me while I thrust out my staff, keeping Liz at a distance.

"You're not a bad person, Liz," I said desperately. "I've seen you sing the theme song to *Frozen*. You change diapers. And you love kids way more than I do."

Liz swatted the staff away and tackled me. She was so strong I could barely hold her off.

"But, Liz, I love you," said Jacob.

"Run, Jake!"

Jacob ran toward the other children. Liz lunged at

him, but I jammed the staff between her ankles, tripping her. I scrambled to my feet and planted the Staff of Destiny on her chest, trying to keep her pinned down.

"You love Jacob!" I cried out. "He's like your family . . . remember?"

Liz grabbed the staff and tried to wrench it from my hands. I held tight, my arms growing weak.

"You're not alone, Liz," I said. "I'm here. . . ."

I saw something flash across Liz's face. Something was stirring inside of her.

"And we can find Kevin. Together."

Her jaw clenched. Her neck muscles strained and pulsed. She was fighting the Grand Guignol's control from somewhere deep inside of herself. From the part that remembered her brother.

"Jacob's here! I'm here! And—and—we're in big trouble, so you better help us!" I pleaded, trying to draw her out of the darkness.

The ground below us shook with the monster's trampling footsteps.

They're coming.

Liz let go of my staff and gagged on a deep, guttural, phlegmy cough.

"We're your friends, Liz!" I looked back at Jacob, urgently encouraging the scared kid to say something.

"Yeah, Liz," Jacob whispered.

Liz gurgled and heaved up a thick chunk of dripping

gray slime. The world's biggest loogie splatted on the floor with a wet *thwack*. Liz gasped for breath. Her eyes blinked back to normal. The blood rushed to her face.

"Liz?" I pleaded.

She gave me a weak smile; her lips looked rose colored, full of life.

An angry grumble sounded between us. Liz's loogie glared up at us with gooey, beady little eyes. I jabbed my staff down at the slimeball, and it quickly scuttled across the floor, like a jellyfish sliding across an ice rink.

"You . . . came back for me?" Liz said.

"Well. Yeah." I shrugged.

"Why?"

"You're my friend, stupid."

Liz smiled.

"You guys!" Jacob called, pointing behind us.

The Grand Guignol and his army of nightmares swarmed up the staircase. The snot-goo creature trickled up the Grand Guignol's leg and stuffed its gloopy body into a small snuffbox the Grand Guignol held in his outstretched hand. The Boogeyman snapped the lid shut and tucked the box into his jacket pocket.

Liz and I stood protectively before the children. Liz cracked her knuckles.

"Ready to throw down, Ferguson?" she said coolly.

Uh . . . no.

"Liz. There's like a hundred of them and two of us."

297

Liz scanned the approaching army of nightmares.

"Okay, maybe you're right," she said.

We turned to the enormous doors, but they slammed shut with an ominous boom. We tried to pry them open, but there were no handles, and each one of them must have weighed a ton. We were trapped, and the smorgasbord of monsters was lurching toward us.

"Boys and ghouls, dinner is served," the Boogeyman called merrily.

Hundreds of wretched mouths, maws, beaks, fangs, and jaws opened as the monsters descended upon us. The children hugged me and Liz. I pressed my back against the massive stone door and swung my staff helplessly. If I was going down, I was going down swinging.

Boom. BOOM. BOOM!

I felt the door shudder. Something enormous was banging on it from the other side. I heard voices. Human voices. My eyes lit up.

"DUCK!" I screamed.

The door exploded. Chunks of rock and stone flew over our heads, wiping out a few monsters. Smoke and rubble filled the palace.

The Grand Guignol and the monsters paused.

"Baron? That you?" he called with a hint of uncertainty.

Something flew through the opening, landing at the

Grand Guignol's feet with a heavy, moist thump.

It was a giant sea monster's tentacle. Severed at the base.

"My Leviathan?" whimpered the Grand Guignol.

Human feet clamored through the hole. A wave of excitement rushed inside me. Through the settling smoke, Mama Vee, Berna, Cassie, Curtis, and Wugnot dropped down beside us. Their faces were covered in sucker marks, and their clothes were dripping wet.

"Vee!" I cried out. "Berna!"

But the babysitters' eyes were fixed on the Grand Guignol's devilish stare. Our happy reunion would have to wait. It was time for business.

"Veronica?" he said. "*Yeesh.* You got old."

"And you got ugly," she said.

The Grand Guignol flicked back his wisps of dead hair. "Thank you."

"Didn't I kill you once?" she sneered.

"Can't kill the Boogeyman, darling. I'm just too pretty."

"Now, Curtis!" she commanded.

Curtis heaved a teddy bear bomb into the snarling horde of nightmares. *BOOM!* Monsters went sailing. As the nightmares scrambled, Mama Vee rolled into a somersault, pouring a ring of blue powder around the Grand Guignol's hooves. She lit it on fire.

WHOOMPH!

A wall of ethereal blue fire raced up around him. Mama Vee stepped back with a contented look, ready to watch the big finale. But the Grand Guignol simply yawned and stepped out of the ghostly flames. Mama Vee's smile sank.

"You really thought a Ring of Angel Fire would work again?"

Mama Vee stared, stunned. Yes. She *did* think that would work again. And now I watched as her confidence melted away, vanishing along with the ring of spectral Angel Fire. The powerful warrior who once stood before me began to back away.

"But . . . That . . . is y-your only weakness," she stuttered.

"*Was* my only weakness, darling," he said, rubbing his fingers together. "But for the past twenty years, I've been sprinkling a bit of it into my tea every evening. Slowly building up a tolerance. Now it just . . . makes me gassy." His tail twitched as he passed wind.

He sniffed the air. "Ah, like roses." He laughed at his little joke and then screamed at the top of his lungs, "DESTROY THE BABYSITTERS!"

I'd like to say we stayed and fought the good fight and won. But we didn't. All of us, even Liz (who seemed a bit out of sorts after being possessed by the snot monster), decided our best—and only—option could be summed up with one single word: "RUN."

With the nightmares stampeding toward us, Wugnot scrambled toward the hole in the door, hoisting kid after kid up and out with lightning speed, like he was trying to win a beanbag toss.

Curtis flung a purple koala stuffed with explosives into the monsters. "Frag out!"

An explosion rocked the entire palace. Nightmares yowled and scattered. The shaking crystal chandelier ripped from the ceiling. It smashed down, sending

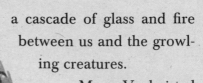

a cascade of glass and fire between us and the growling creatures.

Mama Vee hoisted us up, and we climbed out of the break in the door, slamming down on the sandy ground on the other side. I picked Jacob up and gave him a piggyback ride. The sitters each took a kid, and we ran down the cave toward the distant sound of the ocean.

Moonlight poured through a crack at the end of the rocky tunnel. I squeezed Jacob out and then pulled myself through, scraping my face against the barnacles and starfish. We spilled onto the shoreline of rough pebbles and gray sand at the base of a sea cliff.

Running across the rocks and sand was like running in a terrible dream. Up the winding path, through the brittle tall grass, we made it to the black van. The ground shuddered. Down below, the entire rock wall exploded outward as the Grand Guignol flew from his palace, perched on his flying carriage, whipping his horses. The army of nightmares clamored over the rock, sniffing the air, hunting for us.

302

Wugnot started the engine.

"Go, go, go!" cried Curtis, watching the rising tide of monsters.

"Not until everyone's got on their seat belts," he growled.

"Just drive!" Berna groaned as we buckled up.

The hobgoblin nodded, satisfied, and smashed the gas. The tires shrieked, spewing smoke as the van rocketed off down the road. I looked behind us to see vampires, spiders, and strange unearthly things hunting us. Wugnot pulled the wheel just in time to avoid driving down the gullet of a massive, albino alligator.

The children closed their eyes and balled themselves up, screaming, crying. But Jacob stared out of the window in horror.

"My nightmares," he said. "They're everywhere."

I squeezed his hand and tried to think of something positive to say.

WHAM! Small green things climbed up the back of the van, pounding on the back doors.

"What are those things?!" spat Cassie, pointing to the window.

What looked like stiff green elves with large bushy hair tore at the cage around the van window.

Jacob's jaw dropped.

"It's broccoli," he said with deep dread.

Living pieces of murderous broccoli were scaling the

303

windshield and climbed in through the windows. Wow. Jacob really was afraid of everything. Wugnot turned on the wipers, sweeping off killer veggies. Stalking stalks scrambled under the cages around the windows. They had terrible, cruel eyes and leafy arms and legs. They pulled the children's hair and bit their fingers.

Cassie swung her machetes, chopping the green bushel-heads to pieces.

"Watch it!" cried Berna, ducking from Cassie's singing, clanging blades. "You got broccoli on my—"

One veggie climbed onto my shoulder, and I screamed. It squealed back at me. Liz snatched it from my shoulder and bit its head off as it let out a high-pitched cry. She swallowed the top half and threw the bottom half out of the window. Everyone stared at her for an awestruck moment.

"What? Broccoli's good for you," she said.

Wugnot slammed the brakes. I shot abruptly forward, jerked to a stop by my seat belt. The smell of burning tires filled the cabin.

Up ahead, the nightmares blocked the road. Behind us, the Grand Guignol's phantom carriage scraped against the asphalt. We were blocked in. I held my breath, watching the nightmares and the Grand Guignol slowly approach us. It was quiet and past midnight, so no one was on the street, which was lined with quaint shops and an antique movie theater playing a midnight showing of the classic 80s horror film *The Gyre*. The neon lights of the theater beamed dark red. I felt like a gunslinger in the Wild West facing off against *banditos*.

Liz had the same distant, faraway look in her eye she got when she was thinking about her brother. The fire inside of her seemed to dwindle.

"Total soup sandwich," whispered Curtis.

Berna swallowed and coughed. I slapped her on the back, and she made a huge gulp. "Swallowed my gum," she said mournfully.

"What do we do, Vee?" I asked.

Mama Vee looked back at the demon and his horses, the nightmares, and she nodded to herself.

"We fight."

"Are you crazhy? We're outnumbered!" dribbled Cassie. "We should drive through them!"

"And then what?" Berna asked. Cassie didn't have an answer for that.

I gripped my staff and looked to Mama Vee. I had been afraid of the Boogeyman since I was four years old. I had been afraid my whole life. And I was tired of being afraid.

"The guide says the Grand Guignol feeds on fear, right?" I said. "And that's what we've been giving him. What if we feed him something else?"

"Like poison?" Curtis asked. He fumbled in his bag. "I've got some in here somewhere. . . ."

"No," I said. I looked at Jacob, who was shivering, and then to Liz, who had a haunted expression on her face. I raised the heavy branch in my hand. "Something a lot stronger."

I locked eyes with Liz. I needed her to gather courage if this was going to work. The babysitters held their bizarre weapons. Liz nodded knowingly.

"Okay, then," Vee said. "Kids, you stay in the van."

The four little kids were very happy to hear they did not have to go outside. Out there, it was certain doom.

"Jacob, you're in charge," said Vee. "Look after the others."

Jacob nodded quickly, and the four children clustered around him, who looked a little overwhelmed with his new responsibility. Cassie, Berna, Wugnot, Vee, Liz, and I sprang out of the van and onto the street.

"Semper fi, sitters!" Curtis shouted, leaping from the van.

We stood together, facing the approaching circle of nightmares. The Grand Guignol beat his hooves on the ground three times, and the monster army began slowly walking in sync, stomping their feet together like the drums of death.

Mama Vee clutched her harpoon, waiting for the right moment. Through clenched teeth, she hissed to us, "Babysitters: attack!"

What Was Happening While I Was Battling Nightmares

The dark movie theater was packed.

Victor sat with his buddies, the soccer guys. They were throwing popcorn and shouting with the audience as the blobby monster on-screen swelled from the sea and swallowed its latest victim, a self-centered lifeguard named Chuck. The oily, chunky ooze peeled away from Chuck, leaving only a meaty skeleton. The audience screamed, "Yes! Awesome!"

Victor sighed.

He was the only one who had no idea what was going on in the movie or why people seemed to love it so much. Growing up in a little town in Guatemala, he missed out on a lot of things his American friends took for granted, and a dumb horror film about a floating, swimming, giant mutated blob of pollution, plastic, and trash called "the Gyre" that *somehow* came to life and started eating good-looking kids in bikinis and Speedos with really cheesy eighties, teased-out hair-dos on a beach in Malibu was definitely one of them.

Oh, and it was also a musical.

Looking around, Victor saw that everyone in the theater crowd was dressed up to look like a character from the film: zombie lifeguards, people wearing melted plastic bottles on their heads, Lifeguard Chucks, shy but gorgeous Jackie with glasses, surfer studs, the Big Undead Kahuna himself, and countless spring break victims.

People were wildly tossing beach balls back and forth in the crowd. Victor was the only one not dressed up. He was wearing a sweater and felt really out of place in the sea of sunny reverie. He thought they were going to see a *movie*. Not a so-bad-that-it-was-good movie.

As the ninth victim was pulled off his surfboard and consumed by the floating mass, Victor checked his phone.

Kelly had not texted him back.

"She's negging you, bro," Kent, the preppy soccer kid with white zinc on his nose and yellow sunglasses, said. "Told you not to text her too much. Girls don't like that."

Victor exhaled. All around him, people laughed and cheered as the surfer's skin was sucked off his bones while his girlfriend stood on the shore and shrieked at the top of her lungs.

Kent elbowed Victor and pointed at Deanna and her friends in the front row. Deanna had changed outfits and was in full neon spring break costume, along with her friends. They were cheering and laughing and taking selfies of themselves cheering and laughing, so they could show the world how much they cheered and laughed at this totally rando movie.

"She's the one you should be talking to," whispered Kent.

Victim number ten, the surfer's girlfriend, was being engulfed by the Gyre. Victor shook his head; the surfer's girlfriend *really* should have run instead of standing there screaming.

Estúpido.

A beach ball sailed into Victor's face, and he punched it away. Maybe candy would cheer him up. Yeah, candy. The only thing he *had* eaten all night. Whatever. He just wanted to leave. He squeezed past a crush of kids dressed in bright swim trunks.

"Don't text her, dude!" called out the soccer guys.

Victor banged through the theater doors into the lobby, shutting out the happy howls of the crowd. It was nice and empty and quiet out here. Victor scanned the brightly lit candy selection of king-sized M&M's, Twizzlers, Goobers, and Raisinets with disgust. He had eaten so much sugar the whole night he felt like he was going to be sick.

He didn't want candy.

He didn't want to watch a movie.

He just wanted to sit, be alone, and check his phone for the millionth time in ten minutes.

There was a scream and a snarl. Victor ignored it, thinking someone had turned up the volume on the movie. *CLANG! BOOM!* The sounds were coming from outside. Fighting and metal and odd, unholy shrieks.

Was a pack of wolves attacking a Dumpster or something?

Victor curiously walked toward the entrance and looked out of the round window in the door. His eyes widened as he stared in awestruck wonder.

An eerie wind blew around us. Swirls of dream dust twisted into waves, curling into formation. Figures grew from the mist. Where there was just air and nightmare dust, there were now claws, paws, and tails.

The nightmares were re-forming. Soon, we were facing the same savage villains we had just beaten moments ago. Rats, roaches, clowns, goblins wearing goat-skull masks . . .

I knew why the Boogeyman smiled. His army of nightmares was unstoppable.

We stared, panting, gasping for breath. My fingers were blistered from clinging to the staff. My forearms ached and trembled. I could hardly lift my knees, let alone fight these creatures again. It was like running a marathon, getting to the finish line, and being told you had to run back to the beginning.

"How do we stop these things?" Berna warily asked Vee.

Vee shook her head in disbelief. Her posture was bent and tired. She had never seen anything like this either. None of them had.

"We can't get rid of them," Cassie whispered.

We pressed ourselves against the van as the monsters crept forward. I looked through the window and saw Jacob's frightened face peering out at his living, unbreakable nightmares.

His nightmares . . . These were his. . . . They belonged to him. . . .

I blinked with an idea.

"Cover me," I said to the babysitters, rolling open the van door.

I hopped into the gypsy den, where the children were balled up together, like frightened pups in a city pound. I knelt beside Jacob, guiding his eyes away from the horrific things darkening the sky outside until he looked into my eyes.

"Jacob," I said softly. "These are your nightmares. You're the only one who can make them go away. And you have to make them go away, or they're going to eat everyone, and we're all going to die."

"What?" he cried.

"Sorry. Let me try that again," I said, trying to think of a better way to express myself.

I blocked his view of the monsters slogging toward the van, but I could see them out of the corner of my eye, approaching.

"I mean. Hey. Look what you can do. You can literally make your dreams come true. . . ."

Jacob shook his head and swallowed. "I don't wanna."

"But you can."

"It's weird," he said quietly.

"Well, yeah. But it's also pretty awesome. Sometimes . . . we might think something's weird, but actually . . . that's what makes us cool. And you—you're cool."

Jacob's eyebrows raised.

"Jacob. You're a miracle. You might not feel it, but you're stronger and more powerful than anyone I've ever known." I was trying not to cry when I said it, but I couldn't help it; the words coming out of my mouth were more true than any I had ever spoken. "You can stop this, Jacob. They're your nightmares.

Jacob's eyes welled up with tears.

"I believe in you, little loaf."

He smiled thankfully up at me, tears spilling down his cheeks.

"Heads-up!"

CRASH! The jaws of the giant, albino alligator chomped down on the rear of the van, crushing it like a tin can. The windows shattered. The children screamed. We could see down the gator's gullet. And it was not pretty.

"Everyone out!" I screamed, sliding open the door.

The babysitters scooped out the kids as the alligator shook the van like a rag doll. Mama Vee swung a mace, bashing the albino gator over the head until it burst into dust.

"Kelly?" I heard a voice call my name.

Through the monster horde, I saw Victor standing outside of the movie theater with a bewildered look on his face. I was about to wave hi to him when I thought: *Is that the real Victor or is that a mind-trick Victor?*

Before I could find out, I felt myself being yanked back and hurled across the street. My backpack scraped gravel.

The Grand Guignol and a circle of his monster minions loomed over me. Their slimy drool rained down and the smell of their musty feet made me gag. I swear, one of the Grand Guignol's hooves had stepped in dog poo and it was still stuck to the bottom.

"We could've been best friends, Kelly," snarled the Grand Guignol. "Best friends."

His hoof shot down at my face. I rolled away.

CRACK! CRACK! The sidewalk split under his

314

powerful steps as I dodged them. I could hear the babysitters screaming my name, reaching out for me, but this was my fight.

"Kelly!" Victor shouted, running toward me.

It was the real Victor! Before I could tell him to stop, that I could handle this, a flash of brown fur sprang into his stomach. He was sent skidding along the sidewalk, crumbled up into a ball.

"Victor!" I cried out.

"Oops. Crushed your crush," snarked the Boogeyman.

Liz rushed the Grand Guignol in a series of kicks and punches that would have made Bruce Lee jealous. The Boogeyman danced with her, fast as a fiddle. His tail grabbed her left arm and twisted, spinning her into him. There was a dull crack, and a sharp look of pain snapped across Liz's face. She gasped and dropped to her knees, clutching her left arm. The Grand Guignol smiled wickedly down at her.

"Poor little Lizzie," he said. "Still just a scared little girl."

Liz was screaming through her clenched teeth, trying to bury her agony. Her left arm dangled unnaturally at her side. The Boogeyman's tail shoved her to the ground.

Jacob and the other children were hiding behind Mama Vee, who was battling monsters with her mace.

She was slowing down with each heavy stroke.

All around me, I heard the defeated cries of the babysitters at war with the monsters:

"No more teddy bombs!"

"I'm out of throwing stars!"

"We're toasht!"

Nightmares closed around us. Everything darkened.

I clutched the Staff of Destiny. White-hot intensity surged within me. Blisters on my hands cried out in agony, but I ignored them, ignored the pain, ignored my own weakness. I listened to my breath, my heartbeat, and the quiet, still voice that sounded like Maya Angelou spoke to me from somewhere deep within my soul.

"*Now, Kelly,*" said the voice.

I rose to my feet.

My teeth bared. I was panting. My hair was a mess of sweaty red tangles. Electricity crackled along my skin. Every muscle inside of me wound up like an engine revving.

My focus locked on the Grand Guignol. He was all I could see and smell: every hair on his twitchy tail, every wrinkle in his pale face. It was like a bright spotlight shined on him.

It was happening again, the weird thing. Only this time it didn't feel weird or alien. It felt right and good and ready.

"Back off, Boogeyman," I threatened.

The Grand Guignol cocked his head at me. He gave me a cute little smirk. His nails clicked as he beckoned me to come forward and meet my death.

I launched, staff raised. I charged through the flock of evil, sneakers pounding.

I swiftly spun, cracking the staff into his side, bringing it up under his chin. His fangs clacked shut like a rattrap. My staff whacked him in the temple, and he stumbled. Eyes wide with confusion, he felt the tip of his forked tongue. He studied the small, festering droplets of black blood on his fingertips with a look of confusion.

I did that. Me. Kelly Ferguson. Eighth-grade nobody. Come and get it.

His face went from perplexed to really angry.

The Boogeyman scraped his hooves, like a bull ready to charge. He sprang at me with unimaginable speed, claws out. His tail curled over his head, aimed like a scorpion. I brought my staff up, blocking his strike. I don't know how, but I felt it coming before I saw it. I pulled back just in time to feel his long, sharp talons scraping the air an inch in front of my nose. He kicked. My staff blocked it. I met his crimson gaze.

"May I have this dance?" I sneered.

My arms swung into a fury. Back, forth, up, down. Everything was fast and blurred. My mind was sharp and alert, aware of my every move.

Whispering Nanny. Rock the Cradle. Nap Time Headlock.

A flash of claws arced. *CRACK!* Splinters sprayed. The top of my staff clattered on the pavement. I held the bottom of the branch, sliced clean just above my shaking grip. The Grand Guignol's tail flew out, coiling around my neck.

I gasped for breath, feeling my cheeks burn. I grabbed at my throat. My feet left the ground as his tail hoisted me up, hanging me. My throat bloated. My legs kicked helplessly.

The Grand Guignol fished out a little box from his jacket and flicked it open. The green snot-goo monster that had infected Liz oozed from within it, stretched toward my nose. I clamped my mouth shut and tried to turn away, but the Boogeyman's tail forced me to face him.

Dizzy spots formed in front of my eyes. I looked around the street, swarming with monsters and nightmares. Liz staggered toward me, holding her limp left arm. Victor gulped for breath against the shattered glass storefront he had been thrown into. Berna was pinned down by a ten-foot-tall spider, its sharp pointy legs playing with her hair while its fangs clicked hungrily.

The babysitters were fighting with every last ounce of strength they had while the children cowered under the van. I blinked. There were only four children.

I felt the dripping sludge creature trickle up my nose, and my consciousness slipping away.

Where was Jacob?

"Hey." I heard a little voice behind me.

I fought to stay awake, blowing air through my nostrils to keep the slithering slime out of my nose.

The Grand Guignol kept his eyes on me, enjoying my pain.

"Hey!" shouted the little voice.

Jacob! He was standing behind the Grand Guignol with his little fists balled up. He was standing straight, shoulders back.

"I . . . ," Jacob whispered.

The Grand Guignol glowered down at the boy. "Quiet, child."

He bore his fangs and hissed. Nightmares closed around Jacob: life-sized dolls, centipedes, and ghoulies.

But Jacob didn't run. The little kid just stood there, facing his fears.

"You're just nightmares . . . and . . . and . . . I'm not afraid of you anymore," he said in a quiet voice.

The nightmares laughed, murky and cruel.

That upset Jacob. Children, like the rest of us, do not like to be laughed at. His jaw jutted out, as if he were demanding cookies. He stamped his foot.

"I said . . . I'm not afraid of you!"

Jacob shook with power. His eyes were fixed on the Grand Guignol. His cowardice had faded into passionate anger. He closed his eyes tight, as if to focus on exactly what he wanted. He wasn't trying to block the nightmares out. He was trying to summon the miracle inside of him.

The nightmares crept dangerously close to him, a dark wall of growls and spooky taunts. A strange wind howled around the boy. Jacob's eyes snapped open. They were blazing with courage and strength.

"Leave me and my friends alone!" he screamed in a strong, deep voice. "I'm not afraid of you! I am not afraid of you." He was no longer the little loaf crying over Halloween candy; he was a strong little human, demanding respect from the things that haunted him.

Inches from his face, claws and fangs melted away into golden embers.

A powerful shockwave radiated from Jacob and raced

through the monsters like wildfire, turning them all into shimmering nightmare dust. Nightmares wailed as they dissolved. Zombies, trolls, and ghostly skeletons vanished.

The goo creature tickling up my nose made a tormented shriek and withered into spectral sparkles. Then total nothingness.

Magical sand floated like snow, like some kind of golden nuclear winter. A strong, warm breeze rushed through the air, picking up the glowing clouds and swirling them around the Grand Guignol.

In shock, the Grand Guignol dropped me.

"No . . . ," he mumbled. "No." He swatted at the twirling cloud of dream dust circling him.

He was all alone. His army of monsters had vanished.

"You dirty, rotten children!"

He lunged for Jacob. I stepped forward, ducked, weaved, twisted, and punched the Grand Guignol right in the chest.

He gasped. Lightning forked in the sky. Storm clouds crashed.

"That's called the Monster Heart Breaker," I said. "Learned it from a friend."

Eyes wide in horror, the Grand Guignol clutched his heart. He let out a tiny mouse-whisper.

I stood beside Jacob, holding his hand. We faced the Boogeyman together.

"That's your real weakness," I said. "Your tiny,

little, selfish heart."

A tear formed in the Grand Guignol's eye. "And you just broke it," he whispered.

The nightmare dust gathered into a tornado as wicked winds launched the wretched creature up, like a piece of trash. His claws caught on to a parking meter. He held it, legs scuttling into the sky, tail whipping up, as if a huge vacuum cleaner hovered over him.

I hugged Jacob in the howling winds. I saw Victor clinging to the theater door, his hair blowing across his amazed face. The babysitters held the other children.

"You'll miss me when I'm gone!" shrieked the Boogeyman. "Life without me is boring and dull. Just like all of you." His nails scratched along the parking meter, etching into the metal. "That's why you all *dream* about me! I'm just too much fun. That's why you can never kill the Boogeyman."

Liz rushed forward, clutching her limp arm. "Wait! Where's my brother, you slime?" she shouted over the whistling gust.

His laughter was slow and satisfied. This was his last chance to pour lemon juice on her wound. His final, tiny victory.

"Don't ask me, darling," he said. "Ask Serena."

He released his grip and soared into the sky, tail lashing at the stars.

"'Ooooh, the gooood liiiiife, full of fun . . . ,'" he

crooned as the tornado of shadows inhaled him into the gloom. His twisted singing grew fainter and fainter.

I held Jacob and Liz. We shuddered in the freezing howl. Bolts of lightning cracked deep within the clouds where the Boogeyman vanished, as if the angry heavens had belched after a satisfied meal.

And then the winds died. Stars twinkled. Peaceful silence settled on the street.

All of Jacob's nightmares were gone. So were mine.

"Way to go, little loaf," I said.

Jacob beamed. The babysitters and the four children rushed to us, hugged, and high-fived us. They danced and sang. Overwhelmed with joy, Cassie grabbed Curtis and kissed him on the lips. Curtis sputtered and pulled away, blinking in shock. Cassie looked surprised by her outburst too.

Berna giggled, unwrapped a fresh piece of gum, and popped it into her mouth.

I looked at Liz. She was holding her left arm, still staring up at the empty, starry sky. I unbuckled my belt and tied it over her shoulder, making a really lame attempt at a sling.

"You okay?"

Liz winced, adjusted her shoulder. She kept peering up into the vast darkness.

"Is Serena . . . Is that who I think it is?" I whispered.

Liz nodded. "One of the seven."

Victor staggered up to me and the babysitters. "Kelly," he said breathlessly.

"Victor, you're okay!" I hugged him. Liz mumbled something to Mama Vee, and she signaled the babysitters to hang back a second.

Victor's and my eyes met. I could hear the orchestra swelling our romantic theme song as he gazed into my eyes.

"Wow. Kelly," he said, wild-eyed. "You. You are so . . . weird."

The orchestra stopped swelling.

Not that I needed his praise or approval, but I was at least hoping for a thumbs-up.

A rumble shook the ground. The doors to the movie

theater flew open, and hundreds of teenagers dressed like spring breakers flooded the sidewalk, laughing and whooping.

"The Gyre's alive! Look out, Chad!"

Wugnot dove into the van, hiding from the human eyes.

Among the crowd, the Princess Pack yawned while Deanna called her mom. They looked awesome, like Malibu Barbies but for real. Deanna saw me, and her eyes bugged.

"What happened to you?" Deanna said. "Did you, like, fall into a gorilla's cage at the zoo or something?" The Princess Pack laughed.

I held back, swallowing my instinct to tell her everything. No, this was mine. And nothing she or anybody said could take that away from me.

"I've been out," I said, chin up. "With my friends." I looked back at the babysitters. They smiled at me.

Victor babbled in Spanish at a million miles an hour. He kept pointing at me and saying, "*¡Monstruo! Monstruo!*"

I glared at him. "Yeah, Victor," I said, waving at Deanna and the princesses. "I'm never gonna be one of the cool kids. And I don't want to be." I put my hands on my hips. "This is who I am."

Saying that made me feel light as a feather.

"I like math. And sometimes I get tingly when I

solve a really tough equation or when my brain hurts after I've read a really good book. I have three Instagram followers, two of whom are my parents. My mom doesn't have a sweet ride. I'm not popular."

I grinned at Liz. She was coming out of her trance. Curtis's crooked eyes were fixed on me as he leaned his head down on Cassie's shoulder with a sigh.

"I'm a babysitter. And if that makes me weird, well, then, buddy, I am a number-one fuh-reak show."

Cassie wiped a tear from her eye. Deanna snorted.

"But that's not what got me through tonight. It was my brains. And the oddballs and the freaks . . . the best friends a girl could have."

Victor stared at me a long while. He reached out and took my hand.

"No—no—I didn't mean weird. My English sometimes . . . I mean, um . . . different. Bizarre. No. *Cómo puedo decir único* . . . unique? Extra. Ordinary! Yes! Extraordinary."

I blinked and smiled. "Oh. Well, that's a better word."

He sighed, knocking his knuckles against his temple. "That's what I meant to say all along."

The orchestra resumed playing our theme song. Deanna huffed a few times, but when she saw there was nothing she could do to break our focus on each other, she marched off, snapping at her friends to follow her.

"It's, like, when did this become the Kelly show?" I heard her ask the princesses.

Victor leaned close to me. He was well within kissing distance. The babysitters all turned away from us, pretending not to notice. I felt his breath on my face. Suddenly, every brave bone in my body turned to jelly.

I felt a tug on my shirt. "Can we go home now?" Jacob asked.

Not now, kid.

"Oh, gross!" Jacob squealed. "You guys are nasty." He pretended to wretch.

That cracked me up. Victor laughed too. Our romantic moment in the moonlight vanished. We stepped back, out of kissing distance, stealing knowing looks.

Liz looked at her watch. "Hey, Kelly. It's almost one."

I blinked. Then I remembered: *The Zellmans are coming home at one!*

"Crud! We have six minutes to get you home!" I cried to Jacob.

We bolted into the van, and I left my Cupid's Arrow for the second time that evening.

"I'll call you later!" I shouted to Victor as Wugnot started the engine.

The half-eaten black van screeched around the corner on its large, whumping tires. Wugnot was blasting a triumphant heavy metal song while Mama Vee applied a salve to his cracked, sore horn. I was squeezed in the back with the babysitters, Jacob, and the four children. Berna and the others wiped the mud and tears from the kids' faces with baby wipes. Liz pulled a spare sweater from the gypsy cabinet and tossed it to me.

We launched down Vanderbilt Lane in Mercy Springs. I yelled for Wugnot to stop in front of Jacob's house, and he stomped on the emergency brake, spinning the van in a screaming arc. Everyone glared at the hobgoblin. He shrugged with an evil grin.

"Hate me all you want, but I got you here in five minutes and forty seconds. Go!"

Liz and I held Jacob's hands and darted across the Zellmans' lawn. The lights were off. Liz snuck us in through the front door, and we crept through the shadows of the long hallway, listening for the Zellmans. They weren't home yet.

"I'll keep watch," Liz whispered to me.

"But–you're his favorite," I whispered.

"Kelly? Can I have some water?" came Jacob's voice.

Liz winked and patted me on the arm. "Go get 'em, Quick Study."

I led Jacob into the kitchen and poured him half a glass of water. He gulped it down. As we shuffled into his room, he kicked off his dirty clothes and jumped into a fresh pair of pj's.

I tucked him into bed, and he looked up at me with warm eyes.

"You gonna be okay?" I asked.

Jacob threw his arms around my neck and squeezed tight. A sweet lump fell into my throat.

Headlights swept the window. I heard Liz make a bird whistle. The Zellmans were home.

"Go to sleep, buddy," I said quietly. "I'll turn on your night-light."

"It's okay," he murmured, nuzzling his face into the fluffy pillow. "I think I'll have good dreams. . . ."

"I think you will too."

I leaned down and gave him a gentle kiss on the forehead.

"Thank you," he said.

I watched him drift away into sleep.

"Thank you, little loaf," I whispered.

I walked out of his room and gently closed the door.

Clack, clack! Mrs. Zellman's heels marched across the marble. I dove onto the couch and turned on the TV just as she entered the living room. Mrs. Z. had removed her Ice Queen headpiece. Her hair was pulled back with a hundred bobby pins. Her husband yawned, gave a tired wave, and waddled off to bed.

"Hi!" I said with a little wave back.

"Well. How was he?" she said, wiping the thick blue makeup from her eyes.

"Great! He's asleep. I'm just watching some *Tears of Flowers and Fish*. . . ."

Mrs. Zellman peered inside Jacob's bedroom door, and I heard his soft snore. She took off her high heels, and I saw she wasn't much taller than I was without them. She padded back into the kitchen and grabbed her purse.

"Here's eighty dollars," she said, handing over four crisp twenty-dollar bills. "I don't know if you're busy tomorrow night, but we have to go to a charity event—"

"I'll be here," I said.

She gave me a look. And then a grateful smile. "You're a lifesaver, Kelly."

I grinned a little.

If they only knew.

"Hank will give you a ride home. Hank!"

"It's okay," I said. "I've got a ride."

The black van pulled up in front of my house.

"That was a doozy, huh?" Vee laughed, looking at me. "I thought we were goners for sure."

"How could we lose?" I said, holding up the broken branch. "I had the Staff of Destiny. Sorry I broke it."

Mama Vee pursed her lips. She nodded for me to hop out of the van onto the street so we could speak alone.

"Here's the thing," she said, apologetic. "The Staff of Destiny is just a branch I had lying around. I said all that stuff about it being powerful 'cause I thought it would give you confidence—"

I laughed. "I know, Vee."

Her eyebrows raised. "Can't fool a fooler. So look.

Now that the SITs have graduated to full-time babysitters—"

From inside the van, I heard Berna shriek, "We have?"

"Not nice to eavesdrop, you guys," said Vee.

"The window's busted. We can hear everything," called Curtis.

"Shut up, you guysh! Preshident Preston, you were about to shay shomething," encouraged Cassie.

The babysitters climbed out of the van and looked up at Vee with eager grins.

"You've all proven yourselves in the line of duty," said Mama Vee. "So it gives me great pleasure to officially promote you three to the role and rank of babysitter."

"Aweshome!"

"Oh, thank you, thank you, thank you," said Berna, hopping up and down, hugging Vee.

Sitting in the van, Liz gave a quiet nod and a cool thumbs-up to the SITs.

Curtis clicked his heels and swiftly saluted Vee. "Madame President. It's been a real honor serving with you."

She returned an amused salute to Curtis. "At ease, dude." Vee faced me with challenging eyes. "So. We're going to need some new blood."

Butterflies danced in my stomach. "You want me in

the order?" My spine straightened, and I stood tall.

"Yep."

"Yes!"

"But"—she held up her finger—"there's a whole test you have to pass, and believe me when I say it is brutal."

"Oh, yeah!" agreed Curtis. "There's fire and monsters; a lava course; this half-dragon, half-dog thing. All sorts of craziness!"

"You up for it?"

I blinked, suddenly overwhelmed with the task before me. Was this my purpose? My truth? Could I really rise to the occasion and do this?

"On one condition," I said with a smile. "You gotta get me one of those business cards with my name on it."

"Deal." Mama Vee winked. "Oh. Almost forgot. There're also dues. Ten bucks a month."

She held out her hand. I looked at it, confused.

"I know you got paid tonight," Mama Vee said. "Fork it over, sister."

I grumbled and handed Mama Vee a twenty. She gave me a ten back. At this rate, Camp Miskatonic was going to have to wait a while.

I crouched down to hug the little kids. "You were all so brave."

Cowgirl begged me to come visit her, and I promised

I would. The nubby end of Wugnot's tail bumped into my hand like a hobgoblin high five.

"See you at school, Monday," said Berna with a big smile. I beamed at her. I couldn't wait to hang out with these three lunatics again.

They were about to drive off when Liz had Wugnot stop the van. She slid out to stand beside me, away from the others. Liz had been quiet for a long while, like she was lost inside of herself, thinking about everything.

"That test is pretty serious," she said, handing me her babysitter's guide. "Copy it. Learn it. Live it."

I held the battered notebook in my hands. It was heavy with responsibility but filled with possibility and strength. Liz stared at the ground and adjusted her makeshift sling.

"And uh . . . sorry I almost killed you," she said into her chest.

I shrugged. "Happens."

Liz shifted back and forth. Something else was on her mind. Something she wasn't normally used to feeling, I guess. Tears fell from her eyes. She quickly brushed them away. "And uh . . . thanks. For not giving up on me and stuff. No one's ever done that. I know I can be a real pain."

She flung her right arm around me and pulled me into a powerful hug that bordered on a headlock, squeezing the breath out of me. "You're the best associate I've ever had," she said, her face pressed against my hair. I could feel her hot breath on my neck. My arms and hands clutched her as firmly as she was clutching me.

"We're going to find your brother," I whispered with steel in my hushed voice. "Even if we have to hunt down every single Boogeyman on this planet."

Liz knew I meant it, and she knew just how far I would go to get Kevin back into her arms. A grateful look spread across her face, and she nodded.

"Get some rest. Gonna need it," she said, slipping back into the van.

As Wugnot drove off, the last thing I heard was Mama Vee's voice asking the little kids if they all wanted pancakes before they went home. "Yes! Yes! Yes! Yes!" they said happily. I watched the black van bend around the corner at the end of my block and disappear into the night.

I crept into my house, careful not to wake my parents.

I checked under the bed. No trolls. Looked inside my closet. No pale Boogeyman. Outside my window there was only a quiet moonlit street.

I plugged in my phone. While it charged, I flipped through Liz's red babysitter's guide and thought of all the unseen monsters and wisdom waiting inside of it. I couldn't resist. I flicked on the lamp at my small desk and started to read it, cover to cover. From "anthropoid" to "zurgler." Then I dug through my desk and found my mostly blank Camp Miskatonic notebook.

My phone erupted with texts from Victor.

I laughed as I read them. I was about to text him back, but I decided it could wait a little longer. No need to rush anything. Besides, I had work to do.

I peeled off the "Camp Fund" label on the cover of the notebook, wrote "A Babysitter's Guide to Monster Hunting" on it in big letters, and started copying down everything from Liz's guide onto the fresh, blank pages.

And that's how I started writing the guide you're reading. I hope it's been helpful. There's so much I want to share. Like how to tell if your local librarian's a witch. What to do when you're bit by a demonic child. And how to saddle a white dragon.

All in good time.

Monsters are real. But so are we. And kid by kid, we're going to change the world for the better. So stay safe. Stay brave. This job's worth it. Trust me.

Kelly the Babysitter

ACKNOWLEDGMENTS

This all started with a really, really bad health scare, and I thought, *Well, if I live, what do I want to do with my life?* Remarkably, the tiny voice in my heart didn't come back and say, *Ski Mount Everest or surf the English Channel*; it said, *Write a kid's book.* So I did.

Along the way, there were those who helped and encouraged and kept the fires going. The first is my beautiful wife, Cara. She was there by my side, encouraging me to keep it scary (kids like scary, she said). Dana Spector at Paradigm was the first pro to read it, and she helped push it forward, giving me wonderful advice and access to my now book agent, Alyssa Reuben. Alyssa provided me with incredible inspiration and detailed notes, the likes of which I had never seen, but most of all she believes in the babysitters and is still a great guiding force. The luminous Maria Barbo, my editor at Katherine Tegen Books, HarperCollins, with a keen eye for words and spooky illustrations, worked these pages over and over with me, patiently guiding me along the way, while giggling about the frights and chills we were dishing out to all of you. Our illustrator, Vivienne To, for bringing to life the guide in all its horrific and swashbuckling glory with such style and originality. Rebecca Aronson for her tireless work and who helped me through my first rodeo. And I am forever grateful to the big boss, Katherine Tegen, for taking a chance on a lousy, first-time babysitter named Kelly.

Meanwhile, on the West Coast, David Boxerbaum, my agent, snappy dresser, and man with a plan, set up the book to become a movie. High-five. Enter Montecito and Walden Media. Ali Bell and Naia Cucukov, two producers who I am happy to call friends, developed the screenplay with me, which greatly informed the final book you just read (unless you've cheated and flipped to the very, very end).

I have to thank my parents for listening to a kid with a head full of stories and encouraging him to go for it. And last, my little boy, Theodore. You're too young to read this right now, but I just wanted to say, Thanks, kiddo.